Thomas S. Gaines

BURIED ALIVE BEHIND PRISON WALLS

e-artnow 2018

Thomas S. Gaines

BURIED ALIVE BEHIND PRISON WALLS

The Inside Story of Jackson State Prison from the Eyes of a Former Slave Who Was Punished for Killing a White Man in Self Defence (Black History Series)

e-artnow, 2018
Contact: info@e-artnow.org

ISBN 978-80-268-9157-4

Contents

PREFACE	13
PART FIRST BURIED ALIVE LIFE OF WILLIAM WALKER	15
CHAPTER I SHARKS FED ON HUMAN FLESH — IN THE SLAVE PEN AT NEW ORLEANS	17
CHAPTER II DICK FALLON, THE DEVIL'S BROTHER — NANCY, THE OCTOROON GIRL — THE COTTON FIELD — THE MURDER	19
CHAPTER III THE ESCAPE — PURSUED BY BLOOD HOUNDS — THE CAPTURE — THE PUNISHMENT	23
CHAPTER IV NANCY'S DREAM — A TERRIBLE BLOW — GLOOM — BELLS TOLLING IN THE SKY	33
CHAPTER V A FLASH OF LIGHTNING KILLS FALLON AND WRITES HIS NAME ON STONE	39
CHAPTER VI IN OLD MISSOURI — THE ESCAPE — ARRIVAL IN DETROIT, MICHIGAN	43
CHAPTER VII FARMING — THE SHOLTZ FAMILY — THE MEETING WITH NANCY — THE QUARREL — THE MURDER	45
PART SECOND LIFE IN JACKSON PRISON	51
CHAPTER I IN SOLITARY CONFINEMENT — ABOLISHMENT OF THE SOLITARIES — "FRENCH JOE"	53
CHAPTER II THE CONTRACT SYSTEM — ESCAPE AND CAPTURE OF TOM BARTOLES — DIED WITH HIS SHACKLES ON	57
CHAPTER III THE REIGN OF TERROR — DRAWN FROM HIS CELL WITH RED-HOT IRONS	61
CHAPTER IV A NEW ADMINISTRATION — A CHANGE FOR THE BETTER — A WOMAN PHILANTHROPIST	67
CHAPTER V USE OF TOBACCO PROHIBITED — THE HAUNTED ROOM — THE LIGHTNING BOLT	71
CHAPTER VI PRISON LIFE AT MIDNIGHT — SHAVING ON SHORT NOTICE — HORRIBLE FATALITIES	75
CHAPTER VII CUNNING ESCAPES — WASHINGTON'S BIRTHDAY BANQUET — CONVICT McLOUD KILLED	79
CHAPTER VIII THE STRETCHING MACHINE — RECORD OF MISCONDUCT — FATALITIES, MURDERS AND SUICIDES	83
CHAPTER IX WARDEN HATCH AND PRISON REFORM — THE INDETERMINATE SENTENCE ACT	87
CHAPTER X THE LITERARY MEETINGS AND RELIGIOUS SERVICES — THE PRISON CHAPLAIN	93
CHAPTER XI GUILTY AND INNOCENT — CANFIELD, THE SLAYER OF LITTLE NELLIE GRIFFIN	95
CHAPTER XII DIED FOR WANT OF WATER — WILLIAM WALKER'S PETITION FOR A PARDON	99
CHAPTER XIII PRISON LITERARY MEETINGS — ESSAYS BY EDWARD HANLAN, IRVING LATIMER AND WILLIAM BUTLER	105
CHAPTER XIV LOVERS OF PRISON LIFE — BEGGING TO BE RETURNED TO PRISON	111
CHAPTER XV SUNDAY IN PRISON — MUSICAL PRISONERS — THE DYNAMITE EXPLOSION	113

CHAPTER XVI DESPERATE PRISONERS — MACHINERY DEMOLISHED WITH A SLEDGE HAMMER — PRINCE MICHAEL 117

CHAPTER XVII CANDIDATES FOR THE HOSPITAL — CAPITAL PUNISHMENT — SINGULAR MURDERS 123

CHAPTER XVIII THE SUNDAY SCHOOL — PAPER READ BY IRVING LATIMER AT A SABBATH SCHOOL EXHIBITION 129

CHAPTER XIX EXPIRATION OF WARDEN HATCH'S ADMINISTRATION — A CHRISTMAS PRESENTATION 131

CHAPTER XX WARDEN DAVIS' ADMINISTRATION — EMANCIPATION DAY ADDRESS — CONCLUSION 135

Footnotes 139

PREFACE

In presenting this volume to to the public I do not intend that the convict shall pose as a martyr. And as sensationalism is almost invariably incompatible with the truth, I shall also avoid that. Far more eloquent pens than mine have exhausted the subject of contract labor, showing the world the injurious effects it had on the workingman. It is now my aim to show the misery it causes to his more unfortunate brother on the inside of the walls. I make no comments, I merely portray the facts. I am the artist. You, reader, are the critic. But in sending forth this little book, should it gain the attention of some of our public benefactors, and through them be the means of bettering the condition of those bound to these modern despots, I shall feel that I have not written in vain.

**PART FIRST
BURIED ALIVE
LIFE OF WILLIAM WALKER**

CHAPTER I
SHARKS FED ON HUMAN FLESH — IN THE SLAVE PEN AT NEW ORLEANS

I WAS born in Southampton County, Virginia. I do not know my age, for I was born a slave, and all of my ancestors were slaves. But as near as I can judge, I was born in the year 1819 or 1820.

I do not know either the month or the year of my birth, and it would not be an exaggeration for me to say that there is not one human being in a thousand who was born a slave who knows his exact age; and it would have been much better for me if I had never been born. The true meaning of the words "born a slave" will never be known only to those who were born and nurtured beneath its dismal shadow. Fifty or sixty years ago, slavery in America was in its zenith, and it was the most unrighteous burden ever imposed on a race of people, black or white, civilized or uncivilized. Until I was nineteen or twenty years of age I belonged to Dr. Seaman, who also owned my father and mother. In the month of August, 1841, I was taken from home and confined in the slave pen at Petersburg, Virginia, where six hundred other slaves were awaiting transportation to different Southern cotton farms. The slave pen where we were kept was a one-story shed or building about one hundred feet long and fifty feet wide, and was used as a store house for slaves.

It was a partnership building, owned by Natt Blake and General Downs, and was a dismal looking structure, its swaying roof and sunken corners, its sun-warped sides, in fact, all of its appearance seemed to be in sympathy with the echos and groans of slaves which were continually shaking it.

I have never seen or heard of my father or mother since the day I stepped inside of that slave pen. But nature has sown an imperishable germ in the hearts of all children, black or white, bond or free, and the memory of my old mother will ever be perpetuated. And to-night it is just as fresh and green as the day I was separated from her, which was more than fifty years ago; and I am well aware, as the days flash by and the older I grow, I am being drawn face to face with my father and mother who died in Old Virginia long before the war. Why, what power can equal that which confers existence and reason? and what recollections can last so long as the remembrances of mother and father?

You can rob man of his love, friendship, honor; you can deprive him of his liberty, justice; rob him of the light of the sun; rob him of the gentle zephyrs that kiss the wildest flowers and sway the forest oaks; but you cannot rob him of his parental memory.

After remaining six weeks in the slave pen at Petersburg, we were all marched on board a boat called the "Pelican," and started for our destination, New Orleans. It would be impossible for any man to draw the faintest idea of the horrible position in which we were placed while on the boat. It is indescribable.

Men, women and children were packed beneath the hatches like cattle. Think of six hundred human beings living six weeks in the hold of a vessel 180 feet long, 40 feet wide and 10 feet high. There was no air to be had, for the only means of receiving air was by three small grated windows on either side of the boat, two feet long and eight inches wide; and when sea sickness began among us it was surely one of the most horrible places ever visited by a human being. I believe it would have been dangerous for any boat to have anchored within rods of us or traveled in our wake, for the odor from that filthy boat was poisonous to breathe — — cholera and sure death. Surely the "Pelican" was a floating carcass on the sea. Thirty-one of our number died before we reached the southern coast of Florida, and the last five that died were thrown into the ocean just before we reached Florida Straits, and the sharks that were in swarms around us soon had the surrounding water red with human blood.

Six weeks from the day we left Petersburg we arrived at New Orleans, where we were again placed in another slave pen; and it will never be possible for me to speak, write or by any means adequately explain the horrible condition of that slave pen. It was worse than any cattle yard I have ever seen north of the Ohio river.

It was a sickening place! No wonder Louisiana is the hot bed of the terrible disease called yellow fever. But I suppose the black race is the only race on the globe that cannot, or will not, let their grief and adversities completely overwhelm them. They will sing and dance in the midst of famine, as well as in the midst of abundance; in chains as in liberty. Nearly the entire length of Grand street, in New Orleans, on either side, was one solid row of buildings where human beings were incarcerated waiting for a purchaser.

Some of them were singing and praying; while others were drowning their sorrows by dancing or telling funny stories. Very frequently you could see a woman sitting on one of the old rough benches, with her elbows resting on her knee, her hands supporting her chin, and her eyes staring at the floor. It was not necessary to inquire what was the subject of her meditations; for in her countenance was depicted the very thoughts of her soul; and it was visible to all that her mind was in the old log cabin way up in Old Virginia, where she left her little babe; insanity's cold glitter had already began to curdle in her eye. I believe that every supernatural cause is equally as impenetrable to man; and just as sure as the thunderbolt trails in the wake of the lightning's flash, those Southern cyclones, earthquake shocks and yellow fevers that are daily haunting Southern soil are only the re-echos of many slave groans-just retribution from on high. Man is the only sensible being who forms his reason by continued observation. His education begins with his life, and only ends with his death. His days would pass away in perpetual uncertainty, unless the impression of different objects and the various scenes and flexibility of his brain in early life gave to the impression of his memory a character not to be effaced. At that period are formed ideas and observations which may influence his whole life. Man's first affections are likewise his last. They accompany him amid all the events with which his days are checkered. They re-appear in old age and revive the recollections of his infancy with still more force than even those of mature age.

After remaining about three months in the slave pen at New Orleans, my purchaser arrived. And it seemed to me as though I knew the very minute he was coming by my feelings. I am not superstitious; but yet it seemed to me as though I could hear his voice, and was in his presence long before he arrived. The night preceding the day I was sold I had a presentiment that something was about to occur which was of a character I did not wish to meet. The dreadful feeling completely unnerved me. In twenty-four hours I became a physical wreck, and was mentally tortured until I must have been on the very verge of insanity.

Oh! how I did long to be with my father and mother in the old log cabin 'way up in old Virginia. And in my dreams I was in old Virginia, on the same old plantation, using the same old hoe.

But it was only a dream, and the last one that I ever had in New Orleans, for the shrill blast of the watchman's bugle bade us rise up; for it was five o'clock and we must get ready for our daily rations of corn-meal and bacon.

It would have been impossible for me to have tasted of the most delicious meal that was ever prepared for a king. Why, I felt as though some unseen hand was ready to grasp me; even my own shadow seemed to be breathing and watching me; my own footsteps seemed to rattle like the hoofs of the Negro driver's horse on the distant turnpike.

The uncontrollable hallucination did not deceive me; for the very hour had arrived which was to determine all the joys and sorrows of my future life. Before eight o'clock I heard the keys rattling and the door swung open, and the overseer of the slave pen called the following names: Will Clark, Henry Jones, Sarah Tompkins, Nancy Day and William Walker.

The last name was my own, and on going forward I was brought face to face with Dick Fallon, my purchaser, and the worst human being that ever drew bloody groans from a slave. The four other slaves had been bought for John Porter (an uncle of Frank Porter, now living in Detroit, Mich.)

CHAPTER II
DICK FALLON, THE DEVIL'S BROTHER — NANCY, THE OCTOROON GIRL — THE COTTON FIELD — THE MURDER

BUT I was the property of Ed. Purgoo, and Dick Fallon was Purgoo's Negro driver. The very name of Dick Fallon was terrorizing to all the slaves from North Carolina to Texas.

He was a man (or perhaps we had better call him a demon) about thirty-five years of age, Irish by birth, sandy complexion and a short stubby mustache, small glittering eyes that seemed to sit too far back in his head and which made them glitter like the eyes of a deadly serpent. He could also boast of being the possessor of a small round, head, large neck, very broad shoulders, and he was six feet in stature.

Although he weighed one hundred and eighty pounds, yet he was as supple as a cat and possessed extraordinary strength, and always carried two big horse-pistols, with which I have often seen him, while riding horse back, shoot a crow on the wing.

If ever a fiend walked this earth in human shape, Dick Fallon was the man. I have often heard it said that the wildest animals in the jungles of Africa, when captured and caged, have been known to quail and tremble with fear when confronted with trainers of long experience. I do not know whether it is false or true; but I do know that no other name in all the Southern States was so alarming to the slaves as the name of Dick Fallon, better known before the war as Red Dick, the Negro tamer.

When we emerged from the jail we were commanded to ascend a raised platform, called the auction block, in order that we could be better inspected, which was always customary when buying slaves. We were commanded to walk up and down the platform in order for them to see if there were any defects in our limbs. We were commanded to go through a complete process of gymnastics, and after being thoroughly examined by the planter and his physician that accompanied him, I was pronounced as sound as a rock, as hearty as a buck and as strong as an ox, and nine hundred and fifty dollars in pure gold was counted and paid for me; and I was in the hands of Dick Fallon. He commanded me to come down from the auction block and asked me if I knew who he was. I replied that I did not. He said: "I am Dick Fallon, and I have just paid nine hundred and fifty dollars in hot gold for you, and g___d d___n you, if you do not skin enough cotton in three days for me to get back my money I will skin you just the same as I would any other black squirrel."

John Porter owned three thousand acres of land at a place called Monroe, situated about one hundred and twenty-five miles north of New Orleans. His plantation was stocked with five hundred Negroes; and adjoining his place was the plantation known as the Purgoo Kingdom, owned by E. D. Purgoo. Purgoo himself lived in Paris, France, and his plantation was conducted and run by Dick Fallon, and a half dozen other Negro drivers on the plantation who strictly obeyed and executed the orders of Red Dick.

The Purgoo Kingdom consisted of eleven thousand acres; six thousand five hundred acres was the cotton farm. This mammoth plantation was stocked with one thousand and fifty. Negroes and one hundred and thirteen as ferocious-looking blood-hounds as ever tracked a panting slave. John Porter had justly earned the reputation of being the most humane planter in the State of Louisiana. He would not abuse his slaves nor allow them to be ill-treated by any one else. He lived on the same plantation until the black cloud of rebellion began to settle over Southern soil, and then he sold a few slaves and liberated the rest and moved to Arkansas, where he died with yellow fever.

I did not have long to wait before I was convinced that my new master had justly earned the name of being the most cruel man in the State of Louisiana. Surely he was the most inhuman being that God ever permitted to walk the earth. I will not relate all the many acts of cruelty which I have seen performed by him, or by his command.

The world has long since seen the folly of trafficking in human bodies in America, and a quarter of a million men freely gave their lives for the extirpation of Negro slavery, which was surely the greatest curse known among men.

It would be a crime against my conscience and a sin against God for me to revive the wrongs committed fifty years ago, and not by a human being, but by a fiend in human form. But I shall be compelled to relate one or two incidents in order to connect a link to the chain of circumstances contained in this book.

During the first four or five years that I had been on the plantation I had frequently seen my fellow slaves hanging to the whipping-post — which was made in the shape of a cross — by one hand and one foot, while the other hand and foot was made fast to the ground by a chain running through a post driven into the ground. And although blood was streaming from a hundred gashes made with the lash, yet I have known them to remain hanging for hours in the heat of the burning sun in the month of July. During the summer of 1847 I saw Dick Fallon perpetrate a deed which, perhaps, for cruelty never was equalled in the State of Louisiana.

It is just as visible to my mind now as the day it was enacted, although half a century has passed; and I often wonder why the just retribution which was so swiftly pursuing him, and so close on his heels, did not overtake him before he committed that dreadful act.

One day, just before the blowing of the dinner horn, there were three hundred slaves picking cotton in the field where I was working, and the most of them were women. Women are more expert at picking cotton than men, for their fingers are naturally more supple and not so large as a man's, and their fingers will enter a cotton pod much more easily than a man's. It was customary among the women who had children to carry their nursing babies strapped to their backs, in true Indian style, while picking cotton; and when the child would begin to cry for the want of food, the mother would hasten to her work and get a few rods ahead of the rest of the gang and nurse her child. All of the cotton pickers were compelled to keep in line and side by side while at work; and if any one of them fell behind the gang, even the distance of ten feet, they would feel the keen cut of the Negro driver's lash. It often occurred that one mother who could pick faster than another one, would nurse the other mother's child. Planters were always anxious to have their slaves marry, and would compel them to marry the one of the master's choice, thereby increasing his stock of slaves. Among our number was an Octoroon woman by the name of Nancy. She was married to a Negro on the place by the name of Peter. Slaves were only called by their first names; their last name was the same as that of their masters.

Nancy was a beautiful girl, twenty years of age, always vivacious and full of fun, and made the field ring with her plantation melodies. She had been married about a year, and her child was about two months old. She was called the swiftest cotton picker on the place, but since the birth of her child it had been somewhat of a burden for her to perform her daily task. It seemed as though she had not gained her natural vigor and strength.

The day we now refer to, Nancy's child had been fretting and crying for the want of care; and, in fact, it only lacked a few minutes of the time to hear the blowing of the dinner horn, which was sure to be heard by the time we could reach the end of the row, which was only a few rods away. Nancy was doing her level best to reach the end of the row and care for her hungry child. In fact the whole gang were doing their best to reach the end of the row before the blowing of the dinner horn. Not a song was being sung; not a word spoken; not a sound could be heard, only a steady click, click, click, click of the the fingers of three hundred Negros splitting cotton pods, with the heavy tread of half a dozen Negro drivers just behind them. Nancy was a few feet in the lead of all of us, earnestly struggling to reach the end of the row and nurse her hungry child. Dick Fallon came riding by the plantation from Monroe, where he had been on one of his usual debauches since early in the morning, and on hearing the cry of Nancy's child he leaped from his horse, and came stalking across the field toward us, and the fearful glitter in his eyes and the smell of his breath was a signal that his mission was one of blood. Walking up to the Negro driver that was in the rear of the gang, just behind Nancy, he thus addressed him: "What in h — — l have you got that d — — n little nigger squalling that way for? I could hear it before I left the city;" and before the overseer could answer him he snatched the heavy bull-whip from the overseer's hand, and, approaching Nancy, said to her: "D — — n you; I will stop that brat's crying and set you to squalling in its place;" and as he spoke a blaze of fire seemed to follow the copper wire lash as the heavy whip whistled in its lightning descent upon Nancy's child. The terrible blow even severed the strap by which the child was bound to its mother's back and the infant fell to the ground, and as the mother was bending over it to raise it to her bosom, Fallon snatched the bloody corpse from the ground and threw it in her face. Yes, it was clay! it was a corpse! for the wire lash had plowed its way deep into the left side of the young child's neck and severed its jugular vein as complete as if cut with a razor. Just then the dinner bell was heard, and Fallon went stalking across the field, mounted his horse and went riding homeward to his "dinner," after shedding innocent blood. A complete murderer — — Cain and Abel. Little did he dream, or care, that in all the walks of life, "Thou God seest me." Little did he dream that Justice, the swift and sure messenger of God, was making long and rapid strides and drawing nearer and nearer.

The young mother raised the lifeless form to her breast and turned her eyes toward heaven, as if to catch one glimpse of its ascending spirit, and then she fell into the line with the three hundred other slaves that were slowly wending their way toward their cabins for an hour's rest and consume their scanty meals.

It was a complete funeral procession, silent and speechless; not a voice could be heard, not a word was spoken; there were no Negro melodies, no passing of jokes. The only voices heard were the sweet notes of the mocking birds echoing from the surrounding tree tops-for even the birds seemed to realize our sad situation and were chanting a funeral song while the spirit of the little one rose and was speeding its way to God, from whence it came. It was on the day of that terrible event and standing in the presence of that lifeless form that I swore, in silence, a righteous oath — — that I would have my liberty or die; and from that very hour I began to manufacture different plans by which to make my escape, but I was merely building castles in the air. To think of escape was merely to meditate on performing an impossibility. Little did I dream of what a tremendous task I had before me, ere I eluded the vigilance of my master's Negro drivers and human. blood-hounds. I had not calculated on what a vast tract of land there was for me to cross ere I was safely beyond the reach of Dick Fallon's grasp, and beyond the keen scent of old master's hounds. I had not calculated on the many adversities and calamities that beset the pathways of pedestrians in a free land; much less the dangers and accidents that are ever haunting an escaping slave. I did not know that since black slavery was inaugurated that not one slave in ten thousand had made their escape from Louisiana and successfully reached the land of free soil and free men, Canada, which forty years ago was the only safe place of shelter for a negro on the Western Hemisphere.

The only effectual means for a human being to foil blood hounds when being pursued by them, is to saturate your foot prints with water, thereby erasing the scent and makes it impossible for them to keep your trail. Water has the same effect on deadening the scent from foot prints on any kind of soil, as it does on erasing the smell from any kind of clothing. It is a false idea to believe that by rubbing pepper and other articles on the feet and keeping them in your stockings will make it impossible for the hounds to follow you. There is no possible way to thwart those well trained blood hounds, only by leaving water in each foot print. I have know refugees to bore small holes in the bottom of their boots or shoes and keep them well filled with water, and by so doing sprinkle their tracks and make it impossible for the hounds to follow the trail.

Escaping slaves always choose a rainy night. About three weeks after Fallon committed that horrible crime, my plans were complete by which to make my escape, and I determined to execute them at once. It was one of the darkest nights I ever beheld, and the rain was pouring down as though a river had burst its banks in the heavens and was determined to drag or wash the whole State of Louisiana into the Gulf of Mexico. Blinding flashes of lightning seemed to run along on the ground, and the ground was rolling from the effects of thunder shocks, like the water rolls on the ocean. It was a night like the beginning of Noah's deluge.

CHAPTER III
THE ESCAPE — PURSUED BY BLOOD HOUNDS — THE CAPTURE — THE PUNISHMENT

THIS was the night I selected to start on my journey to that free land of Canada, which I knew was somewhere under the North Star. About ten o'clock at night I selected the swiftest mule on the plantation and started for Lake Providence, which is about ninety miles north-east of Monroe, and situated on the Mississippi River.

My intentions were to ride that mule until nearly day light, and then turn him loose and let him go back to the plantation as he often did when taken from home and turned loose. And then my intentions were to secrete myself in the swamp during the day, and resume my journey at night.

The mule traveled like a deer for more than four hours, and it must have been very near three o'clock in the morning, (for the roosters were crowing) when the old mule changed his mind. All at once he stopped, and I kept straight on over his head for about ten feet, and landed on my stomach in six inches of mud and water.

When I regained my footing he was standing just where I had left him when I went over his head. I again climbed on to his back and told him to go ahead, but he never moved no more than if he had been a dead mule. I patted him on the neck awhile and then again urged him to go ahead, and he turned around and looked me in the face, as if to say:

"I know just what you are doing; you are running away," and all at once he turned around in a perfect circle for about five minutes and then started like the wind.

I have often believed that mule circled around in order to make me lose my bearing, for it had been running for some time before I was aware he was carrying me back over the same road which I had come; and I never saw any living animal run as that mule was running, and all my endeavors to check his speed were of no avail; so I leaped from his back and I have never spoken to a mule since, and I do not care to have anything to do with mules again.

Dear reader, you cannot even imagine what a predicament I was in. To return to my cabin before the blowing of the horn was impossible, for I was more than thirty miles away. It was Fallon's edict that every slave that failed to form in line ten minutes after the sounding of the horn, at four o'clock, should receive one hundred lashes.

My clothing was completely saturated with mud and water, which made me look more like a big mud turtle than a human being. I was in a land where every white man was a Negro catcher, and every black man was worth his weight in gold.

But something was to be done, and at once, for the rain had ceased to fall and the clouds were scattering in every direction; and by the morning star that was slowly moving up the horizon I knew day was breaking. I left the highway and waded through mud and swamp land until I reached the dense forest, and then continued my journey for a mile or two back in the forest and climbed a cypress tree. The fringe on a cypress tree is sufficient to make it impossible to discover a man except by close observation, after he has climbed twenty-five or thirty feet from the ground.

I was not afraid of being captured that day, unless by mere accident, for I was satisfied that the rain had not only made it impossible for the hounds to follow my trail, but it had also erased my foot prints on the main highway. I selected the forks of a tree and lashed myself to the limbs with cypress bark and was soon fast asleep. In my dreams I was again with my father and mother in my log cabin 'way up in old Virginia.

During the day I remained in my hiding place and I was greatly refreshed by my day's rest, and the dry atmosphere had completely dried my clothing, and it was an easy matter for me to rid my clothing of the greater part of the mud and dirt, by pounding and shaking them, and as soon as darkness began to settle over the forest I cautiously began to look around for a sweet potato patch, or some other means to satisfy my stomach. And after having filled up on googer nuts (or peanuts) and sweet potatoes, I re-filled my water bottle and started on my journey toward the town of Lake Providence, but my progress was very slow, as well as irksome, for I was compelled to keep clear of the highway, and traveled across fields and swamps that were filled wit insects and poisonous serpents. Compelled to travel under the cover of darkness, with no guide except the Mississippi River, and no light but the North Star. I did not dare to venture near a habitation of any kind, for fear of arousing all the blood hounds in the neighborhood, and I was also aware that Dick Fallon and his man eaters were at that very hour scouring the country for my capture. You who live in palaces and sleep in a feather bed, can never imagine the hardships of the man who is traveling through mud and swamps in the dead hours of night, with no shelter but the canopy of heaven, and was startled at the rustle of every leaf, and the chirping of every cricket seemed to cry out "Stop him, there he goes!" and imagine he could hear voices whispering in the still midnight air. I knew it was useless for me to think of venturing near the public road, before I reached Lake Providence, which was the safest place for me to cross the river, and get out of the State of Louisiana. It was a beautiful starlight night, not a cloud was visible, and I traveled as rapid as possible, until the morning star arose high in the heavens. Then I again retreated to the forest, and selected the forks of a tree for my hiding place during the day. On the third night of my escape I arrived at Lake Providence about one o'clock in the morning, and securing a row boat, I safely crossed the river into the State of Mississippi, and continued my journey a few miles along the banks of the river, and then, concealed myself in the swamp.

I was unaware of the vigilance kept along the banks of the Mississippi river between Vicksburg and Memphis for the capture of runaway slaves. I was not aware that both sides of the river was being patrolled night and day by those who made their livelihood by capturing escaped slaves, and thereby securing the rewards, which were frequently as high as five hundred dollars if captured alive, and one-half that sum for their dead bodies.

I did not know that blood hounds were let loose at all the accessible places of crossing in order to scent the tracks of any one who might have crossed the river during the night unobserved. But I was soon made aware of these facts. About nine o'clock in the morning, while snugly perched in the forks of a tree, I heard the old familiar howl of hounds, and although the sound was a long distance from me, yet I was sure a human being was being pursued.

But whether it was myself or some one else I was not able to determine. Blood hounds are not fleet until within a few rods of their game. About five miles an hour is their ordinary gait when following a cold trail, or when their game is two or three miles ahead of them; but as they draw nearer they double their speed, and they never tire and are as unerring as time itself. I have known them to follow a trail for five consecutive days and win their game. The owners of them generally follow on horseback and about a mile in the rear.

About ten minutes after hearing the first echos of their howls it was repeated, but was much nearer and more distinct; and then I knew that it was myself that was being pursued, and I determined to foil them if possible. I at once left my hiding place and started for the river, which was about a mile away, and when having run about two-thirds of the distance they gave me another one of their terrible warnings that they were not more than a half mile behind me.

The thoughts of freedom and the dread of Dick Fallon renewed my energy and doubled my speed in my superhuman efforts to reach the river. It was a race against time, a run for my life. I knew that if I could reach the river it was possible to elude them by wading into the water along the bank, and then retracing a few miles of my journey. The canebrake and underbrush that grew along the banks would conceal me, and the water would cover my trail. But it was a task beyond human strength and human speed to execute, for as I neared the river the ground would not bear my weight only by slow and cautious tread. I was wading in six inches of mud and water, and the bogs and mounds were trembling and sinking beneath my feet, and another tremendous howl from a score of those pursuing man eaters made my blood run cold; for they were not more than one hundred rods behind me, while twice that distance must be traveled ere I could reach the river. It was sure death for me to be run down by that swarm of hunting tigers, for the men on horseback were perhaps a mile away, and I knew I would be torn limb from limb before they could possibly arrive.

I knew I must leave the ground, and very speedily, for as I cast one backward glance, I saw the grass swaying and splitting and the canebrake was cracking and falling, as the hounds came rushing after me, and not more than fifty rods away. A small cypress tree stood about ten rods to my left and my life depended on my ability to reach it.

Reader, picture the scene, if possible, of a man running for his life and a score of mad hounds pursuing him to drink his blood. There were no chasms, no cliffs, no places of concealment, no possible chance of escape, except by reaching that cypress tree and ascending beyond their reach ere they came sweeping down upon me. It was the crisis of my life, and although it happened nearly fifty years ago, yet it startles me, even now in my old age.

I succeeded in reaching the cypress tree, and had not a minute to spare, for before I was ten feet from the ground I was surrounded by twenty-one of the largest and most ferocious looking blood hounds I ever saw; and I was still in great danger, for the tree was not more than six inches in diameter, and I was afraid of its being uprooted or torn down before the men on horseback could arrive. They would have succeeded in doing this had I not begun to throw my clothing among them. First I threw my hat and coat, which they tore into shreds in less time than I could relate it. Then I hurled my old shoes at them, which only deterred some of them for perhaps a minute; and at last I hurled my pants among them, which they consumed as speedily as they had the rest of my clothing. And then they at once began digging and tearing at the roots of the tree. Then I began to realize that the end was near, for the tree had begun to reel and totter just as the men on horses hove in sight; and one shrill sound of the bugle was sufficient to cause those well-trained animals to cease their efforts to devour me, and it also caused them to form a complete circle at the root of the tree. It may not be generally known that well-trained blood hounds can be called from the chase by the sounding of the bugle in the hands of their owner, and the same means is also used as a signal for them to renew the chase, and they will readily obey the bugle at any distance within its sound.

When they were within a few rods of me I observed they were seven in number, and I was greatly relieved to see that Dick Fallon was not among them; but, as I have previously stated, it was a party of men that make their living by catching runaway Negroes.

They all dismounted and the one that seemed to be the leader of the party thus addressed me:

"Hello! up there, you black gorilla; what are you doing up there? Don't you know that cocoanuts don't grow on cypress trees? Come down from there, d___n quick, too."

And I immediately obeyed them.

When I had descended to the ground the following conversation passed between us:

"Where is your clothing?"

"The dogs tore them up, master."

"Yes, and you are d___d lucky they did not tear you up. Who are you anyhow? Who's nigger are you? Why, you look like Adam in the garden of Eden. Where do you hail from, and where were you heading to?"

I replied that my home was in old Virginia and I was on my way to Canada, for I did not want them to know that I belonged to Dick Fallon and I was in hopes they would send me back to old Virginia.

I was asked a great many questions concerning Virginia; all of which I was able to answer, for it was the land where I was born and nurtured; but when I was asked why I was in Mississippi if I belonged in Virginia and on my way to Canada I could not make a satisfactory reply.

It was only a matter of time for them to find my owner, for it was customary with them, when they captured a runaway slave, to advertise for the owner and also give a general description of the captured Negro, a process which made it almost impossible for the master not to know the whereabouts of his property.

Of course I was to be kept in jail during the time of the inquiry. They were somewhat puzzled in regards how to supply me with clothing suitable to convey me through the streets of Lake Providence, for the dogs had torn my clothing so fine that there was not enough left to cover the back of a good-sized rabbit, and one of the men suggested that it would be well to take enough skin off my back to make a suit of clothes for me. Finally I was supplied with a horse blanket and was commanded to wrap it around my body in true Indian style, and we all began to retrace our journey toward Lake Providence, which was perhaps some five or six miles away.

I was confined in jail at Lake Providence, with twenty-three other runaways that were held for identification by their owners and the offering of a satisfactory reward, and all of them had been captured by the same party that captured me.

There was one man held in confinement, of whom I will relate a circumstance that happened while I was in jail and of which I was an eye witness. He had escaped from a planter in the northwestern part of Louisiana by the name of Robert Johnson, and was captured while crossing the Mississippi river at Lake Providence and was jailed at that place. His master had seen the advertisement and had come after him. I had frequently heard him say that he would never be carried back alive; and surely he was justified in his declaration, for from the crown of his head to the sole of his feet it would have been impossible to have found a square inch that was not gashed with the lash, and his clothing was glued to his flesh with the exudation from running sores.

About three weeks after I had been confined in jail I was standing at the grated window talking to him. It was just before twelve o'clock noon, when we observed two men coming up the street toward the jail. One of the men was the Sheriff of the jail and the other was his old master; and the minute he saw his master a stream of a fire seemed to leap from his eyes, and he said to me: "Yonder comes Master Roberts after me and he will take his dinner in h — — l; for I shall kill him the minute he steps inside of this door;" and as he spoke he seized one of the railings of the bunk on which we slept and with the strength of a tiger he wrenched the solid scantling from its place and glided behind the door, which swung inward when opened.

The keys rattled, the heavy door swung on its rusty hinges and his master stepped inside the jail without the least suspicion of harm or that death was at hand. Why, there crouched near Robert Johnson a human lion, with the scorching thoughts of wife and babe, who had been sold only a few days before.

There was a man near him whom he had robbed of his wife and child, robbed of his freedom, robbed of his God-given rights; yes, and even robbed him of the skin that covered his back, and then had come to return him to that caldron of misery that was boiling with the white flame of despair. What comes next? Why, what do you expect to hear?

Like a lion that springs from the mountain cliff, the slave leaped from his hiding place and a trail of smoke seemed to follow his uplifted club as it came rushing down upon the head of his cruel master. It was an awful blow. I don't believe so powerful a blow was ever struck before or since by any man. The solid beam, or club, was torn into shavings, and Robert Johnson was a *headless* man, for his head had been swept from his shoulders as completely as if struck by a solid rock shot from the mouth of a volcano.

There was more sympathy manifested in behalf of the Negro than might be expected, considering the crime and place and the vast distinction between slave and master. But it must be remembered that, with the exception of Dick Fallon, Robert Johnson was the most inhuman Negro driver in all the Southern States, and had incurred the ill-will of many of the surrounding planters by his cruel treatment of his Negroes, for his cruelty was the cause of frequent escapes of his slaves and thereby inciting the slaves of surrounding planters to follow their example, and living in the northern part of the State and near the line made it possible for many of their escapes to prove successful. Therefore when he was slayed by one of his own Negroes there was an unusual amount of sympathy manifested in behalf of the slave; and at his trial he was stripped of his clothing in order to impress upon the jurymen the justification for the deed.

And surely he was a pitiable sight to behold. In many places on his back the bare bones were glistening, for his skin was entirely flayed from his body. One of the jurymen exclaimed: "Why! that Negro must surely be Lazarus raised from the grave.

But public opinion was too strong against the Negro those days to let a slave slay his master and then go unpunished. It made no difference in regard to the justification of the act in behalf of the slave.

The jury concluded that if they exonerated the Negro in this case it would be the cause of inciting others to follow his example. He was found guilty and sentenced to be hanged.

There was a very strong petition presented to Governor Palmer, who was then Governor of the State, for the commutation of the sentence to life imprisonment. The petition was formulated and presented by many of the most influential planters in the State. It was finally successful and the Governor commuted the sentence. But when the documents arrived that was to save the life of the condemned man, John Knox, who was then jailor and sheriff, had hanged the Negro just twenty-one minutes before the messenger came.

I was in jail nearly two months before my master was aware of my whereabouts, although I was less than one hundred miles from him. The facilities for conveying news throughout the Southern States were not so great fifty years ago as they are to-day. But at last the advertisement had the desired effect, and two months after my confinement in jail I heard the hoofs of a horse rattling in the street, and on looking out of the window I saw Dick Fallon dismount.

My identification by Fallon and his men was speedy and complete, and I was brought back to the same old home of misery and distress. I was well aware there was a terrible punishment in store for me, and my only desire was to have it over with as soon as possible, but the thought of it was neither alarming nor frightening. Even death itself would have been a cherished friend. For the gaunt specter of disasters and misfortunes had haunted my path until their horrible appearance had become familiar, and I no longer had either fear or trembling while crossing their dismal plain.

We arrived at Monroe about three o'clock Sunday afternoon, and in less than an hour thereafter I was chained to a post a few feet from a bee-hive and given one hundred and twenty-five lashes, then I was blindfolded in order to protect my eyesight, and the swarm of bees was irritated by throwing sand upon them and immediately my bare and bleeding back was completely punctured by their stings. The pain was terrible; it was as though my whole body was on fire; I was in more torment than Dante ever depicted in his frightful illustration of Inferno. My pain was beyond mortal endurance and human strength had forsaken me, and I became insensible to pain or torture.

It is a blessing that human beings are so constructed that when being tortured they are only sensible to pain until it reaches a certain degree of severity, and when that limit is reached they elapse into a comatose state, and for the time being they are invulnerable to pain.

I must have remained in a state of insensibility for hours, for when I aroused from my stupor the night was far spent and I was lying in my cabin, having been carried there soon after dark by Fallon's command. I was in a horrible state; my back was swollen until I looked as if my stomach was on the wrong side of me and gave me the appearance, when moving around my cabin, as though I was continually walking backward.

More than a month elapsed before I was capable of performing any kind of manual labor, and during all of those days of my confinement and torture I never relinquished my desire and intentions to escape at the first opportunity that was offered me. But time doth glide so swiftly by that to-day and to-morrow seems only to change their places. To-day we are born and to-morrow we are buried. Having lived our three score years and ten, in one swing of the pendulum of time, and only one glance at eternity's dial. From the day of our birth it seems as if the thought of the cradle and the grave have been our only companions.

* * * * * * *

Ten months swept by, which were more perplexing to Fallon than all the previous years of his life; for from the very day he committed that inhuman and bloody act, gloom and disasters began to hover around the old plantation; his own soil frowned on him and refused to pursue its natural productiveness. One-half of the cotton seed, when planted, refused to spring into life and would remain in the same condition as though it had not been sown. It was like sowing pebbles; and that portion of the seed that sprung up might just as well have remained in the ground, for all the cotton worms in the State left their accustomed places of destruction and congregated in Fallon's cotton field, while premature frosts and whirlwinds would play havoc with his cotton and leave adjoining plantations undisturbed.

His plantation could justly boast of possessing a thousand head of the finest blooded stock that could be found in all the Southern States; but they seemed to wither away and die, and in less than one year nearly one-third of his stock died from disease or accident.

During this grand carnival of just retribution he was in a terrible rage. There is no mode of expression known among men that could possibly portray his acts or definitely express his disregard of the warnings of God. He was simply a demon roaming the earth, with the huge billows of his coming destruction lashing around him. Thus it is that men go rushing on to sure death, deceived by the very prudential warnings that speak with all the voices in nature's chest and whispers in our ear.

The thought never occurred to him that he was in the red channel of the long prepared destiny of his own construction. The thought never entered his mind that the All Seeing Eye is ever discerning the affairs and acts of men. He believed the affairs of the world to be abandoned to chance, and all his hopes and meditations were centralized in accumulating wealth and recreation. He delighted in tears and groans and immolated human beings without mercy. He was beyond the voice of his own conscience and was incapable of seeing the limits of the acts of men and the mercy of God. His religion was that men could only be governed by fear and cruelty; it is a wicked and terrible opinion and is sure to recoil with a tremendous force on those by whom they are diffused or executed.

The cabins were built on three sides of the plantation, thus forming a complete hollow square around it. There were about three hundred cabins all told and each of them contained two or three rooms, with an average of ten inhabitants per cabin; and for years it had been a practice to congregate at different places on the plantation in the evening and enjoy themselves, as is customary with the black race under all circumstances. There were frequently as many as eight or ten different dances in progress the same night. These dances were called "dusty shuffles," for they were usually performed on the ground in the open air. Where they were held the ground had become beaten as hard as a rock and smooth as glass. They were usually held on moonlight nights, although frequently held on dark nights by the aid of the lights from pine tree knots fixed to an iron rod driven in the ground.

There were many fiddles, banjos and tamborines on the place, all of which were made by the Negroes themselves; bone players were numerous and in great demand, and scarcely was life extinct in an ox or horse before their ribs would be hanging up to dry for the bone players.

The favorite dances were the "Old Virginia Reel" and "Old Jim Crow," and frequently the music would be furnished by many horny hands patting and singing something like this:

"When I lay down to take a little snoot,
A flea and bull frog slid in my boot;

Quick time — —
Bull frog holler, flea he sting;
Den I rise and cut the pijin wing.

Chorus — —
Den hustle and shuffle and sift, sift, sift!
Den hustle and shuffle and sift, sift, sift!

Den I lay down in de middle of de night,
'Long come a skeeter and take one bite,
He wipe him lips and begin to sing,
Den I rise and cut the pijin wing."

Dick Fallon delighted in having such sports among his slaves, for it gave the impression to the score of his contemporaries, whom he brought to see them, that he was just and kind to them.

Some of his serfs would congregate in sacred worship, and they were imperatively commanded not to forget to pray "O Lord, make us obedient servants," a command which they strictly obeyed, not only to satisfy the demand of their rulers, but to satisfy the demand of their consciences. Filial duty was born in them, and human affection had been taught them from the lips of babbling brooks and from the fragrant smell of lilies and roses. To them all nature was a prayer-book and every day an eternal sermon.

Wherever they were, whether in the fields or in their cabins or hanging to the whipping posts, they raised toward heaven innocent hands and pure hearts, filled with the love that makes the whole world kin.

They followed the golden rule, "Do unto others as you would have them do unto you." All their study was how to please and assist all of those around them, whether master or slave, and they did solemnly kneel in prayer for those who were spitefully using them. Mutual affection was the anchor of their hopes and the pillar of their soul. These sentiments were the guiding star of their fathers and had been transmitted to them from time immemorial.

They knew no other philosophy but universal beneficence and resignation to their fate, which seems to be the will of God. But during the last year all of their evening sports and hilarity had disappeared and their religious meetings seemed to be on the wane. There was less fervency in their prayers and vacancy in their numbers. Their nights of worship became scarce and unwelcome. Like the children of Israel they began to wander away and worship strange gods.

The natural and inevitable result followed. They became morose and even suspicious of each other, and many of them were contemplating whether a providence ever existed at all. Their actions were neither strange nor inconsiderate, for there are times in this life that our adversities seem so dreadful and unmerited, that the confidence, even of the wisest, is frequently staggered. They no longer looked to nature and surrounding scenes for their guide and sympathy. Sleep was no longer their balm. Food neither revived their decaying hopes nor stimulated their vanishing pleasure.

It is not surprising that those illiterate people, who were born and raised on the plantation, and many of them never were beyond its limits, should become spiritually depressed until they were atheistical in their opinions and beliefs; and being naturally superstitious, all manner of horrible imaginations took possession of their brain. Superstition is diffused all over the world; but it is more prevalent among the atheistical and illiterate masses than in the intellectual lands of Bibles and spelling books.

Religious opinions and beliefs are an absolute necessity in order to make men strong, vigorous and intelligent, as well as courageous. If it was possible to make all men in civilized America forsake their beliefs in a deity, then every mother's babe that now sleeps in its crib would be weighted with charms to scare away witches and magpies, and every school urchin would see ghosts and hobgoblins lurking in every corner.

Before the days of Wesley, Guttenberg and Luther all Europe was overrun with witches and fairies.

These facts were verified among Fallon's slaves. Their superstitious thoughts augmented in their minds until they became veritable facts; and at last horrible sights were so numerous that none would venture out after nightfall, but would huddle together in their cabins and converse in whispers, and the whole plantation became as silent as the grave.

Many of the slaves began to believe that Dick Fallon was not an ordinary being, and verified their beliefs with many fabulous sights and tales concerning him. There was a magnificent fountain on the place and at its base there was a small-sized lake or pool, and if the plantation tradition concerning its waters were true, then it must have possessed the most miraculous qualities known since the days of the famous pool of Siloam and other Oriental places of bathing; or else Dick Fallon possessed the power of bodily transformation.

By the aid of science and experience we are forced to believe there are times when the air possesses mirrorizing qualities or power of reflecting different objects. Navigators on a large body of water have frequently seen cities that were hundreds of miles away distinctly photographed in the clouds over their heads. Perhaps it is an inexplicable phenomena, and is simply called a mirage.

Many of us have frequently noticed, when standing on a river's bank alone, that a perfect double mirage, or two shadows of ouselves were distinctly visible in the water's depths. These facts just related, may somewhat clear up the mystery concerning the pool, for it was customary with Fallon to bathe in this pool, and it was a prevalent belief on the plantation that when the fog was rising from the fountain at a certain hour in the morning that he was frequently seen floating in mid-air in the center of the fog, and his face was often seen reflecting on the surface of the water, when he was known to be miles away. The plantation was ten miles long, and Fallon was frequently seen at either end of it at the same time. Many other such stories were whispered in the cabins in the evening, and they were told with true sincerity and candor. Although the tales were all ignisfatuus and unfounded.

The dimensions of this gigantic plantation called the Purgoo Kingdom have frequently been stated in this book; and all over its vast domain Fallon's iron hand was felt. In order to make the governing process systematic and complete, Purgoo, the owner of the plantation, had four large bells manufactured. These bells were made in Paris, the planter's home, and were of the finest quality and had been used on the plantation for nearly a quarter of a century. They were so located as to be in hearing distance of each other; and at the necessary time, such as working and meal hours, etc., the overseer that lived near the first bell would signal for the ringing of it by blowing a silver whistle, and immediately the man selected for that purpose would ring bell No. 1, and it was a signal for the next one to it to ring, and in this manner only a few seconds elapsed between the first stroke of the bells on either end of the Purgoo Kingdom that they all seemed to ring together, and three thousand human beings moved around the farm as though they were only one. They all dropped their hoe or bundle of cotton at the same time and filed into line and went marching to their cabins.

All four of the bells had in the course of time received a nickname applicable to some peculiarity connected with them. Hence one of the bells was known by the name of "Weeping Mary," simply because it had such a lamentable sound. Another was called "Whistling Dick," deriving its name from its keen and piercing tone which was so keen and clear it was frequently heard all over the Purgoo Kingdom. But the most comical name among the bells was the one called "Stuttering Tom." This name had been applied to the bell from its peculiar sound caused by a split near its base and gave a suppressed or a smothered sound. But the last bell and the sweetest sounding bell in the State of Louisiana was called "Singing Nancy;" it had derived its name from the fact of its being situated near Nancy's cabin and its charming sound; it was surely a musical sounding bell, and was worthy of performing a more sacred mission. It was somewhat amusing to hear the many jests made concerning these bells just prior to meal time.

At one end of the plantation some weary and hungry soul would cry out, "Oh, weep Mary, weep," and away in the distance could be heard another voice shouting, "Oh, whistle Dick, whistle," "Oh, stutter Tom, stutter," "Oh, sing Nancy, sing." Echos from such voices could be heard ringing over fourteen square miles.

Old Uncle Joe, was the most aged human being on the plantation, and perhaps the oldest in the State, his age was not accurately known, but he was certainly an octogenarian, if not a centenarian. His flesh had entirely withered away until there was nothing left of him but shriveled skin and bone. But his hearing and eyesight were clear and unclouded, although the many years of his life had annihilated him physically. His daily labor consisted in ringing and polishing "Whistling Dick," the first bell, and by his occupation he had gained the sobriquet or nickname of "Bell Ringing Joe," a title he considered as eulogistic as that of General in the army.

"Bell Ringing Joe" was a very devout and a conscientious man, and unshaken in his belief of immortality. But his theory of life in the next world was that all mankind will pursue occupations in the next life which will correspond with their general pursuits in this life. And when questioned in regard to what occupation he expected to pursue in the next world, he was sure to reply: "Ise gwine to polish and ring Whistling Dick," and by what followed many were forced to believe his prophecy was correct and fulfilled.

CHAPTER IV
NANCY'S DREAM — A TERRIBLE BLOW — GLOOM — BELLS TOLLING IN THE SKY

WHAT is a dream? Who can answer? We are told that man is the offspring of his own meditation, and his thoughts constitute the basis of his soul. We know that frequently our dreams are the substance, or the reflection of our thoughts upon the brain after the body is asleep, and we must admit that we are more liable to dream at night concerning the vocations of the day.

Who can tell but what a man's thoughts or his soul steals away while the body is slumbering and wanders back through the channels where the body accompanied during the day, and further still. A man's thoughts are a commoner of the universe and wherever it wanders it is still on its own domain.

Life begins and ends in dreams, from the sleeping smile in the cradle to the babbling over the death bed as worn out nature sinks into the last sleep of all. Whoever thinks they can solve the mysteries of a dream, let them try and they will fail. The fountain formed a ring in the center of a grove, and its borders were strewn with various kinds of flowers and roses, and it was a place where Nancy was frequently found on the Sabbath day watching the sprays from the fountain gracefully curving in the air and forming rainbows in the glare of the midday sunbeams. It was on this Sabbath day while reclining beneath a rose bush she went to sleep, and dreamed that Dick Fallon rose out of the pool, and his head was a solid coal of fire and the rest of his body solid ice. And from the tremendous heat from his fiery head was reflected his face in the depths of his body, but the body still retained its original and icy appearance with Fallon's solidified face glittering within its depths.

All at once there was a crash in mid air and a meteor came rushing downward upon the statue, and fell with an awful crash; and she leaped to her feet, for her sleep had been broken by a deafening thunder peal. One glance toward the sky was sufficient to satisfy her that the impending storm was not one of the ordinary kind. The twisting and circling of the clouds and blue flashes of lightning mingling with a thousand confusing noises and the thunder peals plainly predicted the re-appearance of a Southern cyclone, the king of storms, which for years have been more destructive to Southern property and is more dreaded by the inhabitants than all the combined epidemical diseases inherent to Southern clime.

Nancy started to her cabin with her natural speed, which characterized her the queen of athletes among her sex. And surely she was the queen. I can truthfully assert that she was the most agile damsel on the plantation, and perhaps unequalled in all the Southern States. Her athletic movements may have been the only shield that protected her life, for lagging at her heels was the most destructive cyclone that ever horrified the Southern States.

The storm came from the southwest and swept across the plantation in a northeast direction, thereby cutting it in half from the southwest to the northeast corners. It left death and destruction in its wake. Only those who have witnessed a Southern cyclone can form any adequate idea of its destructive power. Its awful fury was not more than one-half mile in width and everything within its path was forced to disappear. The air was filled with flying debris, and huge trees that had resisted the storms of centuries were wrenched from their places and lifted high in the air; and many of them were reduced to kindling wood. Many slave huts were raised to a dizzy height and then hurled back to the earth again with a tremendous force, and the lifeless forms of forty slaves were buried in the wreck.

The storm continued to rage from four o'clock Sunday afternoon until near midnight. But the greatest damage was wrought during the first half hour.

Monday morning the sun rose bright and clear and Dick Fallon gazed at the ruins in complete silence, and then with an oath remarked, "that he could not see how in h — —l the sun can dare to shine on his premises to-day, when it would not shine yesterday." He immediately issued an order that every human being on the place should begin at once at clearing away the debris and wreckage caused by the storm.

And in fact there was nothing else to do, for all the agricultural products had disappeared; not a stack of grain or bale of cotton could be found on the Purgoo Kingdom.

After issuing the order, Fallon entered his palatial studio, and began writing the following letter to Paris, France.

MONROE, LA., October 1st 18 — —.

Mr. W. H. Purgoo: — —

DEAR SIR: — —I am compelled to covey to you a missive, the contents of which I would like to have of a different nature. But your presence is surely needed here, for your plantation has been baptised with the d — — — — storms on record. If you was here at present and could behold the farm you would be forced to believe it had been raining dead horses, mules and dead niggers for a month. A cyclone passed over the plantation yesterday and it was loaded to the very muzzle with all manner of rubbish and carcasses it could gather between here and the rocky mountains, and it dumped its whole load on this plantation. Whole trees are stacked on the farm that were uprooted in another State, Mississippi. Forty of your niggers were killed, and more are dying, and two-thirds of our blooded stock are buried under the debris. "Bell Ringing Joe" was killed and "Whistling Dick" was carried away in the storm. I can't give you the accurate account of our loss until the wrecks are moved. I shall look for a reply, so please remember I am, truly yours,

D. K. FALLON.

A few weeks later he received the following reply:

PARIS, FRANCE, October 29, 18 — —.

Mr. D. K. Fallon: — —

DEAR SIR: — —Your letter, which arrived to-day, not only surprises me but even surpasses my imagination. You will please receive my sincere condolence and sympathy in your hours of sad misfortune. The loss of our blooded stock and "Whistling Dick" is not only a priceless one, but irreparable.

The loss of the darkies is only a secondary matter of consideration. Niggers are a very cheap article at present, and the sentiments of your Northern Yankees are daily depreciating the value of slaves. It is strongly advocated and predicted in Europe that the United States will ere long have an Abolitionist President, and I have been thinking of selling about one-half of my niggers before there comes a permanent depression in the slave market.

The day before I received your sad letter I promised to Tuebor & Co., manufacturing establishment, ten thousand bales of cotton at a pretty fair figure, and it was to be delivered by the last of the year. So you will please purchase all the available cotton from surrounding planters on the quiet, for the cotton market is rising very rapidly in Europe.

I will come to you the latter part of next month and have another bell cast which I will bring with me, but do not expect that it will replace "Whistling Dick."

Please have ten thousand bales ready for shipment by the time I arrive there.

Remember I am yours as ever,

W. H. PURGOO.

The work of clearing away the debris was a herculean task, and it taxed the combined energy of the plantation for many weeks, for it was strewn with all kinds of rubbish imaginable. The place was covered with carcasses and drift wood to a depth that in many places covered the roofs of the cabins. Huge trees had been brought from miles away and hurled to the earth with their limbs downward and with sufficient force to bury them to a depth that left them standing inverted.

Bell Ringing Joe lived beneath the roof of the building that supported "Whistling Dick," and the roof and bell were blown away in the cyclone and Uncle Joe was found bleeding and dying beneath the wreck.

The whole plantation was one solid mass of desolation, and can only be pictured when the mind reflects upon the appearance of the Garden of Eden the morning after the receding of the waters of Noah's deluge. More than a month was earnestly devoted toward making any visible impression of restoring order on the place. Fallon was very anxious to have it regenerated before the arrival of Purgoo, for already the foul air arising from the damp earth, and the humid atmosphere was heralding the approach of that epidemical king of contagions, the yellow fever.

All manner of tools and means of strength were brought into action. Fires illuminated the heavens night and day as they were slowly consuming the fallen trees, underbrush, etc. Spades, pick-axes and shovels were kept busy, and all the remaining beast of burden on the farm were constantly on the move. Perhaps, never before was a like number of human beings encumbered with such premonitions and laboring under such foreboding circumstances. For since the storm, both masters and slaves were confirmed in their convictions that the Purgoo Kingdom was being surrounded with all the plagues and accidents in the invisible chamber of horror, and that other mysterious and black shadows were slowly creeping down upon the place.

And their surmisings were well-founded, for misfortunes and disasters traveled the earth in pairs, and the familiar tones of "Whistling Dick" was heard in mid air and Fallon's name written on stone with a pen of flame.

For more than a month his time and attention had been occupied in a manner that prohibited him from purchasing the thousands of bales of cotton that Purgoo ordered in his letter, and during that time the news of Purgoo's disaster had been conveyed all over Europe, and all the great cotton establishments and manufactories had despatched their agents to America to buy cotton to tide them over the impending cotton crisis. All the cotton dealers in New Orleans, and in fact, Louisiana, had been divested of their cotton by these foreign agents. And when Fallon began to look for cotton bales, he found it was impossible for him to purchase only that of a very inferior grade, and unfit for shipment to a foreign market.

All the cotton crops had been harvested and sold and not a score of bales could be purchased by Fallon and his men. When Fallon found out the situation he was in, cold drops of sweat poured from his brow, for he was aware of his financial position and knew that by his habitual bacchanaling and damage wrought by the storm, that Purgoo's financial ruin was inevitable. Fallon's inebriety and licentiousness alone had reached to an enormous figure during the last few years. He had frequently lost ten thousand dollars in the club room in one night, and had often flipped coppers for a thousand dollars a throw; and there was great discontent between the Northern and Southern States and the value of slaves was daily on the wane.

* * * * * * *

A few days prior to the time for Purgoo's arrival the plantation had begun to assume a more presentable appearance, although only a fraction of the cyclone's work had been eradicated; but many cabins and huts had been erected and the plantation had been supplied with stables, sheds, etc. All the buildings upon which the bells were hoisted had been rebuilt upon the same spot they had previously occupied. The three remaining bells were uninjured and "Whistling Dick" was to be replaced with the bell that Purgoo had spoken of in his letter.

The day Purgoo arrived he looked steadily upon his place of ruin and said: "I was aware that a great damage had been done; but never had the least idea it was so thorough and complete as it is. Why, my plantation, when I last visited it five years ago, was the diamond of the Southern

States; but now it is only an African swamp and filled with all manner of filth and rubbish, even to hooting owls and croaking frogs."

Ever since the storm there had been considerable irregularity and delay in the progress of the work by being deprived of the most convenient means of signalizing the working hours. Consequently it was a few days after Purgoo's arrival before the bells were hoisted to the places which they were to occupy.

The bell that Purgoo had brought was larger than "Whistling Dick," and had been detained at New Orleans on account of its cumbersomeness and weight, and was to be conveyed to Monroe by the first up-bound boat. "Weeping Mary," "Stuttering Dick" and "Singing Nancy" were swung into their places in the evening and in the morning their charming echoes were again heard on the farm.

For more than a quarter of a century "Weeping Mary" had pealed forth its sad, sad tones; but never before had such lamentable echoes and complete strains of sadness been heard over the plantation. For a number of years "Whistling Dick" and "Weeping Mary" had been answering each other, and never before had the sound of "Weeping Mary" been heard when "Whistling Dick" did not follow. These bells had been answering each other until their echos seemed to be instantaneous and voluntary. Uncle Joe had frequently said that when you hear "Weeping Mary," "you is certain to hear 'Whistling Dick,' for if your Uncle Joe is not dar to rung him, den 'Whistling Dick' done gone and rung heself."

It was a beautiful day; not a cloud was visible between the green earth and the blue sky. The air was balmy and so clear that it seemed possible for the eye to wander upward until it pierced the very heavens. The noon hour was drawing near, and the silver whistle would soon again be heard and the bells signal the hour of rest. Three thousand human beings were anxiously waiting to hear the lamenting tones of "Weeping Mary," but they were unaware that the first peel of "Weeping Mary" would be answered by "Whistling Dick" in mid air.

Imagination plays a very conspicuous part in establishing many of the inexplicable occurrences that torture our minds and frequently make us unhappy during life. But by our own experiences we are forced to believe that things do occur which are certainly extraordinary. There is nothing which could create such disquietude and make us more unhappy for the time being, than the mysterious or unaccountable sounds and echoes the origin of which we can neither demonstrate nor satisfactory fathom.

Perhaps a sound could not be produced which would seem more strange and miraculous, than the tolling of a bell in mid air. The ordinary tolling of bells always create a feeling of awe and nervousness, and when heard from an invisible height would naturally create as great a sensation among a superstitious people, as the red finger when writing on the walls of the palace, create among the kings. It is not for us to assert, whether there is any basis to verify the belief in a supernatural power being connected with bells which are cast for sacred use. But tradition tells us, that during the middle ages, two church bells were being transported across the sea to a temple on the the Mediterranean coast and one of them was lost during a storm, and it is authentically stated that when the remaining bell was hoisted and began tolling the hours of sacred worship, that any one standing on the waters' banks could hear the lost bell answering its mate from the bottom of the sea.[1] In the year 1737 the hundred ton bell, "Monarch," at Moscow, did peal forth three of its deafening tones, three days prior to the tempest of flame that consumed the city. In ancient times it was a prevalent belief among superstitious people, that cymbals and hand bells had the power of driving away evil spirits.

> Get thee gone, and dig my grave thyself,
> And bid thy merry bells ring to thy ear
> That thou art crowned, not that I am dead.

The custom of tolling bells grew out of the belief that it dispersed the evil spirits that were hovering near the death bed to afflict the soul the moment when it escaped from the body. And from a remote antiquity, the tolling of bells has been regarded as a token of a soul passing out of the world. Although none of the incidents we have named may not have any direct bearing toward explaining the mysterious bell heard on the Purgoo Kingdom, but they do sustain the theory of inexplicable events.

On the day we now refer to, only a small white cloud was hovering between the earth and sky. Fallon and his Parisan visitor were sitting on the veranda considering their situation, and comparing the beautiful day with their surrounding adversities. The sincerity of their thoughts and arguments prohibited them from noting the nearness of the hour of noon, but three thousand slaves were aware that the sun stood direct over their heads, and only a few minutes separated them from an hour's rest. The noon hour arrived, the silver whistle was heard, and the solemn tones of "Weeping Mary" went crashing through the air, and all at once, dong, dong, dong, the sound of a bell was heard echoing from the etherial blue sky.

"Why, what is that?" exclaimed Purgoo as he leaped to his feet, pale and trembling and stood by the side of Fallon, who had also arose and was looking toward the heavens. "I will swear by my life," he exclaimed, "That that sound was the echo from "Whistling Dick." The invisible bell was distinctly heard, not only on the plantation, but by many of the inhabitants of Monroe.

The first peal from the invisible bell seemed as though it speeded downward from the clouds and came rushing upon the ear all at once, producing a trembling sound like the bells of a cathedral. The minds of masters and slaves received a new baptism of awe and superstitious dread.

The planter declared he would return to France as soon as possible, and said that he would not remain twenty-four hours on the plantation, not for the whole State of Louisiana, and his companion declared he could manage all the niggers on top of the earth, and did not fear any of them under the earth, but when bells began to toll over head it was more than he could stand, and said that he also would leave the old plantation and let old Joe and "Whistling Dick" run it.

Many theories and explanations were used in attempting to account for the mysterious sound, but all of them were countered with skepticism and universal doubt. But perhaps the most plausible explanation that will ever be given was the one attributing it to a bell bird, which may have wandered from its proper latitude and was returning from one of its aerial voyages to its native land.

The bell bird is found in some of the warmer parts of South America and is remarkable for the metalic resonance of its cry, which distinctly resembles the tolling of a bell. From its forehead protudes a strange tubular appendage or bag, which, when empty, is pendulous, but which can be filled with air by communication from the palate and then it is raised erect to the height of six or eight inches. Its tolling occurs at intervals varying from a minute to several minutes and can be heard to the distance of five miles and resounds through the forest not only at evening and morning, but also at midday, when the blazing sun imposes silence on all other creatures; and many travelers, when lost in the jungles of that tropical clime, have been known to perish by wandering from their proper course, by mistaking the tolling of the bell bird for the sound of a bell from some distant habitation. This is the most plausible explanation that can possibly be given in solving the problem of the tolling of a bell echoing from the sky.

The tolling of the mysterious bell was only another link in the superstitious chain of beliefs that was prevalent among the slaves on the plantation. And, although it was somewhat out of the ordinary channel of their superstitious occurrences, yet to them it was a visible event and easily solved, for many of the leaders in beholding unnatural sights, declared that at the the time the bell was heard tolling in the sky they distinctly saw "Bell Ringing Joe" seated on the edge of a snow white cloud and by his side was "Whistling Dick."

The year was rapidly drawing to a close and Purgoo was very desirous of returning to France, for it has been previously stated in this book, that he had promised to deliver a cargo of cotton to Tuebor & Co. by the first of January, and he had already received a partial payment in advance of its delivery. But it was impossible for him to procure it. The recent destruction caused by the cyclone had necessarily left him in financial straits and bankruptcy seemed inevitable. Furthermore, it was about the time that public sentiment in the North was thoroughly aroused against the slave traffic, and the Northern and Southern States were engaged in hot dispute and frowning at each other, and the financial valuation of slaves was rapidly on the decrease. Even the plantation itself had diminished twenty-two per cent. in the real estate market during the last year.

The effects of the cyclone added a new obstacle for consideration. Eight weeks of diligent work of thousands of slaves and many beasts of burden had only succeeded in the partial erasure of the evidences of destruction wrought by the cyclone.

Purgoo was in a more precarious position than he was aware, for Fallon had not divulged to him the extent of the incumbrances that had accumulated during the last five years. He was yet unaware of the vast sums of gold that had been daily squandered by that maudlin demon and ruler over the Purgoo Kingdom. Neither was he aware of the many enormous bills of credit which must be paid the first of the incoming year.

The planter and his overseer held a long and earnest consultation on the evening of the day the mysterious bell was heard, and the result was the beginning of the end of the Purgoo Kingdom. The predestined struggle that was inevitable between the Northern and Southern States, as well as the many perplexities and adversities hovering over the plantation had been the basis for an agreement to the immediate sale of the place. The inhabitants were startled when the following advertisement appeared in all the morning papers published at Monroe and New Orleans:

NOTICE-FOR SALE-The "Purgoo Kingdom" will be sold at Public Auction December 29th. The purchaser will have the right to retain as many of the present stock of slaves as desired, and the remainder of them will be sold at Public Auction December 31st.

CHAPTER V
A FLASH OF LIGHTNING KILLS FALLON AND WRITES HIS NAME ON STONE

Beyond the starlit paths untrod,
A soul draws nearer to the face of God.

THE life of man, with all of its conjurations and projects, with all of its wealth and pleasure, rears itself like a little tower to which Death adds the finishing stroke. Among all the walks and pursuits of life, the ever alert sentry, Death, challenges the echoes of every approaching foot that steps upon the sinking sands of time. Let man pursue any course he may for a livelihood in life, Death will add the finishing touch, and all his accumulated stock of wealth and pleasures vanishes the moment that Death pronounces its verdict that henceforward, oh "man, thou art clay."

The Purgoo mansion was of gothic design, built of white marble and granite, with a veranda on either side of it, and it was the finest home in Louisiana and the most elaborate dwelling in all the Southern States. The reflection of the sun's rays upon the granite rock gave it a dazzling appearance, magnificent to behold. When first built, it received the appellation of "King Solomon's Home." It had been constructed about fifteen years and was the abode of Purgoo until the ill-health of his wife made it expedient for him to remove to France six or eight years prior to this time. Then began Dick Fallon's complete reign of terror.

If it is possible for a human being to foresee the arrow of coming doom, then Dick Fallon must have foreseen even the shadow of his own death. In the afternoon of the day to which I now refer Fallon was standing on the west veranda gazing at the threatening clouds, before starting to Monroe on business connected with the coming sale. During the day he had not tasted a morsel of food, and for one day during his life he had refused to taste of liquor, and perhaps this was the first day since he left the cradle that burning oaths had not escaped from his lips. Since early morning his conversation had been conducted in whispers; his very looks presented grief and woe, and misery was strongly depicted in his countenance.

Surely Dick Fallon was shivering under the cold and puny shadows of his coming death. With all of his undaunted courage he was aware that he was marching just in front of his own funeral procession. He was standing upon the veranda examining the storm-threatening clouds, when all at once a long flame of fire leaped from the clouds and volumes of smoke seemed to form a circle in the air and a white streak of lightning came rushing downward and illuminated the granite building. Dick Fallon made one step backward, reeled and fell dead.

The lightning flash that killed Dick Fallon forged another link in the mysterious chain of circumstances that was so rife on the plantation, on account of the fact that on either side of the granite column against which he was leaning the initial of his name was indelibly carved in the solid rock. The bolt of fire, in its zigzag course, burned the letters "D. F." in the stone from the top to the bottom of the building.

The sale of the plantation was delayed one week, during which time many of the dark methods of Dick Fallon's financial squanderings came to light. For five years Purgoo had given the control of the place into the overseer's hands, and also the conducting of the financial and agricultural transactions. He had the power of buying and selling slaves, stock, etc., and the legal right, just the same as though he was the sole owner. During the week prior to the sale it was found out that there was an indebtedness upon almost every thing on the kingdom. All of the stock and more than two-thirds of the slaves were covered with mortgages, and the most of them were due, and his creditors came in swarms.

This was supposed to be the largest cotton farm in the world. All the leading manufacturers of goods in Europe was supplied with cotton from this plantation, and when the Purgoo cotton crop was light and insufficient for their annual supply, then enough was purchased by the agents at New Orleans to fill the yearly orders.

The year previous to this time Fallon claimed that his cotton crop was light and gave his note for thousands of bales of cotton which he secured from surrounding planters on pretext of being short on his foreign orders; but the purchased bales never reached Paris, for they were sold at New Orleans and the money was squandered by him.

The damage to the plantation wrought by the cyclone and the many mortgages and bills of credit made it impossible for Purgoo to realize from the sale more than enough to satisfy his creditors. The plantation was purchased by John Lynden and William Perry, two well-known planters from New Orleans.

Most of the slaves were purchased by Lynden & Perry and retained on the place. Only those that were considered as incorrigibles and had manifested a disposition to make their escapes were sold.

The law required all slave owners to keep a record of those who had made, or attempted to make, their escapes. A heavy fine was imposed upon any one who sold a slave without disclosing all the prior attempts to run away. It was an old and well-founded proverb among slave owners that "a nigger that had runaway once would try it again;" and it had a depreciative effect upon the value of the slave, for he was liable to instill the love of freedom in the minds of the others.

My previous record was made known, and although I was young and endowed with wonderful strength and was one of the swiftest workers on the place, yet I was rejected by Lynden & Perry and was sold for six hundred dollars, which was three hundred and fifty dollars less than Dick Fallon paid for me.

I was purchased by Stephen Cary. He was a planter from Missouri, who had been in New Orleans to dispose of his cotton and was returning to his home at Booneville, Missouri, and stopped over at Monroe to attend the sale. He also purchased another slave by the name of Tom.[2] We were confined in jail at Monroe until our new master was ready to continue his journey home.

I was not at all discomforted by being sold, for I had not relinquished my desire for freedom and was unshaken in my opinion that Missouri would confer upon me better opportunities of escape than Louisiana.

On the 10th of January, 1849, Purgoo started for New Orleans, on his way to Paris, and was a passenger on that ill-fated boat "Senegal," which foundered in the Bay of Biscay within five hours of its destination. And thus ended the career of two men that had enjoyed more unmerited pleasure and squandered more ill-gotten gold than any other two men connected with all slave history.

Nancy (the Octoroon) was retained on the plantation, and I will ever remember the words spoken to me by her on the day I was sold. She was an extraordinary domestic and was frequently employed at the Purgoo mansion. On great occasions, such as banquets, balls, etc., Nancy's aid was indispensible. Since Fallon's death she had been steadily employed at the mansion, and during the week prior to the sale, the Purgoo mansion was overrun with transient visitors; and all manner of discussions and arguments were rife in regard to the final end of the threatening attitude then existing between the Northern and Southern States. They were almost unanimous in the opinion that a conflict was focusing in the camera of time, and during the coming melee thousands of slaves would make their escape, and perhaps Negro slavery would receive its final overthrow.

Nancy overheard many of their discussions, and on the day I was sold I bade many of the old plantation slaves a long good bye; and when I came to shake hands with Nancy she whispered in my ear these words: "We will all soon be free." I never had the least idea that her prediction would ever be fulfilled; neither was I aware of the source of her invisible hope upon which were founded her words of encouragement.

The unnatural tone of her voice and the stealthy manner in which she spoke was convincing proof that there was a basis for her information. But I could not believe it was possible for us to be free; for I thought our freedom was the result of our escapes, and it was useless for us to even think of making such an effort.

But I was not aware that we were yet to meet again, and in a strange land. Many years after our cruel servitude was dead and buried. I was yet to learn that the kernel of our freedom was swelling in the bosom of the future, and our hope, long buried, was peering over the brink of time.

I was unconscious of the upheaval of coming events.

* * * * * * *

Years elapsed before we met again, and the virtue of her words had long been graven in the hearts of every Southern slave.

CHAPTER VI
IN OLD MISSOURI — THE ESCAPE — ARRIVAL IN DETROIT, MICHIGAN

IN the latter part of January I was taken from jail where I was confined at Monroe, and in due time arrived at our new home at Booneville, Missouri; and there was a vast difference between our old home and the new one.

The former one governed his plantation by means of torture and fear, and was known to be the most cruel master in Louisiana. But the latter had the reputation of being the most humane planter in the State of Missouri. Stephen Cary would not torture his slaves, nor suffer it to be done by any one else. His plantation was situated about two miles from the Missouri river, and was very small in its dimensions when compared with the Purgoo kingdom. It consisted of two thousand acres, which was cultivated by 220 slaves. Many of them were married and were living with their families on the place. Many of those with large families were allowed twenty acres of ground, which they cultivated on shares.

They cultivated it after working hours by the voluntary aid of the plantation help. The products when gathered were sent to market with the yearly produce, and the owners thereof received their financial share accruing from their extra toil. Many kind and humane acts might be attributed to Stephen Cary which concurs with his reputation of being the most sympathizing slave owner in the state. Many of his aged slaves only worked on their allotted plats of ground and received an equal share of the produce. The new master had never been known to sell a husband from his wife, or a mother from her child, and nearly all of them were born and raised on the plantation. Some were old and gray, and became his property by the legacy of his father.

He was a man in the prime of life and very wealthy, but neither gaudy nor ostentatious. His mansion was a wooden building of the old French style and very neat and perfect in its construction. It occupied a commanding position overlooking the Missouri river. There was a superb fountain on each side of his dwelling, and in the rear of it was an old fashioned fish pond gleaming in the sun.

He delighted in luxuries and pleasures and frequently gave magnificent banquets at his residence. He concurred with his slaves in their many dances or dusty shuffles and often supplied them with the old brown jug and extra refreshments. As a slave owner, Stephen Cary might have been considered a kind and humane master.

Perhaps it was the model treatment of his slaves that made them so contented, for he was living in a place that was more convenient for them to make their escapes than from most of the slave states, and I was told that not a slave had ever been known to attempt to escape from his plantation. I have asserted that his kindness might have been the basis of their contentment, but it must also be remembered that the most of them were born and raised in their old log cabins, and there is a natural love that links us with the place of our birth.

> Men should only count the moments in life
> That's united in pleasure, and divorced from bondage gains.

But, there were two of his slaves who were not contented and were longing for their freedom. They were the two men that he had purchased from the Purgoo kingdom — Tom and William. Tom was born on the Purgoo plantation, and his father died when he was merely a child; his mother was sold by Dick Fallon a few years prior to his death. She was purchased by a planter in Memphis, Tenn., and she succeeded in making her escape with three other slave women. They received their aid from the society called "The Underground Railroad" and their escape was accomplished by dressing in male attire and secreting themselves among the bales of cotton on board the boat, during the season of shipping cotton from Memphis to Cincinnati. They were successfully conveyed to Woodstock, Canada, the place where Tom's mother was residing. Ever since the escape of his mother he had secretly manifested an uncommon desire of being free. Nine years had passed since our arrival on his plantation, and many were the evenings that we were engaged in planning our escape.

Very near two decades had elapsed since I was separated from my parents in old Virginia, and I knew not of their fate, for I had never heard of them since I left Virginia's soil. "Do they live and where are they?" were my torturing thoughts that augmented until they assumed human form of colossal terror. What crisis of thoughts can be more startling and more terrible than meditating upon the limited period of life, and after being absent many years from our aged parents — to be incessantly wondering whether they are living or dead. Tom was a fitting companion for me and we were coeval in years and experience, and similar in our desires of being free. For more than a year we had been making stealthy preparations for our escape, and one night of the first week in June, 1859, we put our plans into execution. We took our master's row boat in the early part of the night and by the aid of the rapid flow of the Missouri river we succeeded in reaching a point called Clark's Fork (about thirty miles from Booneville) before day break, and after having sent the boat adrift in order to elude all pursuit, we continued our journey for a few miles in a different direction and secreted ourselves during the day in the elders and tall grasses that grow in the low lands along the banks of the Missouri river. We resorted to the old and familiar slave tactics of hiding during the day and traveling at night. Our necessary cautiousness was a great obstacle to our speedy progress, and nearly a month had passed before our arrival in the suburbs of St. Louis. We secured a row boat and went across the river into the State of Illinois. We continued our journey for nearly a week, and being completely exhausted by our five weeks of nightly tramping, we halted at a farmer's house near a village called Brownsville. It was during the time of wheat harvesting and we informed the farmer that we were harvest men looking for work. He gave us employment for nearly three weeks, and we were greatly strengthened and recuperated during harvest, for we were blessed with regular meals and regular hours of rest. After harvest was over we continued our journey, although the farmer exhorted us to continue our labor during the year, but we believed it was hazardous for us to delay in reaching Canadian soil. After having walked until we were out of the state of Illinois we purchased tickets and arrived in Windsor, Ont., by railroad, on the 8th day of August.

In October I came over from Windsor to Detroit in pursuit of work. I was employed by Hon. John J. Bagley, a man that was well known as a friend to colored people, and an honor to the state. I frankly informed him of my escape from bondage and my long separation from my mother and father. He gave me advice and instructed me what course was best for me to pursue under the circumstances to make a success in life. He gave me work and admonished me to adhere strictly to the irrefragable laws of industry and integrity, for they were the only and direct paths that lead to wealth and happiness. He advised me to proceed at once in securing a home of my own and was very positive in asserting that a conflict was brewing between the North and South that would only culminate in the destruction of negro slavery and then I would have a shelter for my aged parents, providing they were living, for they would surely be found. I was benefited by his instruction and was zealous in my intentions of being guided through life by his precepts.

CHAPTER VII
FARMING — THE SHOLTZ FAMILY — THE MEETING WITH NANCY — THE QUARREL — THE MURDER

AFTER having completed my labor for John J. Bagley he recommended me to Mr. James F. Joy. I was engaged by him to work on his farm, which was about four miles northwest of the city of Detroit. I was in his employ for more than two years, and with the money that I had saved I bought ten acres of land of John Holmes. I was greatly elated and encouraged by my success in life since my arrival in Detroit and I only regretted that my parents were not with me to enjoy the fruits of my prosperity.

John Harris (my companion) was successful in finding the whereabouts of his mother, and she accompanied him to Windsor. I frequently visited them and was ever interested in hearing his mother rehearse her perilous escape from Memphis. She never wearied in relating the manner in which the three other female slaves (besides herself) were clad in male attire and stored away among the bales of cotton on board of the boat, and of their many circuitous routes of reaching Canadian soil after having left Cincinnati. Tom's mother remained with him until her death, which occurred in October, 1862.

The death of Tom's mother was only a renewing of my insatiable desire of seeing my own mother. For although many years had passed since I last beheld her, yet, she was ever lingering in my mind, like light lingering in the air. I knew not whether my parents were living or dead, and I was aware that all my attempts to ascertain their whereabouts was fraught with impregnable obstacles, for it was in the latter part of the year 1862 and the North and South were engaged in a deadly combat, and old Virginia, my native land, was the seat of their arena of blood.

The first of January, 1863, will ever be a memorable day with me, for it was the day that Abraham Lincoln emancipated the slaves, and it required an unlimited amount of tuition for me to recognize the virtue of the Emancipation Act. It was impossible for me to perceive how one man could release the many millions of slaves from their inherited servitude. But at last it was made plain to me and I was rejoiced at the thought of soon again greeting my aged father and mother. I immediately began making preparations for their future welfare and comfort. I erected an humble dwelling and purchased a number of fowl, stock, etc., and began the cultivation of my small farm. But I had only been basking in the blissful showers of my own imagination. All of my future hopes were only the passing shadows of my own conjuration.

Hope is a powerful stimulus and often unburdens our minds of its weary and fatiguing load; it excites us for the present to such a degree of invited pleasure that it seems almost desirable for us to hope, even after the last echoes of its vanishing tread has disappeared from the precincts of memory.

Soon after I had made such extensive preparations for my father and mother, a man by the name of Dick Sholtz rented the twenty acres of ground adjoining to mine. He was about thirty years of age, of German birth; his wife, Susan, was born in Ireland and was ten years his junior. The day of their appearance in the neighborhood was the knell of my hopes and the birth of new adversities and perplexities which have hovered over me for a quarter of a century. It was the beginning of the blackest chapter in the history of my life, so dire and perpetual, that a quarter of a century behind prison walls has neither cancelled a day of my burning misery nor enkindled a hopeful gleam of its amelioration.

Dick Sholtz was one of the most indolent and selfish men that I ever met. He was an enemy to labor and envious of the prosperity and progress of the industrious neighborhood. His natural negligence and aversion to work would necessarily demonstrate to an industrious man that he anticipated the products of his land to vie with all others around him, regardless of his indisposition to work. And he was the possessor of one of the most brutal and unfeeling dispositions which it is possible to conceive. I have frequently seen his wife plowing in the field while he was lying intoxicated at home.

A rail fence was the dividing line that separated his corn field from mine. One morning in June he and his wife came into their field and began hoeing corn, and before noon the heat was excessive. He manufactured a plausible excuse for returning home, but his wife kept steadily at work until the middle of the afternoon, when he returned, and scanning the progress of her labor he was dissatisfied with the amount she had performed. He raised his huge fist and knocked her down with as little compunction as though she was not a human being.

The beginning of the year 1864 was the most momentous in this country that time has ever produced. It was the year that right and wrong, hope and despair, were in the heat of their death struggle for the supremacy. But the North and Southern states were longing for the termination of their bloody conflict, but they were heart and soul engaged in the complete annihilation of each other rather than concede to the demands of their dispute. The life of this nation was swaying over the chasm of destruction and seemingly only suspended by a hair. It was a national strife, and every loyal man was a soldier and every woman was a soldier's friend, and they were zealous in their attributions of something toward the preservation of this nation's life. Even the boys and girls were wearing tin swords and muskets and were marching with military tread when going or returning from school.

I was deeply interested in the vanquishing of the Southern States, for I was told that the rifles of the North were firing in defense of Lincoln's emancipation, and I knew that my mother and father were yet beyond the evoking hand of freedom. And at the despairing thought my heart sunk within me. It was one of those inexpressible feelings, for there is a feeling of hope and despair that is indepictable, for language can not speak it nor ears can not hear it, and is only interpreted when being transmitted from the mind to the heart.

Another year was consumed in settling their bloody dispute, and one morning in the month of April I was informed that the Southern States had surrendered and the Nation's long and bloody strife was at an end. I began to meditate upon the best methods to pursue in ferreting out the whereabouts of my parents, and was preparing to go in search of them, but was advised to defer my journey for a time for the country was overrun with soldiers, horses, cannon and implements of war as they were being transferred to different places, and my contemplated journey was more liable to meet with success after the rush for the relics of war was over. Furthermore, Old Virginia was like a huge furnace when once fired to a white heat and cooling off. It was dangerous to tread upon.

During the year I made a great improvement on my place. I enlarged my dwelling and built a barn and a granary, and my home was scrupulously neat and presentable. And persevering industry had been amply rewarded, for in November I received four hundred and twenty dollars for the produce I had raised during the year. The next summer after the war was over I came to the city market with a load of vegetables, and a middle aged colored lady approached my vehicle for the purpose of purchasing and I was startled by the familiarity of her countenance. Her face and general appearance seemed to be very familiar to me and I was convinced that I had seen her somewhere, but where was more than I could tell, and I concluded by her scrutinizing manner that my face was not unfamiliar to her. She concluded her purchasing and paid me for her vegetables, and I was returning the change due her when she gazed intently at a scar upon my left hand which I received by Dick Fallon's wire lash while on the Purgoo kingdom more than fifteen years before. After having noticed the scar on my hand she exclaimed, "Great heavens, can it be possible that this is William that was sold from the Purgoo Kingdom?" I replied, "Yes; and I believe that you are Nancy the Octoroon." For a few minutes there was complete silence between us, and then she said these words, "God is good." The explanation of our singular meeting is soon explained. All the slaves on the place were manumitted about the time of Gen. Sherman's march to the sea, and Nancy and her husband were employed in caring for the sick and wounded soldiers in the hospital at Savanah, Ga,, where her husband died from the effects of being constantly in the midst of contagious diseases. After his death she was employed by the wife of a colonel of a Michigan regiment, who had brought her to Detroit a year prior to our meeting, and she was recognized as one of the family and was contented and happy. The approaching hour of noon made it necessary for her to defer our conversation for the present, but ere long we would meet again and relate some of the things that happened on the old plantation. After she had disappeared from my sight I became intoxicated with the meditations of the past until my mind ran over the black pages of my life and mingled with the horrors of the Purgoo Kingdom. The forms of the mysterious fountain and Dick Fallon loomed up before me as visible as if an artist had sculptured them from solid marble.

A few days after my conversation with Nancy, Dick Sholtz came to my house and requested (perhaps it would be better to say that he demanded) I should sell him one dozen (of my fifteen) turkeys, and for a price which he had already concluded to pay. I informed him that none of my poultry was for sale, and he insisted in a manner that was almost imperative that I should gratify his demand. I reiterated my former statement, and then he became very wroth and hot words followed and I told him to leave my premises, and after having showered upon me a storm of anathemas and sordid names he reluctantly took his departure. The third morning thereafter I found forty-eight of my choices poultry lying dead in their coop, and among the number were all of my turkeys but one. They had been poisoned, and perhaps I would not have had a fowl left on the place if the one turkey and six chickens had not been hatching, for they were on their nests, I was satisfied that Dick Sholtz was the only person in the neighborhood who would perpetrate so dastardly an act, and I immediately went to Justice Harbough to enter complaint against him. But the Justice informed me that if Sholtz was not seen on my place on the night in question my suspicions were insufficient to sustain a warrant for his arrest and advised me to wait awhile and something more valid and sustaining might occur. I was satisfied that my suspicion was not without a cause, and did not think in the future it would be wise nor safe for me to leave my home unguarded. And my livelihood was the unavoidable means of my home being frequently left without a protector. Furthermore I was anticipating a trip to old Virginia during the fall of the year in search of my parents. Therefore I hired a man by the name of Abel Piney to work for me, also a housekeeper by the name of Elizabeth Kelly, for I was desirous of leaving my home amply cared for and protected.

Mrs. Sholtz and my housekeeper very soon became intimate friends and often visited each other after working hours. Her husband not approving of their intimacy became more severe in the ill treatment of his wife and renewed his envious and malicious actions toward me. I admonished my housekeeper, and for the sake of peace told Mrs. Sholtz not to visit my house so frequently.

Her husband had been very adroit and persistent in his efforts to obtain a milch cow of mine. He frequently offered me a price for it which I considered was not more than half her value. His pleadings became so constant and irksome that I finally told him to give me $25 and take the cow. The next day after this offer of mine, and while I was in the city, he came to my place and left $15 with my housekeeper with the understanding that he had bought it of me. He took it away and sold it to some one for whom he had been so desirous of buying it. When I returned and was told of his stealthy work, I speedily went to him and demanded the immediate return of my property, or else he would suffer the just process of the law. He replied that he had purchased it for a butcher and that it had already been slaughtered, and said he would give me another $15, which was $5 more than my estimated value of the cow. This was satisfactory and I returned home, but he did not keep his word and I never received the money.

The last Saturday in October, 1866, Abel Piney and myself went into my corn field and began cutting corn. Dick Sholtz and his wife were doing the same in their corn field, and as usual, he was under the influence of liquor. A quarrel arose between them, and with an awful oath he raised his corn knife and struck at his wife's head. As the knife descended she sprang aside and ran toward us for protection. He pursued her, but she succeeded in reaching us before she was overtaken by him. My hired man was very powerful, quick as a cat and fearless as a lion, and together we succeeded in disarming him of his deadly weapon and saving the life of his wife. It required considerable time and patience before we succeeded in pacifying him sufficiently for it to be safe to return him his knife. In the meantime his wife had fled to my house and said that the trouble arose from an insinuating remark her husband made about her when he saw Abel Piney and myself enter the corn field. His reflections were unfounded and she had promptly called him a liar, and he, being in liquor, become wroth and sought to slay her. After having returned him his corn knife we all returned to my house for the purpose of making a reconciliation. Mrs. Sholtz was naturally of a nervous and timid disposition and very reluctantly consented to depart from her protectors and go home with her husband, thereby putting herself at his mercy. The quarrel originated on Saturday afternoon and the twilight was hovering around us before she consented to go with him, but would not until he consented to leave his knife at my house, which he did, and she went home with him.

SUSAN SHOLTZ'S STORY OF THAT TERRIBLE NIGHT.

Once at home my husband did not have a word to say in regard to what had passed between us during the day, but he was sullen and seemed unnaturally reticent, and the steadily increasing frown upon his countenance and the cold glitter in his eyes plainly predicted that the long hoarded jealousy and malice was on the eve of its culmination.

During the night he frequently left the house on pretense of being sick, but the odor of his breath became so strong with liquor that I was convinced that he was making trips to a jug which he always kept concealed when on his drunken sprees. I had a presentiment that trouble was near and concluded to be on my guard, for the night was far spent, and if attacked it would be a very easy matter to escape from him when once in the open air.

(Neither of them closed their eyes to sleep during the night, for the husband was only waiting for his wife to close her eyes ere he would take her life, and the wife was on the alert to prevent it.)

It was the longest and most terrible night I ever passed through during my life. Just before daybreak he asked me why I did not go to bed. I replied I was not sleepy, and as he went out doors he muttered, "You will be d — d sound asleep before daylight." As soon as he closed the door I raised the window as a way of exit in case of being attacked and prevented from the door. The open window was concealed by again dropping the window curtain. This time he remained out of doors nearly an hour, and daybreak began to appear in the eastern sky, and I was in hopes of passing the last night under his roof undisturbed, for early in the morning I intended to go to the city of Detroit and visit my sister and then go back to my mother in Canada and remain there. But my frail hope was of short duration, for at that very moment my husband came staggering in the house and locked the door. One glance toward him was enough to account for his lengthy absence, for in his right hand he carried a hickory club about the size of a base ball bat, and in his left hand was a huge butcher knife which he had used in whittling his club. As he entered my bedroom horror was depicted in his countenance and murder engraven on his soul. I said to him, "Why, Mr. Sholtz, what do you mean?" He replied, "Get ready to die, for you will be in h — l in five minutes." As he turned to lock the bedroom door I jumped, or rather tumbled, through the window, and fell close under the window, for my clothing had caught on a nail that was driven on the inside of the window sill. He was taken by surprise by my sudden means of exit, but struck at me with his knife whilst I lay upon the ground. But I was too far from him and so close under the window that he only succeeded in gashing my clothing, and when he saw that they were fastened he at once grabbed them; but I had regained my footing and tore away from him, leaving part of my dress in his hands. It was now broad daylight and there was no way to elude him only by being protected, and I at once began running toward my nearest neighbor, William Walker. My husband came through the window and ran after me. William Walker's house was only about eighty rods from ours, but it seemed to me as though it was ten times that distance, and I soon found out that my great struggle for my life had over-taxed my physical powers, for I felt that my strength was failing me. But a human being can accomplish much when their life is at stake, and fright gave me wings. Walker's house sat only a few rods from the brow of the hill, and when running up the hill I looked back and saw that my husband was only a few rods behind me and then I began to scream. On reaching the house I ran against the door, but it was locked for it was early in the morning and no one was up. My husband was not yet in sight, for he had not reached the top of the hill, and I ran around to the back of the house and hid in the woodshed.

Early on the last Sunday morning in October, 1866, I was aroused by something being thrown heavily against my door. I got up and opened it just as Dick Sholtz came running up to it. I stepped back from the door and he ran in the house with a heavy club in his hand. I asked him what was the matter, and he replied G — d d — n you I will show you, and shouted you are intimate with my wife and G__d d___n you I will kill you both. He raised his club over my head and then I seized my gun and fired. He staggered to the door of the woodshed and fell, and then I discovered his wife crouched in one corner of the shed, which was the first I knew of her presence, for she came in the woodshed through the outside door, and at first I thought she was dead, for she had fainted.

It is Sunday morning and my home, instead of being a place of worship and prayer, was wrapped in eternal gloom and perpetual misery. Justice and Truth whispered in my ear: "Was not either your life or his on the altar of sacrifice?" Conscience and Mercy answered: "Might it not have been averted?" All hopes of greeting my mother and father were consumed in the white flames of passion that had so suddenly flared in self-defense.

Susan Sholtz, on recovering from her swoon, exclaimed: "Great heavens! I would much rather for my husband to have slain me than to have been the means of jeopardizing my liberty and staining your conscience with blood." But Abel Piney was of quite a different opinion, for he declared that man was ever and completely justified in taking a life in self-defense, although the laws of our land may succeed in extinguishing justice and banish the slayer to perpetual servitude. I was of the opinion that the best course for me to pursue was to give myself into the hands of the law and state the facts, and let justice take its course. But Abel Piney declared that such a course would only involve myself and all those under my roof into an inextricable situation, which would only end in the imprisonment of us all, consequently the best thing to do was to conceal the body and keep our mouths closed.

After considerable controversy, Susan Sholtz being undecided in mind, and from dread and fear of implication, concurred with Piney in his proposal to secrete the body, and she would go to her mother's in Canada on a visit and on her return she would make inquiry for her husband and convey the idea that he had deserted her. Under the circumstances I believed it was the proper course for me to pursue, for I was not familiar with the laws of our land and knew not whether it would be possible for me to prove it was murder in self-defense.

We concealed the body in the woodshed during the day and at night Abel Piney and myself carried it about two miles away and covered it over with underbrush in a swampy place, and not a great distance from the main road, for it was impossible for us to go very far in the swamp, the recent rains rendering the soft lands insupportable of our weight.

But murder will out just as sure as the grave will yet uncover its dead. In less than one week his body was discovered and Mrs. Sholtz was arrested while packing her clothes to go on the visit already spoken of. When she was charged with being implicated in the murder of her husband, her countenance assumed an aspect of horror and misery seldom seen in the aspects of civilized people. She confessed all and told the truth of the whole circumstance, and related all that happened during the day while cutting corn, and told of the death struggle with her husband on that fatal Sunday morning.

When brought before the court I related all that had occurred from the time Dick Sholtz came in the neighborhood until he came into my own house and attempted to take my life. I told of the inducements and my reasons for concealing the body, but the prosecuting attorney (Mr. Patchen, the prosecutor of Wayne county), reversed facts and supplemented fiction and used the concealing of the corpse as a weapon of our premeditations and murderous plots. He succeeded in making it appear to the jury that Susan Sholtz arose from her bed in order to decoy her husband to the premeditated place for his death.

Lizz Kelly, my housekeeper, went to the city of Detroit on Saturday evening after Sholtz and his wife left my house, and she remained in the city visiting her aunt until Monday morning. She had informed me on leaving that she would spend the Sabbath with her aunt. And the prosecuting attorney made the jury believe that that visit was concocted by the prisoners in order to make the way clear and secrecy complete. He manufactured many other cogent and logical reasons for our conviction, and the jury brought in a verdict that William Walker, Abel Piney and Susan Sholtz were guilty of murder in the first degree.

At the announcement of this terrible and unjust verdict a cold chill ran through me as speedily as a lightning flash can riddle the green and thriving oak, when its heart is left bleeding and bare, as a target for winter's blasts and the sport for summer's zephyrs. I was aware that capital punishment had long since been abandoned in Michigan, but a far more dire and torturing penalty awaited all men convicted of murder in the first degree, for the penalty was solitary confinement for life, which is by far a more dreadful thought than those which canker the hope and fleck the brain of the culprit while standing on the scaffold, or chose of the assassin while under the guillotine, just before his head rolls from the chopping block and falls into the bloody basket.

On the 23rd day of December, 1866, all three of us were sentenced to Jackson State Prison for the term of our natural life, and the day before Christmas we entered within its dark and gloomy walls. When I entered my narrow cell and rockbound grave, I simply said, "At last I am buried alive, I am buried alive." All future hope vanished and the wrinkled and fading countenance of my gray haired mother disappeared from my memory, the future and the past changed places. I had wedded those horrible twins — misery and despair — christened ruin and woe, and give love and hope their winding sheet.

PART SECOND
LIFE IN JACKSON PRISON

CHAPTER I
IN SOLITARY CONFINEMENT — ABOLISHMENT OF THE SOLITARIES — "FRENCH JOE"

IN perusing the remaining pages of this book, the reader will find many things that would naturally make the sceptical shake their heads, and may cause those with more humane feelings and Christian love to wonder with amazement and holy horror. Nevertheless, the incidents which we shall relate are not all fiction, but are based on facts, and many of the participants are yet living; although the most of them have long since taken their final leave of this brief life. It's an old adage, that one-half of the world does not know how the other half are living, and it can righteously be said that one-half of the living never heard of the tortures of some who fill the unmarked graves in the convict's burial ground.

On Christmas day, 1866, I was placed in solitary confinement, at Jackson prison, for life. I could distinctly hear the sleigh bells ringing and the voices of little children as they were shouting, "I wish you a merry Christmas." On entering my dark and dismal cell I heard the hoarse and sepulcheral voice of an inmate cry out: "Say your prayers, for those who enter here all hope is lost! In one year you will be a lunatic! And in three years you will be in the hog pen!"[3]

It would be impossible for any man to accurately describe the interior of that den of misery. There has been a remarkable change in the treatment of convicts during the last quarter of a century, and within recent years a complete revolution has taken place throughout the penal institutions of the civilized world.

Twenty-five years ago the solitary was disconnected from the rest of the prison and was standing in the yard, a few rods from the female department, and a high board fence separated them. At that time a life sentence in Jackson meant a much different reception for the convict than it does at the present time. Then the old "life solitary" cells meant the worst kind of a living death. The cell in which the convict was then placed was just large enough for an iron bedstead. Here a hole twelve inches long and two in width was cut slantingly through the top of the cell door, which was the only means of furnishing air and light, and to see the light at all, the inmate was compelled to lie upon the stone floor and look straight up.

I shall ameliorate the horrors of the solitary, for the facts, if related, would shame canibals and hottentots, and would outrage the belief and conscience of the most sanguine advocates of prison torture.

Furthermore, a cloud of public sentiment is gathering around the convict's home, and the very air is ablaze with Christian love and energy in their untiring effort to elevate and reconstruct the minds and hopes of all men who go forth from prison doors with integrity stamped upon their brow and industry written in their countenance. Therefore, I shall only give a short and hasty description of my life while in solitary confinement.

We are told that in solitude, passion feeds upon the heart, and during prison life I have learned that solitude not only feeds upon the heart, but it consumes the mind, dwarfs the brain, destroys the intellect, and leaves the man a total wreck. The most potent faculties in a human being deserts him; even his physical and mental powers are canceled, until only the skeleton of the man is left, for the man himself has disappeared. There were thirteen men in the solitary and some of them had not even seen the sky o'er head in more than ten years. During that long term of complete isolation not a razor had touched their faces, and a comb was a thing unknown. Their hair and whiskers hung down to their waist and was as white as snow — although the most of them were less than forty-five years of age — and some were raving mad; their yells and screams in the dead hours of night were too horrible to mention. Their bed, in most cases, consisted of the stone floor and a piece of blanket, although some of them were supplied with old and rickety cots, which were alive with vermin. Some cells looked like hog pens and were as filthy; bugs and insects were in their glee. A convict brought their scanty meals, and the board of inspectors would occasionally take a hasty look at them. These were all who visited us, except the doctor, who came in time to find his bloodless patient lying on his cot quivering in death, or, perhaps, already dead upon the stone floor; for, as soon as they became insane, everything within their cells was removed.

No light ever penetrated that dismal home, except the faintest rays of the noon-day sun. No lurid light from decaying candle; no blinding glare of flickering lamps; no Bible; no Christian tracts; no newspapers; no books; nothing. No letters ever came. The father never heard from his child; no letter came from mother to her son. They were simply living dead men, isolated and left alone, until the foul air consumed their lungs, or the sledge of constant thought dethroned their minds. Then death came — and was welcome. Do you wonder why some of them at my reception predicted that in one year I would be a lunatic, and in three, a corpse?

When Michigan abolished hanging and substituted solitary confinement she not only made a monstrous stride backward toward the days of barbarism, but took a backward step in suppressing murder. I know that humanitarians will not agree with me on this phase of my subject, but I am speaking from experience and not from any verbal information. I am speaking from the experience of a quarter of a century among men convicted of a capital crime.

Solitary confinement neither deterred murder nor purified society, for the moral sentiment of those who were being tortured by this process reacted upon those who inflicted the punishment. Their christian love and moral sentiment gradually faded away, and ere long all moral feelings of the torturer sank to the level with that of their subjects. The surgeon feels neither pain nor sorrow whilst amputating the limb of his patient. Torturing never had a salutary effect.

Other reasons might be given in support of the assertion that the State erred when she abolished hanging and substituted solitary confinement, for I can call the names of men who have been in Jackson prison more than once, and each time they came for life. Furthermore, men in solitary confinement were not only a dead weight to the State, but they became insane, and is it possible that the state of Michigan gloats in the perpetual torturing of a human being, and by a process that destroys even the power of reasoning?

How long I remained in the solitary I am unable to tell. It was impossible to keep track of the days of the week or the date of the month. However, in the course of time, there were five or six men who made their escape from the solitary by prying up the stone floor and digging under the walls of the building. All of them were captured except two. But, after so many men having made their escape in one night, the Board of Inspectors became somewhat alarmed and concluded it was insecure and condemned it, so the men in solitary confinement were placed in the main prison with the rest of the convicts and were subject to the same rules and regulations. We were permited to work, and work would have been a pleasure to all of us, but many days passed by before some of us were able to perform any kind of manual labor, as nearly all were physical wrecks.

After being released from the solitary I had an opportunity of viewing the faces of those who were confined in that terrible den of misery. I shall only name a few, for some of them have long since been pardoned and are now engaged in the legitimate pursuits of life, and I do not wish to cast any reflections that would be detrimental to their social connections, or mar their happiness.

The oldest inhabitant of the solitary was a colored man by the name of John Moss. He was sent from Detroit about the year 1850, and remained in solitary confinement until it was abolished by an act of the Legislature in 1872. In 1883 he became blind and insane and was conveyed to the convicts insane asylum at Ionia, where he still remains. He is now an old man and a complete physical wreck. I shall ever believe that the loss of his eyesight is the result of his long confinement in the solitary, and his insanity is the natural consequence of long imprisonment. Nearly half a century has elapsed since he began life in Jackson prison.

The next oldest inmate of the solitary was Billy Hitchcock. He also came from Detroit, in 1854, and was greatly elated at the idea of being released from solitary confinement after having remained therein for so many years. He was pardoned by Gov. Luce in 1885.

Another of the prison veterans was Joe Duquette, better known by the name of "French Joe," who came from Sanilac county, April 27th, 1857. He has made several attempts toward getting a pardon, but none of his requests have been granted. His last effort to procure a pardon was in the spring of 1891, when the Legislature was in session. Edwin B. Winans was then Govenor of Michigan, being the first democratic Governor in many years. "French Joe" was anticipating clemency in his case after thirty-three years of constant torture. But as soon as his application for a pardon was made public many of the leading newspapers of the State became hostile toward him, and in glowing language recalled the day of his crime and pictured his three-year-old step-child in her screams and misery when dying from the effects of being internally seared with a hot iron in the hands of him who was seeking for a pardon. The reader can imagine the vindictive feeling toward Duquette by the following article that appeared in the Jackson Weekly Citizen of May 5th, 1891:

THE HORRIBLE CRIME FOR WHICH DUQUETTE WANTS A PARDON.

The convict whose piteous appeal for pardon has recently been printed in nearly all the papers in the country makes no statement of the horrible crime for which he was incarcerated, which is described as follows by the Lansing Republican:

Duquette married a handsome, loving wife, who thought much of him, and cared for him as none but a loving wife could; but she had a child, his step-child, who was only three years old. A pretty, prattling babe, who gladdened her mother's heart and was a living joy to all but Duquette. His hatred became morbid and he wanted the child out of the way. One day while the mother and grandfather were away he was left alone with the little one. Duquette was poking the fire absent-mindedly, and he thought of how he would like to be rid of the step-child. The poker was in his hands. He jabbed it among the glowing coals and the iron rod was heated to a white heat. He took it out and called caressingly to the innocent child, who ran to him with all the faith of babyhood. Duquette seized the little one, tore off its clothes and thrust the white heated poker into the child clear up to the hilt. The babe screamed and moaned, the sickening smell of burning flesh filled the room, but Duquette never relented. He twisted and turned the red hot poker within the little one's stomach until it was burned to death internally.

Who is there that wants him pardoned? Who thinks that solitary confinement for a thousand years could expiate such a crime? Let the state press examine the other side of the story and see how long sympathy will hold out for convict Duquette.

―――――

He is known as No. 7 on the prison register and has spent thirty-five years of his life behind that silent, somber, significant looking monument to the civilization of a great state. When one reflects upon the significance of being out of the world and still in it for a period of thirty-five years, it must naturally result in the query: "What would be the impression of the little old man if restored to liberty." To approximate an answer let one endeavor to conjecture his own impression and sensations if thrown a half century in the future with all its possibilities. Born in Montreal, Canada, in 1830, at the age of five years he came with his parents — French Canadians — to Detroit. Soon after his mother died, and his father, a dissolute character, gave his young son to a Frenchman named Willette, near Monroe. For many years the little lad was subjected to untold hardships and cruelties.

At the age of 12 he ran away from his cruel master and arriving at Toledo, Ohio, he soon found employment and was in many ways befriended by people whose interests were aroused in the waif. Ere long his father appeared and demanded the boy's earnings, which for several years he received and squandered in idleness and dissipation.

For years Joe engaged in the lake service in the capacity of a sailor and fisherman. In 1854 he took up a homestead in Sanilac county, with a view of abandoning the lakes for a less hazardous life. His father continued a "hanger-on" and took up his abode with him.

Under the influence of his father Joseph married, in 1856, a woman of Amherstburg, Ont., who was some years his senior and had two children, although he was her first husband, the youngest six years of age. This child they took with them to Michigan.

They had not lived long in Michigan before Joseph discovered that his wife had no love for him nor her child. In one of his depressed moods, being annoyed by the little boy, he inflicted injuries upon him resulting in his death.

Duquette has always believed that the death of the child was not directly attributable to him, but that his father and wife improved the opportunity offered by the injuries inflicted to consummate their long desire of having the illegitimate child out of the way.

The incidents which he relates would bear him out in his statement. He was tried at Lexington on the charge of murder, found guilty and sentenced to Jackson for life.

In June, 1889, a stranger called at the prison and asked to see Joseph Duquette. The request was granted and he announced himself to the little old man as his son. The old man could not understand the declaration, not knowing he had a son. An explanation disclosed the fact that the wife had given birth to the son some months after the husband's imprisonment. The son was taught that the father was dead, and never knew to the contrary, until just before the time of his visit. He had been informed of the facts by a priest in Canada who was familiar with all the details.

The son, Joseph Duquette, Jr., sought to procure the release of his aged father, and being a prosperous business man in Canada, gave every assurance to Governor Luce that he would care for the old man the balance of his life, but, as yet, it seems the sunset of his life will be passed within Jackson prison walls, for such feeling of prejudice as was aroused by the different articles in newspapers throughout the State at the time of his application for a pardon, will remain an obstacle that may prevent his freedom until-released by death.

CHAPTER II
THE CONTRACT SYSTEM — ESCAPE AND CAPTURE OF TOM BARTOLES — DIED WITH HIS SHACKLES ON

A few weeks after having been released from solitary confinement, I was sold to the Austin, Tomlinson & Webster Jackson Wagon Manufactory. I say I was sold. The Jackson wagon is made by convict labor, and it may not be generally known that convicts who work for contractors in Jackson prison are the contractors' slaves. Contract labor in Jackson prison is, by far, a worse system of slavery than ever existed on Southern soil. I was born and raised a slave, and have also done contract labor for a quarter of a century and know whereof I speak. The convict's labor is bought by the contractors, just the same as the Southern negros were bought who stood on the auction block prior to the war.

The contractors buy the convicts' labor from the State by paying the insignificant sum of fifty or seventy cents per day for each convict, and out of that paltry sum the State must feed, bed, clothe and pay the medical expenses of the convicts; for this the contractor compels his serfs to perform from three to six dollars' worth of work each day. It frequently occurs that some are not physically constructed in such a manner as to possess the muscular strength and energy to perform what a contractor demands for a day's work, and then — woe betide the convict. Some of them frequently fail to turn out the required amount of work each day, and failure means a swift and thorough punishment.

A more complete and minute description of contract labor will be given before the reader shall have finished this book, and then he can form some idea of contract labor in Jackson prison, and he must be his own judge as to whether the convicts have any basis for their abhorrence of contract labor.

H. H. Bingham was warden and John Martin deputy warden of the prison when I began working on the wagon contract. There are many men in Jackson prison today who frequently speak of the Bingham and Martin reign of terror and we shall name many acts of severity perpetrated by John Martin, which have not occurred since he ceased to be deputy warden. In those days there was scarcely any thought, or care, in regard to the condition of the clothing worn by convicts during winter months. All of their wearing apparel was inferior in warmth and durability when compared with what they now wear. Convicts in Jackson prison are now supplied with two suits of clothes, also with the same number of underwear, and each convict can obtain a new suit of clothes as frequently as it becomes necessary. One suit of their underwear is sent to each convict once a week, after having been purified at the prison laundry.

But twenty-five years ago there was quite a different state of things. Their outer wear was made of a cheap and flimsy material and underclothing among convicts was unknown. Socks were not in use, and during the winter months we were compelled to wrap old rags around our feet and pieces of blankets around our bodies to keep us as comfortable as possible. Under these circumstances it was only a short time after I began work on the wagon contract before I was numbered among the many invalids in a place where the sick and dying were huddled together.

My illness occurred during the time of the great epidemic in Jackson prison, which is yet remembered, not only by convicts, but also by many of the inhabitants of Michigan.

That disease which created such havoc among convicts during the three months of its terrible rage was called by us, the mutton fever, and its origin might have been from the constant use of mutton, upon which they were invariably fed.

However, I shall ever believe that epidemic was the genuine yellow fever, for all of its features were of the same nature as that terrible southern plague that was so destructive among the slaves in Louisiana.

During its rage here in prison, men who were in their usual health, and in the shops at work during the day, were a corpse the following morning, and in a few hours after their death they assumed a yellowish complexion, which made it almost impossible to recognize or distinguish one corpse from another. As soon as a vacancy occurred in the chamber of death, it was speedily replaced with another victim for the convicts' burial ground, or another subject for the dissecting knife at Ann Arbor.

One would naturally suppose that during dire illness and when standing in death's door, there would be a compromise of severity and a relaxation of unnecessary vigilance, in order that a peaceful voyage might accompany the dying man on the sea of death. But, since my arrival in Jackson prison I have been forced to believe that even a dying man may not be exempt from taunts and torture. For instance, a few months previous to the mutton fever, a convict by the name of Tom Bartoles had succeeded in gaining the displeasure of the prison authorities. He was an Irish boy, with a fifteen years sentence to complete. Tom was not an exception to the Irish race, and was endowed with an inexhaustible amount of wit. In those days Deputy Warden Martin was very much displeased and disappointed if he failed in getting his daily number of eight or ten men to flog the next morning before breakfast. Tom Bartoles' quick retort to contractors and keepers, when being unjustly reprimanded, had been the means of being a weekly candidate for the whipping post. He had been so repeatedly lashed that his back had become a solid mass of welts and bruises.

One morning in the month of June a dispute arose between himself and the contractor. The deputy was sent for, and, as usual, he vindicated the unjust claim of the contractor, and told the convict slave that he would give him fifty lashes in the morning instead of his breakfast. Bartoles made no reply, but a terrible glitter was in his eyes. The quarrel occurred about 10 o'clock in the morning, and during the noon hour he kept his eye on the guard in the east tower on the wall until the guard began to eat his dinner. He then seized a long piece of timber and placed it against the wall directly under the guard's tower. In an instant he was in the tower, and when the guard turned his head from his dinner table he was looking into the muzzle of his own gun, which was being held in the hands of a man with liberty or death written in his countenance. The guard simply stammered, "don't shoot," and then fainted away.

There was a stairway that lead from the outside of the tower to the ground, and by which the convict made his escape.

Twenty-five years ago the City of Jackson only numbered a few thousand inhabitants and very few dwellings were to be seen in the vicinity of the prison. North and east of the prison was a dense swamp, toward which the escaped prisoner rapidly made his way, still clutching the repeating rifle in his hand.

Not more then ten minutes after having made his escape he was being pursued by the guards from the prison, and by many of the inhabitants of Jackson, some of whom succeeded in getting within speaking distance, but his deadly rifle kept them back, and after having gained the heart of the forest he made good his escape.

Deputy Warden John Martin was very much chagrined by Bartoles' escape, for he was one of the targets of his wrath and personal contempt, and a reward of unusual amount for an escaped convict was immediately offered for his capture.

A few months after the convict's escape he was seen in Chatham, Ontario, and two detectives were sent there by the prison authorities, and who very soon became his inseparable friends.

His case was not extraditable, and he could only be captured by strategy. For several days the fugitive and his false friends were having a grand time in Chatham and adjacent towns — the detectives bearing all expenses.

But during their mirth and hilarity no persuasion was sufficient to induce Bartoles to accompany his new found friends on any of their frequent trips across the river. Moreover, the convict had began to be somewhat suspicious of his new friends, and on several occasions declined to accompany them after nightfall.

The detectives became apprehensive at his disregard for their friendship, and were aware that some decisive and cunning method was necessary for his capture. Consequently they told him they were anticipating a trip to Europe and would take their departure on the evening train, and under these circumstances they would dine together. Perhaps their scheme might have failed if they had proposed it at any other time except the noon hour and at a public hotel. Bartoles was well aware he had naught to fear at a public hotel in the middle of the day, and accepted their invitation. And the very moment he consented to dine with his false friends he paved the way to his own ruin and death. He was unaware of the deceit and treacherousness of men. Perhaps he never heard of the adage that every man has his price. The detectives had made their plans known to the proprietor of the hotel, and like Judas Iscariot for a few pieces of silver had consented to deliver the man into their hands. They dined together, and by special request the landlord dined with them. After the feast the proprietor proposed they should join in a game of whist for the cigars, etc. Several games of whist were played, and the proprietor went for the refreshments at the end of each game. All at once the convict reeled and fell senseless to the floor. His last glass of wine had been heavily drugged by the landlord himself. When the escaped convict was being carried to a hack by his false friends, it was supposed by those ignorant of the plot, he was intoxicated and was being conveyed to his home. The conveyance was driven rapidly away, and a few hours later, when Bartoles awoke from his stupor, he was shackled and on board a tug boat, and before daybreak he was on the American side. He had been successfully kidnapped, and the laws of God and man had been successfully outraged. But the tale is incomplete, and the worst is yet to come.

Immediately after having been brought back to the prison he received the most severe punishment ever inflicted upon a convict within prison walls. He was flogged until he fainted, and was left hanging with his hands shackled to the iron door until he regained consciousness. And then, after being shackled to a thirty pound ball and chain, he was set to work. His pitiable appearance would have been sufficient for the wildest Indian to have ceased torturing his victim and dress the bloody gashes of the captured convict. Tom Bartole's physical strength was something wonderful, but the severity of his punishment and the weight of his shackles were a burden that would have worried an ox. It will be remembered he made his escape a few months prior to the mutton fever, which was raging here among convicts at the time of his capture. A few hours after having been so severely flogged his limbs became paralyzed and he was unable to move, and was carried where many others were dead and dying, but his shackles were not removed.

The next morning after being carried to the hospital, the Deputy Warden, John Martin, was standing at the bedside of the captured prisoner, when the dying man thus addressed him: "Deputy Warden, I've only a few hours to live. Won't you please take the shackles off my legs so that I can move them?" The deputy replied: "No, sir; you shall wear your shackles right into h___l." Tom Bartoles was dead before night, and he died with his shackles on.

CHAPTER III
THE REIGN OF TERROR — DRAWN FROM HIS CELL WITH RED-HOT IRONS

DURING the epidemic there was no change in regard to the convicts' food. It was mutton for breakfast and the same for dinner, and during the month of July and August the unrelishable mutton soup, with its nauseous smell, was sure to be found on the dinner table. At one time during the mutton fever the convicts rebelled in the dining room and refused to go to work until they received something more wholesome to eat than the deadly mutton soup. But as soon as their wants were made manifest the guards were called into the dining room with their rifles and the convicts were marched to the hall and locked in their cells. They were then unlocked, one at a time, and given fifty lashes. One convict by the name of Charles J. Forbes refused to meekly submit to the flogging process, whereupon John Martin and his aids took their canes and clubbed him until his arm was broken. He was then handcuffed to his door, with his feet barely touching the floor, and was left hanging in this position with his weight on his broken arm, until severely flogged. Afterward he was unshackled and thrown into a cell, where he remained from Saturday afternoon, the day of the occurrence, until Monday morning, before his broken arm was set.

There were many attempts to escape while the fever was raging, and some were shot dead while trying to scale the wall. Among the number who were shot and killed was a convict by the name of Jim Givins. He was a man about thirty years of age and of fine physical structure. He was naturally of a reticent disposition and was ever brooding and seemed to be in perpetual meditation about the welfare of his widowed mother.

Jack McCoy was shot dead when very near the center of the river which runs a few rods from the wall on the west side of the prison.

The day I received my terrible sentence of life imprisonment, another man by the name of Shields was also sentenced for stealing cattle. He received thirteen years and came to prison in the same chain gang with myself. During the reign of terror he attempted to escape by scaling the wall on the east side of the prison, but fell dead with a bullet through his brain.

A convict by the name of Scott was shot when inside the prison walls, and the reader must determine whether it was justifiable. Convict Lynch was also shot dead while on the north wall.

Another man by the name of Jack Nevells received a bullet when outside the north end of the wall, after he had surrendered. He being one of the most powerful men ever confined in Jackson prison, the guards were timid in approaching him even after he had surrendered, whereupon they shot him, but he recovered.

We could mention many others who have been slain and mutilated with lead, but it is not necessary.

The flogging of convicts during the reign of terror was horrible and indepictable. The lash was ever in the air, and the groans and yells of convicts could be heard from early in the morning until late at night.

There has been a wonderful change in regard to the reporting of convicts since Bingham and Martin's reign. At the present time the keepers are seeking to abstain from reporting a prisoner, unless it becomes absolutely necessary. But twenty-five years ago it was considered a laxity in the vigilance of any officer who failed to report every day a certain number of the men under his care. Consequently it seemed as though the keepers in the shops were striving to see which of them could issue the greatest number of reports during the day. A report in those days most always called for a flogging of the prisoner. They were often called aside from their work, and after being chained to a post, or some other part of the building, they were flogged until the floor was sprinkled with their blood. There are convicts in the prison today who are crippled for life from the effects of the lash, wielded by the hands of John Martin, for some of them had the cords and fibers in their legs and arms so severely ruptured that they lost their natural strength.

The reader is aware that I was born and raised in a slave country, and for many years under the control of one of the most cruel negro drivers that ever drew groans from a slave. Grief and pain have been my boon companions since the days of my childhood. But since my arrival in Jackson prison I've been in the midst of a more severe and systematic style of torture than was ever heard of on southern soil.

During the reign of terror a convict by the name of Tony Brinon had a part of his right ear torn off by the lash. Henry Monihan was a cripple, his left arm being amputated at the elbow, but during one of his heats of passion John Martin so severely lashed him that the amputated spot was reopened by the lash, the blood gushing from the stub until he swooned and came very near bleeding to death.

For some infraction of the rules a convict by the name of Ezekiel Oaks was punished by water being thrown upon his head from the third gallery while shackled to a cell door on the ground floor. Afterwards he was confined in a dark cell, and when released was a raving maniac. Although yet living he is still insane.

Henry Thompson, a colored man, was maltreated until patience ceased to be a virtue with him, and one morning when the bell rang the hour for convicts to begin their daily toil he remained in his cell. Failing to emerge from his cell with the other prisoners, the prison authorities selected a new mode of torture and a complete remedy for his indisposition to come forth. He was a physical giant, and perpetual teasing and unmerited rebuke had incurred his anger, and the guards were not anxious to enter his cell and eject him. But a remedy was soon at hand. Bars of iron were procured, and after being heated to a blazing heat, they were forced through the grated cell door where the convict was at bay.

The iron rods were about ten feet in length and were blazing hot, excepting the end which remained in the hands of his tormenters. This method of ejectment was in progress for some time before they succeeded in burning him out of his cell. His agility in moving and leaping around was not only wonderful, but very annoying to his persecutors. Several times they succeeded in scorching him and the smell of burning flesh was exuding, still the maddened man refused to make his exit through the unlocked door. At last he received a terrible burn, and like an enraged beast leaped from his cell and sprang upon the guards. Then began the most terrible conflict (against such superior odds) ever witnessed within these prison walls. But no man could successfully combat against a half dozen men who were using clubs, hot irons and the butt end of revolvers. He was conquered, and although already scorched and bleeding, was shackled and his burns and bruises reopened with the lash.

The sacred command which directs us when smitten on one cheek by our adversary to turn and let him smite the other also, seems to be neglected or overlooked in these days, for we seldom meet the man who will not strike in self defense. Blood letting, mob violence, lynch law and the free use of deadly weapons have come to be the rule in prisons and out of them. And it frequently occurs that we find processions of men often headed by leading citizens and officers of the law marching to our jails in the light of the noonday sun and demanding the body of the convict, that his corpse may be seen swinging on public highways before the courts of justice can establish his guilt or innocence.

Convicts of a quarter of a century ago, who were living under that regime of misery, were not of more immoral inclinations than those confined in prison at the present time. And if inhuman ferocity is unnecessary for the disciplining of men now, then why was such rigid manifestations of savageness in vogue during the reign of terror?

We are told when reason is wide awake then remorse fastens its fangs. The experience of a quarter of a century among men convicted of capital crimes has produced sufficient evidence that even a touch from the fangs of remorse is enough to fill the cup of human torture, without a fierce system of destroying physical strength and suppressing future hopes and resolutions. During prison life we have strictly observed that the majority of men who return to prison, after serving one term, are those who experienced the most severe trials and tasted its bitterest end during their previous incarceration. While those who are not sold to contractors and are in the direct employ of the State, or fill humane places, such as clerks, book-keepers, etc., their humane positions and daily associations with men of moral and refined temperament conflict with the idea of harsh and rigorous treatment. Such men when once released seldom return. But those who were maimed, bruised and disfigured while in prison, returned.

Thompson, the colored man who experienced such severe trials by so many different means of torture was scarcely out of prison before he was back again.

Another one of those who experienced untold agony during prison life was John H. Proctor. He was one of the main objects of torture and prison virulence; he was branded with hot irons, starved, confined in dungeons and scourged time after time, besides being the victim of many other inhuman acts, and yet he served his third term of imprisonment.

Convict R. Reynolds was incompetent of being saturated with vicious and immoral ideas, for he was young in years and inexperienced in life, and ought not to have been inseparably united with men skillful in crime and guilty of capital offenses. His mother died when he was only twelve years of age and his father was killed in a railroad disaster the followiug year. At the age of fifteen he was battling the world without a friend or guide. Selling newspapers was his daily defense against hunger. The last day in October, 1870, the sky was dark and rain and snow was slowly descending. The streets of Detroit were deserted and young Reynolds' newspapers were left unsold, and during the night, famishing with hunger and shivering with cold, he forced an entrance into a storehouse where rags were kept and went to sleep among the rags. He was arrested and convicted of burglary and his sixteenth birthday found him a convict for three years within these prison walls, where he was looked upon, even by convicts, as a lamb among wolves.

His youthful appearance was no shield for his defense and he was ever tormented by the same harrowing process imposed upon confirmed criminals.

During his three years imprisonment he was immorally graduated — vicious, ignorant of the value of integrity, and nearly void of human feeling — left these prison doors fully competent to commit any crime of the most daring nature. It was only a few months before he returned to serve a ten years' sentence.

Very frequently our face becomes a looking glass and portrays our intentions. There was a remarkable change in his daily countenance, which was very discernible in its progress from the features of a criminal by accident to those of a criminal in perfection. Reynolds' harrowing trials during his second term were only a repetition of the first, and at its expiration the insatiable desire for robbery and crime was the all-absorbing thought and was visibly depicted in his countenance. Three years later he was caught in the act while burglarizing a dwelling in an Eastern state and, during his struggle to escape, committed murder, a crime for which he died on the scaffold.

There are those over whom, even in the cradle, the darkness of a miserable life and a premature death seem brooding in every shadow. We know the pleading of our instances may be like a bird in the wilderness — it sings from impulse, and the song dies without a listener. But truth, when fairly kindled, will burn down all false opinions and consume all unjust prejudice, and even erase the trail.

Let those who read our brief history of Convict Reynolds, the orphan newsboy, and then justify his first conviction and defend his inhuman chastisement during prison life, remember that all men are formed of the same clay and gifted by the same God.

It's far beyond the limit of memory and the intellectual power of man to accurately describe the numerous and inhuman deeds of violence perpetrated upon convicts during the reign of terror. It seems almost impossible for such a state of affairs to exist for so many years, right within the sound of church bells and within sight of the many sacred places of worship, with their spires towering toward the heavens. When you consider the christian energy and human interest which at the present time are being manifested toward establishing a just and moral conduction of the penal institutions of our land and then recall the days of prison life of a quarter of a century ago, why, we are completely overwhelmed at the results of christian neglect and human disregard.

At the present time all men of conscientious thought sincerely believe justice toward both convict and State should be the motto for the governing of our penal institutions, as unnecessary and cruel punishment of convicts has long since been analyzed and declared void of all salutary effect, and detrimental to the prevention of the increase of crime. The color of men's actions — like that of objects — depends on the light. Convicts are of the same nature as the majority of men whom we meet in our daily walks of life, and it is inherent in human nature to protest against any system of a cringing form. Many demoralizing acts of punishment were in vogue during the reign of terror which at the present time are beyond the conception of human reasoning.

It should be remembered that in those days women convicted of crime were incarcerated here. And within these prison walls the deafening scream of women's voices were frequently heard in their unavailing appeals for mercy, while their burning and bleeding flesh was being torn by the lash in the hands of John Martin. In a moral and conscientious light, it seems to be trespassing upon refinement and moral law for men to have the statutory power to have absolute control of an institution for women, even with pure and unblemished records, and it seems unnatural for men to have almost unlimited power over an institution of female convicts. If refinement is arduous and almost imperceptible, and if the moral strides are short and meagre in places of confinement where men govern their own sex, then it is reasonable to believe that depravity will diminish and the products of moral refinement be enlarged where men are empowered with absolute control of an institution for female prisoners?

Which have been the most assiduous and enduring in their efforts toward erasing immorality and vice from our land? Societies and leagues of men, or societies and leagues of women?

We presume that violators of the laws of our land are deprived of their liberty for the purpose of proper chastisement and reflection, as well as a safeguard to society and a deterring obstacle to crime and immorality. Penal institutions are erected for the protection and purity of society, and not with the sole intention of eradicating the last flickering spark of self respect. Experience in prison life has produced convincing proof that men should have control of the penal institutions of their own sex, and women the control of institutions for women. Perhaps there is no institution where some of the inmates will not incur the displeasure and ever be at cross purposes with some of their superiors, and under such circumstances corporal punishment seems inevitable, but it should be administered by one of the same sex as the offender.

At the time we now refer to there were about thirty women in the Jackson prison. Among them were two colored and one Indian woman. One of the colored women came from Kalamazoo county in September, 18 — , and was doing a life sentence, and the other one a long term of years. But like the rest of their race, it was impossible for surrounding adversities to suppress their natural mirth and hilarity. The trio was the life and light of the female prison, and their plantation melodies and Indian warwhoops were music and sunshine for this dismal abode. Their numerous euphonious sayings and jocular ways were the cause of considerable sport and outbursts of laughter among the remainder of the women.

As previously stated, only a high board fence separated the women's department from the men's, and by ascending to the upper story of the building and approaching the windows it was an easy matter to converse with the men while passing through the yard or with those at work in the shops. A severe punishment was in store for the woman or man caught in the act of conversing or attracting the attention of one another.

It is just as natural and the desire quite as predominant to talk as it is to breathe or laugh, and just as impossible to abstain. It was the means of replenishing the daily number of victims for the lash to appease Deputy Martin's insatiable thirst for blood. It was impossible for him to dispel or curb the natural merriment and lightheartedness of those two colored girls, and his fruitless efforts to suppress their glee was a burden of perpetual worriment, and on several occasions the severity of their punishment indicated he was a man devoid of mercy and disregarded feminity.

They were tortured in almost every conceivable way possible to produce human misery. They were starved, cat-whipped and kept in dungeons. But all of his truculent and inhuman acts were unavailable in obliterating their jocular expressions, or extinguishing their sportive inclination. Like the rest of the colored race, mirth and sunshine was engendered at their birth, and could only be divorced by the hands of death itself. The release from their places of torture was the signal for the renewal of comical expressions, plantation songs and Indian war whoops; and again wreaths of smiles and pleasantry were depicted in hourly growth upon the countenances throughout the female department.

Prison life can only be pictured, or even imagined in its mildest form, to those who have slept within prison cells and breathed their poisonous atmosphere. It is just as impossible to form a correct idea of prison life without experience, as to form any adequate idea of the most destructive cyclone of the ocean by verbal information. It must be witnessed in order to be realized.

Under the best circumstances that any prison can possibly afford, or concessions that will ever be made to the inmates, prison life will ever be a living death, and before the close of this book we will produce a convincing amount of indisputable evidence that there is not one man among a thousand who can endure a long term of imprisonment, employed on contract work, without making a sacrifice of some of the mental or physical faculties. We will name many who entered the prison doors that were models in mental and physical attainments, and who in a few years of prison life and contract labor were reduced to human skeletons and raving maniacs. Furthermore, we will call the names of men yet living, who after years of unrequited toil (thereby filling the coffers of contractors) were found to be innocent of the crime that caused their incarceration, and were released by executive clemency, and left these prison doors wrecked in mind and body, no home, no friends. And with the paltry sum of seven dollars and fifty cents tendered them by the great State of Michigan they went forth in the midst of both pessimists and critics to resurrect a new home, new friends, a new life, out of the very dregs and ashes of adversity.

If such obstacles as those are sufficient to palsy the will and energy of strong men, then what evidence can be produced in justification of a similar treatment of women? And, with the exception of contract labor, their circumstances were parallel to those of the men.

On Christmas morning the two colored women, Gosher Revengo, (Indian), and Maggie Karl (white woman), were standing at the window admiring the beautiful snow flakes that were slowly falling upon the earth. As a company of men were marching toward the dining room, they were greeted with the cheering words, "We wish you a merry Christmas," that rang through the air from female voices who were standing at the window in the upper story of the woman's department. For a manifestation of their gratitude and good wishes, their compliment was returned in one unanimous shout from the hoarse voices of the entire company of fifty men. This was considered, (by Deputy Martin) as supreme and irreparable breach of the rules, and the entire day was consumed in dealing copious and blood drenching showers of the lash, and other methods of maltreatment and abuse.

On Christmas, and other legal holidays, convicts expect a day of rest and an extra quality of food. But many were disappointed, and during that Christmas day some were made to forget that it was the birth day of "Peace on earth and good will to men."

The four women were held responsible by the Deputy, as the real instigators of such an unpardonable offense against the rules and discipline of the prison, and each of them was shackled with their hands to the iron door of a cell and severely lashed on their bare back, and during the torturing process their screams evoked the sympathy, and enkindled the ire of some of the most hardened criminals that ever shed human blood.

No one can tell what might have been the result, if this had occured on any day when the men were not locked in their cells, for volumes of oaths and curses re-echoed through the corridors as they were being hurled at John Martin from the lips of every man confined within these prison walls.

John Martin believed the colored women to be the principals of all the hilarity and disturbances that originated in the female department, and the Indian girl, their voluntary companion, so the trio, after a very severe punishment with the lash, was chained together with their hands behind them and with their elbows touching one another, and in this position they were locked in the dungeon from the begining of the afternoon until the next morning.

We believe the many barbarous and inhuman deeds perpetrated during the reign of terror were unequaled in all the prison history of this country from its earliest date. And we are not exaggerating nor overdrawing the iniquitous facts which compelled our decision, and sustains us in our verdict that the governing power of women in our penal institutions should be entirely in the hands of their own sex. And we are unswerving in the belief that our land is overflowing with women who are fully competent to rule and meet all the moral and punitive emergencies that may originate in places wherein females may be incarcerated.

It is not for the purpose of producing public criticism nor creating a sensation, that we have attempted to vindicate our objections of masculine ruling over feminine rights. And our opinion may be considered by some an encroachment upon a privilege which has been exercised and utilized by men, until it became, not only lawful, but their natural and inalienable right. But in reaching our decision we have used truth as our basis, and conscience for a guide. Any law or custom that conflicts with justice and conscience, ought to be abolished.

Many other things concerning Michigan's living tomb we have yet to consider, and must now leave our incomplete description of the penitentiary reign of terror and direct our minds to more recent events, which are equally harrowing and not more creditable to justice and conscience than those of bygone days, and which are yet so indelibly impressed on our minds

CHAPTER IV
A NEW ADMINISTRATION — A CHANGE FOR THE BETTER — A WOMAN PHILANTHROPIST

IN the year 1872 John J. Bagley was elected Governor of the State, and he appointed John Morris to the wardenship of Jackson prison, and George Winans was appointed deputy warden.

A change of any kind was very desirable, for we were thoroughly convinced that our condition would not be made more unenviable, so a change in the management of the prison was welcome and long desired.

From the many alterations made in the rules and regulations at the beginning of the new administration, we were confident that at last our star of hope was slowly ascending. One of the first and most important changes made was in regard to our food. Just prior to this the prisoners were fed in an old brick building that was standing in the yard a few feet from the north wall. The building was about seventy by forty feet and two and a half stories in height. The ground floor was our dining-room, and over the dining-room was a cigar shop, where many convicts were daily employed.

The floor of the cigar shop was strewn with tobacco leavings and cigar dust, and particles were ever falling through the crevices in the floor. Under the old regime, very frequently our mutton soup was flavored with tobacco dust, which was sifted through cracks in the ceiling by the heavy tread of prisoners descending from the cigar shop to partake of their scanty meals. The dining-room was the place where Divine services were held on Sabbath days, although men were frequently chained there and given scores of lashes on Sunday mornings before church time.

For many years six days during the week, right in the midst of odor arising from many bales of tobacco, we had been fed on deadly mutton soup, and then on the seventh day, marched to the same place and stimulated with the sacred precepts — love your enemies and pray for those who wrongfully use you.

The beginning of the new administration was the end of mutton soup and all other unsavory food, and whatever else may be said that is not commendable, yet it is an indisputable fact, that the relishable food furnished convicts under the reign of John Morris has not been equaled during the time of the oldest inhabitant of Jackson prison. His wife was an estimable woman and her desire to cheer us in our gloomy abode was unfailing. She delighted in surprising us with delicacies, and frequently on entering our cells we have found many different dainties prepared by her own hands. She exercised great patience and sympathy among the younger class of prisoners, and her motherly precepts were much cherished by many who never had a mother's care. At noon time she was often present in our dining-room and in her eagerness to satisfy our appetites, assumed the duties of a common waitress. For the first time in the history of the prison the walls of our cells were adorned with some cheering pictures, and religious pamphlets were laid upon our beds. We never questioned from whence these things came, for we all knew.

Preparations for a new dining-room (which is the same that supplies food for the prisoners at the present time) were immediately begun. While digging the cellar we were again reminded of the penitentiary reign of terror. We were startled by the unearthing of three human skeletons, which were buried only a few feet beneath the surface and clad in decayed relics of convict clothing.

The finding of human skeletons would not have created any great surprise had they not been exhumed inside the prison walls. All of them had been buried without box or coffin, and the time of interment could only be determined by one of them, which was in a fair state of preservation.

But why they were buried inside the walls instead of the earth of the hog pen in the convict's burial ground, was a mystery to us and a problem which was only solved in our own minds.

Another commendable act under the new regime, one which was a necessity as well as a benefit in establishing a moral germ in the minds of the majority of the prison population, was the building of a chapel in a place more suitable for religious services than the old dining-room where they were once held. Perhaps there is no structure in Michigan which can boast of filling so many different missions, and is so unique in its history as the old brick building, which was for many years the convict's kitchen, chapel, and workshop. From this building the terrible disease originated which proved so fatal in its results. It was here that convicts for many years were steadily employed filling the overflowing coffers of contractors at the expense of the State. In this building sermons were preached and the echoes of the lash were frequently heard.

Warden Morris manifested a great deal of energy in the welfare of men who were serving life sentences.

By legislative authority he established a rule called the percentage act. By this act each convict at the expiration of the month received five per cent. of the money they had earned for the State, but a fine of one dollar was imposed for each report.

In those days convicts were seldom sold to contractors for less than one dollar a day; thereby it was possible for them to earn some money for themselves. But this rule was abolished by the next legislature, for every dollar that was given to convicts was a loss to the State, although the most of the prisoners sent their money home at the end of each month to aid in the support of their wives and children. But the State chose to take the responsibility and support of these families without the convict's aid.

A contribution box was also placed in the visitor's waiting room for the benefit of life men, and each visitor could contribute something toward the financial interests of men called lifers. By this method, two or three of that class of men were enabled to pursue the proper course which resulted in their successful attempts to procure pardons.

It is seldom we meet those whose energy and determination to contribute something to the uplifting and reconstructing of fallen men, have met with any degree of success. And when present obstacles, which surround convicts, are compared with those with a score of years ago, who will say that a woman who successfully advocated prison philanthropy and held her ground against the scorchings of prison critics and public opinion, until the entire sentiment of the people changed and rallied to her support, is not worthy of an abundance of merit.

We are living in the age of moral and intellectual development, and in our expansion of knowledge it is possible for us to look back a score of years and observe the multiple advantages now for the moral and mental betterment of criminals. In these times many of the barriers that once existed between convicts and citizens have disappeared. Disease and death, sorrowing and suffering, still afflict our prisons as elsewhere, but our prisons are morally, mentally and physically healthier places to live in than a few years since, and there is a wonderful change in public sentiment.

In the midst of all these obstacles a woman, Mrs. d'Arcambal, from Kalamazoo, Mich., visited Jackson prison and at once became deeply interested in the welfare of its inmates. It has already been stated that prior to her advent among us we were not supplied with underclothing, and as a manifestation of her sincerity she began canvassing different towns throughout the State, soliciting articles of underclothing for men in Jackson prison, thereby greatly increasing our warmth, thus promoting health during cold weather. The benefits of underwear during winter months was very soon visible in diminishing the number of men on the sick list. This was the means of underwear being regularly supplied at the expense of the State.

Frequently all assembled together while in plain and reasonable words she taught us the most elementary notions of propriety and decorum and directed the proper course to pursue at the expiration of imprisonment. Perhaps no other woman can be mentioned who has been more successful in seeking clemency for convicts. She was the means of securing a great number of pardons for men, some of whom were convicted on very questionable evidence on which to impose a life sentence.

The case of Tommy Kidd was the most difficult and perplexing she ever had upon her mind. He was a mere boy, imprisoned for life. For many years Mrs. d'Arcambal had been seeking a commutation of his sentence and frequently requested the different Governors of our State to consider the boy's age and previous circumstances. But all of her efforts were unavailing until the year 1884, when she secured his release. Josiah Begole was then Governor of the State. Many of those who were here for many years undergoing life sentences secured pardons by her aid and are now living honorable lives. Among the number is Charley Wright, who served nineteen years, and when pardoned went to the State of Minnesota and secured land under the homestead act. For two seasons in succession his crops proved a complete failure by means of the drouth which proved so disastrous to farmers throughout the state in the summers of 1885-6. During these two years many farmers in that state were bankrupt and famine seemed inevitable. Wright was at last compelled to mortgage his farm in order to obtain food and other necessities for winter. His health failed him and for months he was confined to his bed. The mortgage was due and financial vultures were anxious to foreclose.

The ex-convict wrote to his old companions in Jackson prison and informed them of his condition and they at once authorized the warden to find out if the statement was true. He did as requested and received indisputable evidence that the pardoned man had not exaggerated in his letter to his old associates. In the evening, after working hours, the convicts met together for the purpose of doing something to aid the sick man so far away and in such adverse circumstances. During the meeting several speeches were made relative to the mortgagee who was hasty and eager to deprive the owner of his home. The sentiment of the meeting was an honorable and fitting example for any law-abiding class of men. They all seemed to concur in their idea that any man who went forth from prison doors and was striving to live by the work of his own hands, should not be induced to part from the paths of rectitude, nor suffer during illness and lose his home thereby. As a manifestation of their zeal a subscription was called for and in a very few minutes more than twice the amount of the mortgage was raised and the check for three hundred dollars was immediately forwarded to relieve the Minnesota invalid. On the receipt of the money (much to the surprise and chagrin of the expectant land owner) the ex-convict relieved him of his claim. Afterwards he regained his health and by industry and frugality is now possessor of 160 acres of land well stocked and cultivated.

Mrs. d'Arcambal obtained pardons for convicts Charles Hewlett and Jacob Louie, both life men. Hewlett is yet living, and since his release has ever been worthy of his freedom, and now in old age is the owner of a comfortable home and a happy family. Jacob Louie was of German birth and departed for his native land soon after his release.

At last this woman who had devoted so much time and patience for the betterment of evil doers succeeded in establishing a home for ex-convicts in Detroit, which is a great benefit to men released from prison, they here having a place of shelter until enabled to find employment.

CHAPTER V
USE OF TOBACCO PROHIBITED — THE HAUNTED ROOM — THE LIGHTNING BOLT

THE second term of John Morris' administration presents a very different aspect when compared with his first. Perhaps there are few, however well intentioned or philanthropic, who, taking the responsibility of a prison with its avaricious contract system, would not in time become more or less contaminated by contact with hard and grasping contractors, and would find himself in the most tormenting position of his life.

The contract system is the very basis of nearly all the disturbances which originate during prison life. It is tormenting to prison authorities and a burning sore to the inmates, and we will produce facts which sustain us in the assertion that contract labor is burdensome and a disgrace to the State. Then it is not surprising at the beginning of his second term that the cat o' nine tails was again brought into use and many predicted he was gradually following in the trail of his dreaded predecessor.

The State law which permits us to see our relatives occasionally was entirely ignored, and our mothers, wives and other kindred who came were ruthlessly spurned and compelled to leave without our knowledge of their presence. Mrs. Van Anstell came from Ohio to see her husband John, who was serving a five year sentence for a burglary in Monroe county. He had been three years imprisoned before she learned of his whereabouts, and although this was her first visit since his incarceration, yet the wife and her five year old child were not allowed a glimpse of the husband and father, simply because ill health had prevented the completion of his task the day before she came. The wife in her anxiety to see him fully related the many sacrifices and inconveniences connected with herself and child prior to their journey. But all of her pleadings and reasonings were useless and unavailing. The Warden emphatically stated to this poor woman that her husband was undergoing punishment for disobedience and that it would be impossible to deviate from the established custom of the prison, or to investigate the severity considered necessary in such a case. Crestfallen and disappointed she left the prison doors, and when she wrote to him her letters were withheld and he knew not of her visit until the expiration of his sentence in the following year. We believe it was a malicious intention to wound and torment an innocent human being, and was the most unparalleled act of malevolence ever manifested toward a convict's wife and child by an officer of this prison. Even now the scorching recollection burns and stirs in our minds and gradually brings up horrible thoughts which have long been dormant.

What created the most universal surprise among us, and was considered a direct attempt to usurp our privileges, was the announcement of the Warden's order prohibiting the use of tobacco amongst convicts, and henceforward a severe punishment would be inflicted upon those found with it in their possession. We were aware our tobacco was given us by the laws of the State, and could only be suppressed with the State's consent.

For a few weeks no tobacco was issued, and during the interval the prisoners who worked in the cigar factory stealthily conveyed tobacco to the rest of their companions. By this method there seemed to be as much of it in circulation as ever.

The cigar establishment complained to Morris that a hundred dollars would not cover the amount of tobacco carried away by convicts during the month, and proposed the Warden should supply convicts with tobacco or recompense the firm for its loss. The Warden objected to their proposition and quickly retorted that he was not responsible for the shrinkage. However, he would be more alert, and at the first opportunity would make an example of those who were helping themselves to tobacco and distributing it amongst the other convicts.

The opportunity soon came, and it was the beginning of the end of his administration. Jim Lightfoot, (colored) was sentenced to thirty years imprisonment for a number of burglaries committed in the City of Detroit and in Wayne County. Twenty years ago a gang of bold highwaymen, called the "Break o' day Johnnies," were terrifying the inhabitants of that city, and Lightfoot was known as their leader until prison doors closed upon them. He was physically powerful and was very daring. His frankness and outspoken manner was not soothing to contractors, and was the means of much trouble for him with the prison authorities. The evening of the same day of the Warden's dispute with the cigar contractors the colored convict was seen to expectorate tobacco juice whilst marching in the ranks to his cell, and on being searched any amount of tobacco was found concealed in his clothing.

In the north end of the west wing there was a place for flogging purposes which was called the haunted room. There the screams of human beings and the whistling of the lash was so frequently heard that many of us believed those sounds originated spontaneously, and that their echoes might be heard even when the room was unoccupied. To this room convict Lightfoot was conveyed and received eighty lashes with the cat whip, and left hanging with his hands shackled to the iron door, from Saturday evening until Monday morning, when he was released and sent to work. As soon as he reached the shop, he deliberately selected the best tobacco he could find, and began to chew and expectorate on the keeper's desk, afterwhich he informed his shop mates of his treatment while in the haunted room. Before the hour of noon three bales of tobacco were secretly hacked into shavings and ten thousand cigars destroyed.

This outburst of hoarded malice and intentional waste, brought matters to such a crisis that it appeared as though the very elements had taken an active part. Convicts on the cigar contract declared they would chew tobacco as long as a particle of it remained on the contract, and if their tobacco was not restored, the destruction wrought that day was only the beginning of what would follow.

John Morris was not hasty to make concessions to convicts, but sought to intimidate and submit them to his will by his own dictations. Consequently on the afternoon of the episode, the lash was constantly in the air, and that night the haunted room was over-run. During the banishment of the rioters hot words ensued between the warden and contractors. They severely censured him for prohibiting convicts from using tobacco, thereby instituting perpetual discord between them and the contractors. In their opinion the warden had transcended his authority, and they insisted the new rule be annulled. But he was staunch and imperative in the course he had taken, and not being in sympathy with the contract system, declared his ability to run the prison without their assistance.

Prison disturbances were frequent and complaints to Governor Bagley were numerous. News of the recent outbreak was conveyed to him, and he concluded to make a thorough investigation at once, and sent word to that effect. In the meantime the instigators of the trouble were languishing in the haunted room. The news of the Governor's investigation was a signal for their release from punishment, and then a remarkable event occurred.

In the haunted room was a large iron ring fixed to the wall to which our hands were shackled whilst being flogged. Just prior to their release from punishment, the sun was shining and no clouds were visible. But soon thereafter, a black and angry looking cloud arose in the western sky and moved with great rapidity eastward until directly over the prison, when it seemed to halt. All at once an awful crash was heard and a bolt of fire came darting down upon the haunted room. When the lightning struck the building, the haunted room was filled with fire and smoke and one side of it torn out, the iron ring melted and crumbled to the floor.

Governor Bagley used sound judgment, great patience and was very successful searching for important facts, and a basis for complaints. His methods, on such occasions, were quite different from those of our other Governors.

It was his custom to be entirely alone while passing through the prison and would stop at our places of work, take a box or anything at hand to sit upon and talk of prison life. During these conversations he was often convinced that the prisoner was unjustly convicted, or had suffered enough for his crime, and immediately pardoned him. Henry Green, a colored convict sentenced from Detroit, was serving a term of seven years. One morning Governor Bagley, while passing through the shops, approached the colored convict and began to converse with him of prison life and why he chose a life of crime. The convict frankly admitted his guilt and how he was led to pursue the evil course by his evil associates, but when the remaining three years of his sentence expired he would strive to make an honest living for his widowed mother and himself, and if possible would regain his good character. The Governor replied: "You have no cause to wait three years before you make the effort, for you will have a chance to begin a new life at once." He was pardoned that day. His process of questioning so many of us and then comparing our statements enabled him to discern the facts, and in the tobacco trouble our grievances were sustained by veritable facts and concurred with many other complaints.

At the conclusion of his investigation the Governor was very much displeased by the many uncovered cases of illtreatment of convicts and at the disregard manifested toward our families and friends who visited us. The Governor was his own counselor; justice and conscience were his guide and it was impossible for him to entertain the thought of any injustice. He ordered our tobacco restored to us and severely criticised the Warden's ability to conduct the prison, and was outspoken in his opinion that some other man was more competent to fill that position.

A few days after the investigation Warden Morris tendered his resignation, which was readily accepted by the Governor. But, like many others, Warden Morris was wedded to his position and very much regretted to leave it. When the hour of separation came he was overwhelmed at the thought of leaving us to take good care of ourselves, or perhaps to fall into evil hands, and his heart overflowed with pity and love for our welfare. During his farewell speech to us in the dining room tears ran in streams from his eyes. None of our tears mingled with his at that lamentable fact, although many of our hearts were sad and our minds perplexed at the thought whether our next warden would keep in the present ratio of good victuals.

It is natural to suppose that all men imprisoned here are only paying the penalty of their crimes. But are they all perpetrators of the crimes for which they are incarcerated? We are told sometimes the law may err, but it must judge according to its lights. We believe that the law ought not to err, and our experience in prison life confirms the fact that in most cases circumstancial evidence is dangerous and unreliable and it is better to let ninety-nine guilty men go unpunished than to convict one innocent man. Are there no extenuating facts connected with some of us here imprisoned? There are men here who were mere boys when they entered these prison doors, and during many years of complete isolation with professional criminals they have shown no desire for the company of their criminal associates, and the records of their conduct since imprisonment are clean and unsoiled from reports.

The most of this junior class of convicts never had any intellectual training or heard a religious service prior to prison life. But now their religious opinions and their mental powers are in the common ratio of young men raised among church spires, guided by christian parents and taught within public school rooms. Under such conditions it is even justice to prolong the torturing here of this class of men, and for crimes committed while still too young to realize the enormity of their offenses. People in the outside world are disposed to look upon all men who commit the crime of murder as the very worst criminals imaginable.

Murder, it is true, is a great crime and when it is deliberately planned and executed in a spirit of revenge, or for the purpose of robbery or gain, should be punished to the fullest extent of the law. There was, however, a crime committed called murder, when, in fact, no intent was harbored nor any disposition to murder was entertained, there was no incentive, no preconceived plan for murder, no gain contemplated; only an altercation, strong passion, a struggle and the deed was done. The person who committed this deed was only a boy, and led a life as clean and pure as the most of boys who are raised with a father's care and blessed with a mother's love, although he was an orphan when the current of his hopes changed and wrecked his life. But the law made no distinction in his case; murder was the verdict; life the sentence. But there are analytical facts in this case worthy of great consideration. We know there is a disposition on the part of some in authority over orphans to wrong them, to treat them ill, to tantalize and use them unmercifully because of such authority. Forbearance, after awhile, seems to have been exhausted on the part of the abused one, and in a passion he seized a deadly implement and killed the person who had made his life intolerable.

George Burkhart, when a boy less than fifteen years old, was living with his step-uncle, who would get beastly drunk nearly every time he went to town or market. He would come home and upon the slightest provocation (and often without provocation) would beat and horsewhip the boy in the most cruel manner. The boy was entirely under his uncle's control; he was without another home, uneducated, and no friends to advise, admonish or cheer him. After so much abuse forbearance in his case ceased to be a virtue, and in the midst of one of these scenes and in the heat of passion caused by this perpetual system of dire abuse, he seized a loaded musket and killed the tyrant who had made his life so miserable. For this crime he was arrested and convicted at Ann Arbor, in, September, 1875, and sentenced to imprisonment for life. He received the same punishment that the convict did who boasted he had killed ten people and was very sorry he had killed no more. Hundreds of men who have stood over their victims, robbing their bodies of all their earthly possessions have been pardoned. Hundreds of men who have committed the most heinous offenses have been pardoned out of the prisons of this country, and many in this State.

Still, this boy, who is here for defending, perhaps, his own life at the age of fifteen years, and after remaining here nearly two decades is still behind prison bars. Although he has always obeyed the rules and never even been reported for misconduct during his long term of confinement, yet no human being has ever even made an effort toward securing clemency or investigating his case. This orphan has received but one letter for ten years, and if there is a man here worthy of any commiseration, it is Convict George Burkhart.

CHAPTER VI
PRISON LIFE AT MIDNIGHT — SHAVING ON SHORT NOTICE — HORRIBLE FATALITIES

WHO can imagine an innocent man's thoughts, when behind prison walls and wide awake at midnight. Who can picture the dreams of the cold blooded murderer when sleeping. Many believe that sleep is the counter-part of death, and no pains or penalties can reach the slumberer. For whilst asleep, his spirit lives in an awful solitude, unapproachable like its maker. But we are adverse to such opinions, and will take the convict's dreams for the basis of our disbelief. During the hours of sleep, the spirit is free to soar where e'er it will, and in its flight frequently travels in various places, the memory of which it retains when the body is again reanimated, and which we call a dream. If sleep is the brother of death, then man's spirit never slumbered, nor ever will, and at midnight the ghost of the murdered man comes to the bed-side of his slayer, and while the culprit sleeps, the disembodied visitor engages in hot dispute and argument with the slumberer's spirit.

At nine o'clock the prison gong signals the hour of bed time. Suddenly the electric light in each cell disappears and the inmate is left alone with his conscience. He can then reflect upon his past life and devise new plans for the future. The first night of imprisonment is the longest, and most dreadful to the culprit than any of the remaining nights of his incarceration. It is the first time he fully realizes the severity of the crime, and it is most keenly felt.

In a dark and dismal cell which must be his home for many years, perhaps future hopes sink beneath the despair of present realities. This alone, is sufficient to oppose all somnolent feelings and cancel all desire for repose. But there are other potent reasons for the convict's wakefulness. The slumbers of men imprisoned are more vague and unnatural than in any other condition. It is no exaggeration for us to say that at all hours of the night more than one-third of the men are wide awake, and listening to the mutterings of their fellow prisoners, who, in their troubled dreams, are talking in their sleep. Some are dreaming of home and loved ones and even in the first degree of crime the white searching light of truth and experience is teaching them that only misery exists along the course they have pursued. These facts are being so indelibly impressed on their minds, that they contemplate them in their dreams and repeat them over and over again in their sleep.

These visions are moral sentinels, which if heeded and cherished will yet lead men to pure and happy lives. But if ignored and uncultivated they will soon vanish and their vacancy will be replaced with meditations of deadly revenge and hostile intentions.

Men in the beginning of prison life seldom manifest any great amount of concern for their own welfare, but are very much disheartened and downcast at the thought of the humiliating conditions in which they have placed some other persons from whom they are being separated.

However, there is another class of men imprisoned here who do not care to sleep and, perhaps, could not if they so desired. Some of them have been so long in confinement that their desire for executive clemency seems to have died out, yet the flickering hope of once again breathing free air is ever present in their minds. Their hoarded thoughts of freedom have augmented and in the dead hours of night their imprisonment becomes unreal and imaginary. At these illusive periods very grave apprehensions are frequently indulged in. The son fancies he hears the loving voice of mother whispering his name; the father harkens to the prattling of his child; the cold blooded murderer hears the dying groans of his victim and imagines his blood stained countenance standing in the room. And then a terrible shriek is heard from some dark and lonely cell of the corridors and the night guards only look toward the place whence those noises emanate, and express no unusual surprise or concern, for the many previous nights of such disturbances have long since taught them — it is midnight in Jackson prison.

When John Morris resigned his position Governor Bagley appointed William Humphrey to the vacant Wardenship. At the beginning of his administration the most of his criminal subjects were on the lookout for any changes that might take place in the rules and methods of the prison. Our greatest concern was in regard to our food. And on entering the dining room all eyes were quickly turned toward the dinner plates in the anxiety to observe the least diminution in the amount or quality of our victuals. For a while everything seemed to be moving as well as the most of us expected, and even better than the most sanguine predicted.

Mrs. Morris, who was naturally kind and pleasant and was very attentive to our wants at meal times, had left us, and we were loth to be deprived of her familiar presence. After she had left us many were our misgivings as to future sympathy and motherly care. But the wife of the new Warden was equal to her predecessor, and was as deeply interested in our welfare. There was no curtailing of the many delicacies previously found in our cells at night, and our stock of moral and religious reading matter was replenished.

The most notable and cheerful picture under the new reign was the Warden's little girl, who was always running and playing with her pet rabbits. This little girl racing with her well trained pets was the first attraction ever within these walls which was effective in turning our thoughts homeward. Many of us were forced to think of our own little ones at home. Men who were old and gray would approach the windows of the shops and gaze at the child playing upon the lawn. And as the tears began to gather in their eyes they would turn from the window and walk away with the remark that the little girl playing yonder reminded them of their own children whom they had left at home many years ago.

Convicts are always very suspicious of a new set of officers, and especially the Warden. Although our dinner hour was quite as inviting as under the previous reign, yet it was the opinion of some that good things are not always long lived, and frequently they are only bad ones in disguise.

We had heard that Warden Humphrey had been a great general during the late rebellion, and perhaps he was only waiting to find out all of our vulnerable places of attack, for we were not sure he was entirely cured of his thirst for blood. However, we had not very long to wait before the prophecies of the most correct ones were confirmed. Soon after General Humphrey's appointment, Dwight Hinkley was appointed Deputy Warden, and then misery and trouble for us was at hand. It is the opinion to-day of many of the old timers here that Deputy Hinkley was as cruel an officer as ever drew groans from a convict within these walls. His cruel deeds, the severity of his punishments, were unsurpassed by Deputy John Martin in the times of Warden H. H. Bingham's reign of terror.

At the time our literary meetings were in full bloom under Warden Hatch's administration, it was proposed we should debate the following question:

"*Resolved*, That Deputy Hinkley took more delight in flogging convicts and was more dextrous with the lash than Deputy Martin."

The president of the meeting (Warden Hatch) expressed his opinion on the subject, saying the question was too weighty and prolific for us to accurately determine, and the resolution was laid on the table.

Warden Humphrey, prior to the advent of his deputy, had conveyed the impression that he was a firm believer in the reformation of criminals. He occasionally visited the cells and conversed with the inmates on the subject of reform. But soon thereafter, we were told, he appeared before the Legislature at Lansing and informed that august assembly that men emerging from his command exhausted their money in spiritous liquor and its contingencies, and he desired the annulment of the percentage act. (Which was virtually asking for the reduction of convicts pay on leaving the prison to the paltry sum of seven dollars and fifty cents.) The Warden's suggestion was considered at the State Capitol as a move in the right direction, it being financially of great importance to the State. They could not see any reason for further continuance of the per centage act, and much against our wishes it was immediately canceled. This change was a great discouragement to many of us, for it cut off the means whereby we had been enabled to aid in the support of our wives and children. And when it became generally known that the per centage act was suppressed there was much dissatisfaction.

The unexpected change was very gratifying to the knowing ones, for it was a potent factor in sustaining their previous predictions, and they simply shook their heads and said, "We told you so."

Our new warden, in many respects, was superior to his predecessors, but he was not averse to the contract system. Only two men who have held the wardenship here in a quarter of a century have not been in favor of convict slave trade. We will, however, call the names of wardens who during their term of office have manifested a determination to do justice to convicts as well as to contractors.

Just as soon as a new warden is properly installed, his mind and patience are constantly being harrowed with unending complaints and demands of contractors for more work from their serfs. And from some cause unknown to us, they are generally very successful in their demands.

We shall endeavor to give our readers some idea of the methods employed in the greedy contract system.

The State had a lawful agreement with contractors that their subjects should be allowed ample time for shaving and bathing purposes. Twenty minutes once a week for each man to shave and the same for bath, was the time agreed upon, and the prison barbers came into the shops to shave us. But Mr. Elijah Cooley came into the shop one day and saw three or four men standing by the barber's chair waiting for their turn. He immediately sought the warden and informed him that convicts were allowed to stand waiting and they were taking advantage of it to keep from work. After hearing such information from the lips of a contractor the warden instructed the keeper to take notice of the time when he called a man from his work to get shaved, and when the prisoner returned to his work. The keeper must make a list of the number of minutes thus occupied and forward the same to the warden. Time was so precious that we were not allowed to stop and wash our faces after leaving the barber's chair. Those who were shaved in the morning were compelled to let the fragments of lather and hair remain drying on their faces until time to prepare for dinner. And those who were shaved in the afternoon could not wash-until time to quit work at night, for not a minute could be spared for cleanliness.

On the 27th day of April, 1877, John Patridge was sentenced from the city of Jackson to a term of twenty-five years. He was a new man in the shop and was not cognizant of this rule. After he was shaved he started to wash the lather from his face and out of his ears. But Keeper Gallup halted him and said he must not stop to wash, but go to work at once. The prisoner had taken a drink of water and retained a part of it in his mouth, and with this moistened his handkerchief and wiped his face and ears. The keeper chided him severely for this violation of the rules, and threatened severe consequences if the act was ever repeated. This system of shaving was very satisfactory to contractors, for the average time we were absent from our work was less than ten minutes. After a few months of this rapid kind of barbering its injurious effect was plain to be seen upon our faces, and the warden concluded the rule was neither justice to us nor in accordance with the lawful time allowed by the contract, and he ordered the rule discontinued.

For some reason or other it seems customary for the most unjust and exacting mechanics to be selected for foremen in the contract shops. They are not so numerous here at the present time as they were a few years ago, for some of those we now have are very reasonable with us and always pleasant. But some yet remain who profess to have had a great deal of experience in their trade, and yet they exercise unjust judgment of what should constitute a day's work. On the Withington & Cooley contract the foreman was John Landers. He was a bloodthirsty tyrant when he took control of the shop and a murderer when he left it. It is safe for us to say that before he was compelled to leave he did not have a friend inside of the prison walls, except the contractors, by whom he was employed. Neither convicts nor officers had any use for him. He was of a revengeful nature, and when once displeased at a prisoner he would not let him rest and was ever on the alert for some means to have him punished. Death and accident seemed to be lurking in the shop from the day he came into it until the day he committed murder and was compelled to leave. In those days prison life on the contract was a hard one. One day Convict Donovan remarked to a fellow prisoner that a dead death was preferable to a living one, and the next day he was a corpse. Whether he committed suicide or was killed by accident will never be known. If it had not been for the despondent mood manifested prior to his death it would have been more reasonable for us to believe that it was an accident, for his sentence would have expired in a few days. But in some inexplicable manner he was thrown into the pit where the fly wheel of many tons weight was swiftly revolving and his body was crushed into an unrecognizable mass and was taken out of the pit in pieces.

While this sacrifice of a human life was still fresh in our minds another sad affair occurred. We had long since become accustomed to the crash of ponderous trip hammers and the hiss of whirling machinery, but seeing one of our companions thus rapidly whirled to death was a sad and revolting sight. The death of our comrade Westgate was an accident. His clothing became entangled with the belting while at work and he was thrown many times against the ceiling with tremendous force and instantly killed.

The next horrible death that occurred is surely without a parallel in the history of the prison. The horrible manner in which Convict Vanatten deliberately chose to die is conclusive that he was insane. He was sent from Monroe county and was doing a life sentence for the murder of his wife and daughter with an ax. In order that he might prevent the guards from entering the cell before his deadly intentions were carried out he piled his bedding against the cell door, applied a match and then plunged headlong into the flames. J. H. Purvis, captain of the night guard, was startled in the dead hours of night by the smell of smoke. On examination fire was seen issuing from a convict's cell. The suicidal plan was so laid that it was impossible to enter the cell until the inmate was so severely burned that he died soon after being extricated.

During these fatalities Convict Mix was having a trying time with the foreman, John Landers. Mix was an Irish Canadian, and one of the most stupid and headstrong human beings imaginable. He was very obstinate and quickly angered, but an excellent worker, and with proper treatment might have been easily managed. In him the foreman found a fit subject for dissatisfaction and even abhorrence. Their quarrels and disputes frequently caused Mix to be chained to the whipping post. One day he had finished some work, and as usual, the foreman was displeased with it and commanded him to do it over again. Hot words ensued and Deputy Hinkley took him to the hall and flogged him.

But at last they had reached the limit of his patience, and punishment only made him worse. His perverse attitude was very pleasing to the head workman, and he removed none of the obstacles of discord. One day while being chided by his superior he became angry and talked back. John Landers reported him at once. The deputy took him to the hall and he was severely lashed and then sent to the hospital, where he died a few days thereafter. We were told that the coroner's verdict in his case was spinal meningitis.

Under this foreman's control was James Dougherty, a burly Irishman doing a ten years' sentence. For once John Landers found his equal, for Convict Dougherty was ever ready to resent an insult, and the disputes and altercations between them were frequent. The foreman was very cautious and timid whilst imposing on his well matched subordinate. One evening he went up town and purchased a large jack-knife, and the following morning when showing the deadly looking blade to a prisoner in the shop he remarked to Convict Patridge that when the burly Irishman ran against that blade he would not feel so funny. One of my shop mates said: "Why, Mr. Landers, surely you would not plunge that blade into a man, would you?" With an oath he replied: "That is just the purpose for which it was bought." We will soon see whether he was in earnest or not, and the manner in which his murderous intentions were executed. We at once informed Convict Dougherty of his danger and advised him to consider present circumstances and avoid as much as possible the altercations with his superior. In some manner the prisoner succeeded in getting changed to another contract, and more recent events developed the fact that perhaps the change was the means of saving his life.

CHAPTER VII
CUNNING ESCAPES — WASHINGTON'S BIRTHDAY BANQUET — CONVICT McLOUD KILLED

IT seems as if some men were born to a heritage of misery, exposure and crime; while others are happily nurtured in christian homes, and under so many protecting influences that the path of virtue lies straight and open before them; so plain, indeed, that even the blind could safely walk therein. The latter class may not look upon the unearthed horrors of prison life with any great amount of sentiment or concern; for it may seem to them that we are but undergoing a just retribution in expiation of our sins.

We believe we are about to narrate the most notable incident in our prison history, for we are now within the radius of events not so remote, but that they are easily recalled to our minds, and some of which may have already been partially told by the press. But a quarter of a century behind these walls, with its many vicissitudes, has convinced us that it is almost impossible for the press to learn the true version of a prison disturbance, as it is very seldom that reporters are allowed within these walls, and never within the dungeons — the home of our complaints. The press, in general, receives the prison news by telephone, and frequently it is liable to be much curtailed, and thus conveyed from the lips of an interested official it is taken and given to the world.

In the year 1884 Josiah Begole was elected Governor of the State, and very soon thereafter we had a complete change of administration. E. B. Pond was appointed to the wardenship and Spencer C. Drake succeeded Dwight Hinkley as deputy warden. We shall not give a very lengthy description of this administration, which was short and uneventful.

Warden Pond was with us but two years, during which time we could not but believe him to be naturally just and entirely unbiased, and we have not yet had a warden more frank and open hearted. He made no concessions to contractors nor tolerated prison pets.

During his term of office our food, while not superior to that furnished by some of his predecessors, was always wholesome and well cooked. He was a thorough believer in discipline and held us responsible for disobedience of the rules. We were ever alert and very anxious to avoid being reported, for this meant the deprivation of privileges for a period of six months, during which time no delicacies were allowed the offender.

There were fewer reports and vexations during this administration than in any other corresponding period of time. He was not in sympathy with the contract system, and their complaints were weighed with great discretion, and in most cases were proven to be unfounded. Consequently there was not a premium on contractor's reports. He believed that a prisoner who had labored silently and diligently during working hours had complied with the rules of the prison and also with the demands of the State, and ought not to be punished for having failed to perform a contractor's desired task, which for some men was far beyond their physical strength.

In the beginning of this administration, and before it became acquainted with the shrewd and cunning abilities possessed by some of those herein imprisoned, there occured one of the most daring and unique escapes in the history of the prison.

Marine Smith, a colored convict, was serving a sentence of twenty-five years for a murder committed in the city of Detroit. During the previous administration his many attemps to escape had proved futile. When detected the last time with two other prisoners in scaling the west wall, he attributed his ill success and many failures to the sluggishness of those who accompanied him, and declared that the next time he attempted to escape he would go by himself, and that it would be a success. He kept his word, and it terminated just as he had predicted. At the time of the episode the wing containing the cell blocks was partially roofed with glass skylight. One night in the month of February, 1884, when the prisoners were unlocked for school, Convict Smith remained in his cell until the rest of the prisoners had reached the school room. Then quickly mounting to the top of the cell block, he uncoiled a rope which he had prepared for the occasion, and with great precision he hurled it to the rafters overhead. Then all at once a crash was heard and a shower of glass came rattling down upon the stone floor. The guards, attracted by the noise, came running to the spot and were in time to discover the form of a man vanishing through the skylight. But Smith made so rapid use of his rope that before they could reach the outside of the prison he had decended beyond the walls and had disappeared in the darkness. When we consider the icy condition of the slanting roof from which he made his descent to the ground, fifty feet below, we must admit that his escape was a very hazardous undertaking.

After this daring escape the warden concluded that no more should occur in that manner, and immediately had the skylight removed and the holes roofed over with the same material as the rest of the building.

Warden Pond, skeptical of prison reform, did not place much faith in a prisoner who was ever speaking of his lofty and ardent intentions for the future, unless sustained by his daily deportment. But he was ever ready and willing to aid those who made a sincere effort or were anxious to improve on their former line of conduct. He was not afraid to conduct the prison as his own judgment dictated, and was uninfluenced by the adverse criticism that followed every change in administration.

During this administration very little improvement was made in the dismal appearance of the prison. The only one worth mentioning was the laying of a sidewalk, which proved to be worthless and soon decayed.

Deputy Warden Drake was, generally speaking, liked by the prisoners, although he was considered by some to be ostentatious and inclined to domineer in his official position. Be that as it may, he was powerless to employ any great amount of unjust severity, even if he so desired, for Warden Pond exercised a watchful eye and would not permit any infringement on the convicts' rights.

One day in the month of April, 1884, convict Johnson was reported and the deputy came to the shop and ordered him to go to the hall. The prisoner did not seem in any hurry to comply with the demand, whereon the deputy pulled his revolver and leveling it at the convict said, "Go to the hall at once or take the consequences." This persuasion was sufficient, and the prisoner started for the hall on a run. We do not believe any dire results would have followed, even if the culprit had longer tarried, for, as soon as he had left the shop the deputy laughed at his rapid strides and called him a coward.

We believe the most cowardice was shown by the man that drew the deadly weapon, for it was an uncalled for display of authority over a puny and defenseless prisoner, and perhaps under other circumstances it may not have occurred. Johnson's offense on this occasion could not have been very great, for when investigated by the warden he was exhonerated and sent back to work.

For many years it has been customary for the contractors to furnish prisoners with a dinner which is far more sumptuous than the regular daily food. This banquet occured annually on the 22d of February. The contractors are convinced that we are worthy of extra compensation for our labor, and once in every twelve months we are welcome to what we can eat at their expense. During the banquet speeches are made by invited guests, contractors or convicts. After which songs and instrumental music are indulged in. Very little of the sentiment of the orator on this occasion has any material bearing or reference to the man who is called the saviour of his country and for whom the day is held in commemoration. The speaker generally strives to impress upon our minds the benefits derived from the contract system, and skilfully depicts the bountiful results where servants submissively obey their masters.

In 1885, while enjoying our yearly festival, Mr. E. A. Webster stepped upon the platform and introduced to us Hiram F. Hatch, who had been appointed warden by R. A. Alger, the new Governor. Many of the old timers at once recognized him as a man, who in bygone times had operated a shoe shop here on the contract plan and were satisfied that at last they were at the mercy of task masters. He at once proceeded to address us in a very commendable manner, saying he was well pleased at our healthy appearance and was satisfied that many were merely criminals by accident and not by profession. In glowing words he depicted the future happiness and prosperity in store for those who were determined to live by the sweat of their brow and were convinced of the truth "that it is better to starve than to steal."

Very soon after he assumed the duties of his office many changes were made in the appearance and management of the prison. Some of the alterations were of great importance and much needed for the sanitary welfare of the place. He at once began making preparations for the introduction of an electric lighting plant in order to supply each cell with a separate light, which very soon thereafter was completed and in operation. His first plant for illuminating the cells was a failure, the lights being placed in the corridors in front of the cells, it being impossible by this method to produce sufficient brilliancy for the inmates to see to read, and consequently he had the lights removed from the corridors and placed in each cell. Soon after this he turned his attention to the yard, and for a while many convicts were steadily employed grading, sodding and adorning it with beds of sweet smelling flowers, and the result was a beautiful lawn not surpassed in Jackson.

Many prisoners who were very anxious to make their escape were closely watching him while his time and attention was thus diverted, and while he was so busily engaged in remodeling the prison and improving its appearance and sanitary conditions, there were others who were just as busily engaged in making their preparations to leave it. While he was digging on top of the earth they were tunneling beneath it. The plan of escape was by means of a tunnel constructed under an old unused storehouse that stood about thirty feet from the north wall, and beneath which the loosened earth was secreted. The six men who were so earnestly engaged in this work during the many months required to construct their subterranean passage were all desperate men, whose sentences ranged from seven years to life.

It certainly shows culpable negligence, or a laxity of discipline, for men who were sentenced for such terms to have been able to consumate such a wonderful plan of escape.

Convict Geo. Wilson, was supposed to be the real instigator of the plot. He was convicted in Detroit in March, 1884, for the murder of policeman Bullard, and was sentenced to life imprisonment. During the eleven months of his incarceration he was one of a number of prisoners whose names were on the free list — a list of men who are permitted to go in and out of the shops as their work calls them. Convict Lawson was undergoing a sentence of fifteen years for burglary and assault committed in Wayne County in April, 1884. This was his second term, having previously completed a sentence of five years here for a similar offense. Dakin and Ryan were serving terms of ten and fifteen years respectively for burglarious crimes, and Geo. Murray was doing seven years for pilfering from dwellings at midnight. John Talbot was sent from Muskegon County for fifteen years for manslaugter. He was a big strong Irishman, weighing over two hundred pounds and was the last of the gang who made their exit through the tunnel.

When he attempted to emerge from its mouth he found it was too small to permit the passage of his bulky form, and found himself fastened in the hole, with his head and shoulders in plain view. While struggling to extricate himself from this predicament, he was discovered by the guard on the wall who was only a few rods away. His companions had escaped unseen and before the guard had recovered from his surprise, the man had freed himself, and at once started on the run, but the whistling bullet that grazed his ear was a sufficient inducement for him to stop without further warning. Three days after the out break all the rest were captured while fast asleep in a farmer's barn, near Coldwater, except Wilson and Ryan who made good their escape.

We have already stated that Warden Hatch was once engaged in contract work, and it is not reasonable to believe that he was entirely unmindful of contractors interests. It was now the right time for contractors demands and complaints, and soon after the outbreak it was proposed by some of the task masters, that their subjects should be supplied with more work, and perhaps thereby the time and opportunities for digging tunnels and planning escapes would be lessened. The suggestion was duly considered, and much to our surprise we were informed by the warden, that in the future, heavier tasks would be required. It will be remembered that in these times some of the stronger workmen were enabled by their strength and skill to perform an extra amount of labor, thus daily earning overtime for themselves. But these were generally old timers, of long experience, or men with families for whose support they were willing and anxious to labor. It was not very encouraging news for them, when told by the warden that in future they would be required to perform the extra labor without any compensation. The information was none the less dishearting to those not so skillful in their work, and many were the murmurings against the contract system, which was justly called the blackest form of servitude sustained by law. But it was cheering news for John Landers, the foreman before spoken of on the Cooly contract, for during the during the two years of Warden Pond's administration, he was held in check, and unable to persist in his former persecutions.

The increase of tasks revived discords which had long lain dormant. For some time it seemed that Landers had been much displeased with convict McCloud. His work was frequently complained of and rejected, although perhaps as perfect as that performed by other prisoners, for which they were often commended. McCloud well knowing the savage and quarrelsome disposition of Landers, and not forgetting the deadly threats made soon after purchasing the murderous looking knife, which he yet retained, sought to avoid contention as much as possible by doing his work in the most perfect manner. His efforts to please were unavailing, for the knife was purchased with the intention of staining it with convict blood and its mission must be fulfilled. Convicts are of the same nature as other men whom we meet in our daily life, and are more irritable and easily provoked because imprisoned. At last McCloud became impatient at being so much abused, and boldly resented the unmerited persecutions. One day he had finished some work which the foreman ordered him to do over again. A fierce quarrel ensued. The prisoner advanced in a threatening manner toward the foreman, who, quick as a flash, drew the knife and plunged it into the convicts side, saying, take that, d — you. The convict reeled and fell to the floor, with a terrible gash in his side, from which his life's blood was freely flowing, we knew his wound was mortal. He was carried to the hospital, where he soon died.

Landers claimed that the murder was done in self-defense and the coroner's verdict confirmed him in in this unjurt claim. The only punishment that was imposed upon the perpetrator of this unjustifiable act was his exclusion from the yard by the authorities of the prison.

We were very anxious to have him return to us after the convict died, when we found that law and justice would not interfere. But it was concluded best for his personal safety for him not to be seen again by us. And to-day he is one of the leading lights in a populous city, although the perpetrator of a crime for which many men have died on the scaffold. But it was only taking the life of a prisoner, and the widowed wife and orphan children were only those of a convict, and the death of the husband and father yet remains unavenged.

Perhaps this injustice was the means of creating a burning rage among convicts here that they began plotting to hang one of their own number. It will be remembered that about the time we now refer to, there was great excitement in Hillsdale County, which originated by the heinous offense and murder committed by Daniel Stone upon his little eight-year-old niece. Those who sought to lynch him when the deed was done were were only foiled in the attempt by the rapid steps of justice, and he was soon beyond the reach of lynch law, safe behind these prison walls.

Under this administration it became customary for men sentenced to solitary confinement to be so kept for three months, after which they were released by the board of prison managers and set to work.

When Convict Stone was released from the solitary and assigned to the Webster contract we were still burning with rage at the outcome of the Landers affair, and having heard of this convict's awful crime and narrow escape from mob violence it was proposed that he should act as substitute for Landers, now beyond our reach, and be hung to the rafters in the shop.

Due preparations for the hanging were quietly made, which was to occur on entering the shop in the morning.

One of the main leaders of the plot was a colored convict, whose courage failed him the evening prior to the time fixed for the execution. His shop mates were much disgusted at his cowardice, which was the means of postponing the scheme, and which was finally abandoned.

CHAPTER VIII
THE STRETCHING MACHINE — RECORD OF MISCONDUCT — FATALITIES, MURDERS AND SUICIDES

VERY little credence should be given to reports for misconduct under a reign where the contract system is having full sway. Very frequently many reports are filed against convicts, which give them a record of incorrigibility, when, if it were possible for the world to know the true cause of the insubordination, it would be looked upon in a very different light. The new rule demanding heavier tasks caused more daily reports than we have ever known since Bingham and Martin's reign of terror. The new task being imperative, and failure to comply was quickly followed by punishment. At all hours of the day prisoners were called from the shops and chastised for not having done their tasks. Some were severely reprimanded by the warden and then sent back to work on condition that the offense should not occur again. But there were others who were not so submissive to the will of the task masters. These were consigned to the dungeon for many days, during which their only food was bread and water. During this administration there were many very cruel methods of punishment.

There was a stretching machine, whose frequent use was a disgrace to civilized people. This instrument of torture consisted of a square wooden frame in two parts like the frame of a window. Upon this bed of pain the prisoner was placed with his hands and feet securely shackled to the top and bottom. It was then slid apart and fastened with an iron pin, and its victims have often heard their sinews and muscles crack as if they were being disjointed. Wm. Harris, a colored convict from Cass County, declared that when upon this bed of torture he experienced the most severe pains of his life, and when taken therefrom and set to work his limbs were swollen for many days.

Even the most desperate criminals, on entering prison doors, generally seek to keep their conduct records as perfect as possible, for they are aware that it is for their own benefit to gain the good will of prison authorities. Perverseness and wilful transgressions of rules will only necessitate a more watchful eye over them and thereby lessen desired opportunities for escape. Furthermore, it is but human nature for men imprisoned to ask for commutations and pardons, and they well know that a record of good conduct is of great weight when seeking executive clemency. When these facts are well weighed how can we account for the many reports under a reign when the contract system was having full sway, unless caused by the increase of tasks over those of former administrations.

We give some figures of misconduct which the prison record shows under two different administrations when refractory convicts were in punishment:

	1890.	1891.
October	91½ days.	3½ days.
November	87½ days.	1½ days.
December	28½ days.	5½ days.
	207½	10½

The average monthly reports for 1891 were in proportion to these figures given. Under Warden Hatch's administration in 1890, from the first of September to the first of March, the records of two shops on the Webster contract show that convicts lost 315 days of good time, and yet, during the same month under the new reign they only lost 25 days and the discipline was as good as the prison has ever seen. Who will say that every day of good time lost by convicts on contract work is beneficial to contractors?

During the six years' administration of Warden Hatch there were many fatal accidents, murders and suicides. Convicts became so desperate in their despondent conditions that a plot to murder was fixed for a Sabbath day, in the dining room and at meal time. It will be remembered that in 1879 Isaac Clark, Daniel Graham, Charles Plattner and Enos Girard were convicted of Murder committed in Wayne county. The two former received life sentences, but Plattner and Girard received fifteen years each. The two lifers have ever maintained their innocence and declared that their freedom was forfeited by false swearing of their companions and have frequently stated that neither of the perjured convicts should leave the prison alive. Plattner and Girard were aware their lives were in great danger and by keeping a watchful eye they had succeeded in evading their enemies during eight years imprisonment, but one Sabbath day in September, 1887, during meal time, it seems their minds were otherwise engaged and then did not notice Convict Clark when he quietly left his place at the table and stealthily approached behind them. The prisoner was employed on the shoe contract and Saturday night when leaving the shop he retained his shoe knife, with which to do his bloody work the coming day. The prison authorities were aware of the convict's deadly threats and bloody intentions, and his movements were under surveillance. Scarcely had the desperate man began to use his knife before he was struck down by a terrible blow on the head from a heavy cane in the hands of Keeper Baldwin. This prevented him from accomplishing his end, although one of his victims was badly wounded, the table spattered with blood and great excitement prevailed in the dining room. At this time only Plattner was cut and the other escaped unhurt, but the enraged convict swore he would kill them both before their remaining three years expired, and he partly kept his oath.

The blow from the heavy club was sufficient to cause a terrible wound on the convict's head, and at first it was thought his skull was fractured. The assassin and his victim were carried to the hospital, where they soon recovered and were again set to work.

The two lifers frequently made applications to the Governor for pardons and when their pleadings were rejected it only diminished their hope of freedom and increased their revengeful desire against those who they claim had sworn falsely and caused their imprisonment for life. In the meantime the sentence of the men whose lives were sought were drawing to a close, and the blood-thirsty convict at once began to seek new opportunities to accomplish his deadly purposes. At the time we now refer to we were allowed an hour's freedom in the yard every Saturday afternoon. During this hour the prisoners conversed together, while ball playing and many other kinds of sport were indulged in. While thus together Clark might have easily slashed the man he so bitterly hated, but he was well aware that if a disturbance of this kind occurred our privilege would be discontinued and he did not wish to jeopardize our pleasure.

He bided his time when he alone would be responsible, and it soon came. In the evening of August 20th, 1889, two years after the dining room affair, when our day's work was done and the men were filing into the east wing, the revengeful man spied one of his enemies just ahead of him and, quickly leaving his place in the ranks, with rapid strides came up behind him. Instantly the concealed knife was drawn and plunged into the neck of Girard. But before he could repeat the blow he was seized by other convicts and easily disarmed. But the deed was done — the knife thrust proved fatal and the victim died a few days later.

The prison authorities were now thoroughly convinced that something must be done to protect the man that had had such a narrow escape from death in the dining room. Hence, the assassin was kept locked in his cell until the sentence of the other convict expired, which occurred in June of the following year.

One of the most noted and determined suicides that has ever occurred here was that of Joseph Allen. He was an old man, sixty years of age, from Van Buren county, under a sentence of eighteen years. He was, perhaps, one of the most despondent men that has slept within these walls. From the time he entered until the day he died his life was one of perpetual gloom. A few days after he was assigned to the Webster contract he remarked to a fellow prisoner that he was born a free man and had been loyal to his freedom during three score years of life and would die before he would be made a slave in his old age. At a time when his mind was sorely vexed and his strength well tested with contract work, he received the very sad news that his little girl had been killed by the cars while crossing the railroad track at home. This news was the climax of his despair — the death of his future hopes.

One day when leaving the dining room at noon time, he remarked to the deputy warden that earth's troubles were more than he could bear, and that he would move out of the world at once. The Webster contract was then engaged in their annual inventory and we were taking a rest while locked in our cells. Soon after the dinner hour a groan was heard from the cell of the despondent convict. The door was at once unlocked and the guard, E. C. Nichols, was horrified at the sight of a man struggling in death upon the blood stained floor. The pocket knife that was found lying near him and the deep gash in his side was conclusive that he intended to make sure work and had aimed at the most vital spot.

After the suicide came a death by an accident, and this time to one of our number, who was well liked by officers and men; and what made the sad occurrence still more lamentable was the shortness of time prior to the expiration of his sentence. The unfortunate man, Peter Ackerman, was sent from Monroe county for two years and was employed on the Webster contract, sawing lumber with a rip saw. Those who are posted in this kind of work are well aware of its dangers, especially when cutting either green, wet or knotty timber. The shop where he was engaged is the place where the lumber is dressed for the Jackson Wagon Company, and much of it is prepared while still in its green and rough condition and then it is sent to the drying kiln to dry for future use. Many convicts are thus employed, and so numerous were the accidents in bygone days that it was given the nickname of "The Prison Guillotine." In that place more men have lost their arms, hands, or were otherwise maimed, than in all of the other shops combined. On the 15th of October, 1890, just before the unfortunate man had finished his day's work, he placed a piece of heavy wood on the sliding table in front of the flying saw. Scarcely had it begun to cleave its way through the flinty wood before it came in contact with a solid knot. With a tremendous force the heavy piece was hurled back from the saw and against the breast of him who was so faithfully guiding it. The force of the blow was sufficient to cause almost instant death. He never regained consciousness and died within a few minutes.

Should we continue to relate the many regretful things that occurred during this administration, it would make such a volume of horrors as no one would wish to read.

We will now turn our thoughts to other things of which we wish to speak and which, perhaps, are not so sorrowful.

CHAPTER IX
WARDEN HATCH AND PRISON REFORM — THE INDETERMINATE SENTENCE ACT

ZACHARIAH ELDRED succeeded Deputy Warden Drake, and was the first deputy warden under the Hatch administration. He was a man of perhaps sixty years of age, and was one of the best officers that we have ever had. We were told that his occupation was that of a farmer, his previous residence having been in Cass County, where he was made sheriff just prior to his advent among us.

One of the many good deeds rendered by him was the searching for facts connected with the conviction of Elias Wilson, a colored man who was doing a sentence of fifteen years for arson. Deputy Eldred did not believe the man committed the crime, and by his untiring efforts was at last rewarded by the facts which sustained the correctness of his judgment and secured the convict's pardon. He was firm in his conviction that a day's work behind prison walls should be pro rata with a day's work elsewhere; and he often told us that the State rule required we should work silently and diligently during the day and when the rule was complied with it should be satisfactory to all concerned. It was a great question with him where to draw the average line of men's strength and endurance to perform manual labor, for all men do not possess the same strength and agility, and it would be both unreasonable and unjust to require an equal amount of work from every man.

It was predicted that a man of such sentiments could not long retain his position in a place where contractors were kings. These predictions were verified, for his term of office was short, and greatly to our disappointment he tendered his resignation. We never learned the true cause of the disagreement, but that it resulted from his human endeavors to be guided by the dictates of his conscience, we had not the slightest doubt. Although we felt keenly the loss of such an upright official, contrary to our expectations, our interests did not suffer, for the vacancy was soon favorably filled by a Mr. Tompkins, who was far from being a tyrant, and who, like his predecessor, believed in justice to both bond and free. He was unquestionably competent and as energetic as any officer the prison had had. He frequented the shops daily, and late at night he might be seen passing through the corridors of the prison proper. He was ever on the alert, watching attentively the keepers in the shops and the guards on the wall. The latter were very cautious about smoking or sleeping on their posts, as they all appreciated his unceasing vigilance. Deputy Tompkins remained for three years, until the completion of the Upper Peninsula State Prison at Marquette, when he resigned to accept the wardenship of that institution. On the Saturday evening prior to his departure, while we all were assembled on the lawn, he was presented with a gold watch and chain, purchased by us, and tendered him as a token of gratitude for his fair dealings and friendly attitude to all.

We are now on the fourth year of the administration and at the time when prison reform was at its zenith.

Warden Hatch was known as an ardent advocate in the work of reformation of criminals, and taught us that it was best to remain here under his control (and with the contractors) until prison authorities were satisfied that our reformation was thorough and complete, and proof against temptation. For some cause or other he was well supported in his ideas of criminal detention, for the State Legislature, which was then in session, readily passed the indeterminate sentence act and parole law. A parole system was a long felt want, and would have given a measure of satisfaction and encouragement if it had only been constructed like the parole system in the State of Ohio and that of some other places. But when we consider the many obstacles which must be surmounted under this parole system before we were eligible to our freedom, it seemed to us as if it had instead been made lawful for our retention here even after our sentence may have expired. Prison authorities were vested with the power to let convicts out on parole, to go anywhere in the United States, or to go a distance of five miles from the prison to work and return at night. It silenced courts of justice and defied both the Judge and the jury, for if a convict was convicted of a crime while out on his ticket of leave he must be returned to prison to serve out his first sentence prior to being punished for the last offense. Under that law all convicts were compelled to serve only the least punishment possible for the offense before they might secure their freedom. There are sentences imposed for different crimes, varying in length from one day to fifteen years, hence it was possible for some with friends and wealth to be released after remaining here but one day, while others might be held for fifteen years for a like offense.

Many were the anathemas hurled at the Legislature for passing such an unjust law. Many men who were doing contract work believed it would be almost impossible for us to conduct ourselves in such a manner as to gain our freedom. Our experience had taught us to believe that contractors are loth to give up skillful and willing workmen, and our perfect work might not hasten all to determine that we were entirely cured of our evil desires, while on the other hand our reformation could be established only by industry and good work. We concluded that the indeterminate sentence law was the only legal form of slavery this State has ever had. It was an edict of destruction, a swamping of the object for which some of us were so earnestly striving, a lawful act which might deprive us of our earliest freedom.

It was a humiliating spectacle to see the Legislature of a great State confiscating our rights, although we were only convicts, yet we knew there were some inalienable rights which neither our offenses nor Legislatures could destroy.

What might be the next inauguration of injustice we knew not, but were convinced that the present was the pivot upon which the future must turn. Generally speaking public sentiment is most always against men in prison, let them be young or old, innocent or guilty. Let their term of imprisonment be long or short, public sentiment seldom changes. It would be a most cruel law indeed that society would investigate and demand repealed.

Well knowing these things were true, it was proposed that it should be tested by the Supreme Court at the first opportunity, which soon came. While the validity of the new law was being tested we were being mocked at by the knowing ones for our stupidity in testing the virtue of an act of the Legislature by which convicts must abide. But we will soon see how it terminated.

On the 4th day of January, 1886, Jimmy Moore was pardoned under this act, and was re-arrested and brought back for not strictly observing the condition of his pardon. He at once applied to the Supreme Court for a writ of habeas corpus, and on the 6th of July they demanded his release from prison.

Daniel Cummings was sentenced by a Circuit Judge to imprisonment for a period of not less than two nor more than four years, in the discretion of the Board of Control of Prisons. This sentence was appealed to the Supreme Court and was declared unconstitutional.

Rarely in the history of Supreme Court decisions of Michigan has an act of the Legislature been so severely condemned as the Legislature which provided for an indeterminate sentence for criminals. We believe that the decision should be read by every one, in order that they may understand the injustice of such an act. The following is the substance of the decision of the highest judiciary of the State of Michigan:

"The act provides that, in the discretion of the Court, a general sentence of imprisonment may be given. The term of such imprisonment may be terminated by the Board of Inspectors, but the term of imprisonment shall not exceed the maximum term provided by the law for the offense committed. Neither can the prisoner be released until after he has served the minimum term under the law. The Board of Control is granted authority to release the convict on parole, but may order and secure his return to the prison in case of a violation of his parole, in the discretion of the Board, and when such an order is made the delinquent shall thereafter be treated as an escaped prisoner owing service to the State, and liable when arrested to serve out the unexpired period of the maximum possible imprisonment; and, committing a fresh crime, if convicted, shall serve the remainder of the first sentence before the beginning of the second. There is nothing in the act, however, to impair the power to grant a pardon or commutation."

The Court says: "It is not clear whether the Board has the power to grant an absolute discharge or not. If so it would be clearly unconstitutional. It would be either the exercise of judicial power in determining the term of imprisonment of a citizen or the bestowing of a pardon before the term expired. The judicial power in Michigan is vested in courts, and the pardoning power absolutely with the Governor. If it be considered that the power conferred on the Board is a conditional release or parole (provided the prisoner keeps his parole) the release is an absolute one and the effect is that of a pardon.

"The term of imprisonment is fixed by the Board and not by the Court. No term is fixed by the Judge. It rests entirely with the Board, and may in some cases be one day or fifteen years. The Legislature has the power to fix the term of imprisonment between the maximum and minimum punishment, and this discretion can not be given to any other person without imperiling the liberties of the citizen without any remedy in the courts. The Legislature cannot authorize a Circuit Judge to delegate his power or discretion to another person. The act deprives the court of discretion, and without interference by others the sentence must stand for the maximum term. In manslaughter the sentence may be one day's imprisonment or a fine of one cent, while the maximum is fifteen years and $1,000 fine. The moment the Judge sentences under the indeterminate law, the term of imprisonment is entirely within the discretion of the Board of Control. No court can review their action. When the convict (in whose interest so-called humanitarians have devised the law) enters the prison he becomes the servant and slave of the Prison Board, and no court has the power to reach him. Their power is arbitrary.

In this case Cummings was sentenced to prison for not less than two nor more than four years. The Judge exercised his discretion in fixing the minimum and maximum period, and delegated the rest to the Board, but under the act he must delegate it all or not sentence under the statute at all.

The Legislature cannot confer judicial power upon any officers not specified in the constitution. (Chandler vs. Nash, 5. Mich., 409). It was held in People vs. Brown, (54 Mich., 15), that the pardoning power belongs to the Governor alone, and that no Judge can exercise it by indefinitely suspending the sentence of a convicted criminal. Yet, under this law the Judge, by his sentence, may delegate the power to the Prison Board, and in effect, pardon him in many cases, the first day he is imprisoned.

The act authorizes a parole, and the Board may fix the distance that he may go from the prison at five miles, within the County limits, the Congressional District, the State, or the United States. Or does the law," Judge Morse says, "contemplate that this parole shall be, in fact, a release from prison with only the condition that the Board may bring the person or parole back again if they see fit to make him serve his whole unexpired term within the prison walls. In any event, this parole system is as opposed to the constitution, as an unconditional release by the Board would be, and if they have the power to release on conditions, those conditions may be made so trifling as in fact to be no condition at all. If such power can be exercised by a Judge, it incorporates into our administration of the criminal law the 'ticket-of-leave' system of English Judicature, without its surveillance and checks, and places the criminal at the caprice of the Judge, subject to be called up for sentence at any time. If the Judge can delay the the sentence one year, we do not see why he may not for fifteen years. An exercise of such power in this age would be no less revolting to our sense of justice, than was the exercise of such power in the reign of James I, when he sent Sir Walter Raleigh to the block fifteen years after his conviction. This law introduces the 'ticket-of-leave' system and places despotic power in the hands of the Prison Board over the persons sentenced under this statute.

In the case of Jimmy Moore it was held that the agent or keeper of a prison, could not arrest or bring back into prison a convict pardoned by the Governor on conditions for a violation of such conditions, unless such convict was arrested, held and tried, for such violation in the same manner as other offenders against the criminal laws. The Governor has the undoubted right to pardon. He may pardon on conditions. But neither he nor any other person can have, under the laws, the sole right to determine whether or not such conditions have been violated. This must be determined by the courts by the usual and proper proceedings.

The act of the Legislature in that case authorizing the arrest of such a pardoned convict without a warrant for an alleged violation of the conditions of his pardon, was held unconstitutional and void.

When a person has been set at liberty under the pardon or commutation of his sentence by the Executive, he becomes once more a full citizen, clothed with all the rights, privileges and prerogatives that belong to any other free man. He cannot be sent out half free and half slave. He is not to be let out with a rope around his body, as it were, with one end in the hands of the warden, to be hauled back at the caprice of that officer. He must go out a free man, and remain a free man until he breaks the condition of his pardon. He must enjoy the blessing and benefits that belong to an American citizen until he has violated the law of his release. His character may be tarnished and his reputation soiled by his imprisonment, but his rights as a citizen are unimpaired. He is clothed as he passes out of the prison door with the same garb of freedom that was removed from him when he went in. He has the right to his liberty the same as any other citizen, so long as he keeps the conditions of his pardon, and he cannot be deprived of his liberty, save in the mode prescribed by the constitution and laws of our State as applied to any other citizen. If the breaking of the condition is in the nature of a crime, or punished as such with penal consequences, that crime, or act, punished as a crime, must be established as any other crime would be.

By the operation of this statute the person pardoned and absolved from the penal consequences of his crime (we must presume for a good cause) is not free upon his release. He is subject to the will of a master. The warden, or other official, can reach out his hand at any moment and pull him back into prison, governed by no restrictions save the will of the officer. When the warden's hand is laid upon the released convict he becomes his absolute servant and prisoner until the prosecuting attorney gets time, or sees fit to move. This arbitrary power over the liberty of another is possessed by no other officer of our government in times of peace. It cannot lawfully exist in a free country. This law is subject to the same infirmity and has more viciousness than the ticket of leave law in England. And any convict thus released on parole can at any time be brought back into the prison upon the written order of the board, which all officers must obey. All that is necessary is for the board to enter the formal order that the convict is a delinquent; has violated the conditions of his parole, and that is the end of it. The convict is not to have a hearing and no court has power to interfere in his behalf if this law is constitutional.

Nor is this all. He is to be treated thereafter as an escaped prisoner, owing service to the State, and loses the time, even, that he has earned by keeping the conditions of his parole, perhaps for years. And if he commits another crime while he is at large upon his parole, and convicted thereof, his new sentence is deferred until he has served out his old, meting out to him double punishment for his last crime.

We have not sufficient words at our command to use in condemnation of this statute. It would fill our State with convicts; they could not be called free men, running at large outside of our prison walls, all liable at any moment to be taken back inside at the will of four individuals, no better, probably, in their impulses and caprices than the average man.

These people, thus at large, would not only be subject to the will and pleasure of their masters without hope or redress if wronged by them, but they would be out of prison under various conditions, and such as the board might impose upon them without regulation or restriction from any other power or authority. One under the conditions that he shall drink no intoxicating liquor, and another that he shall not chew tobacco, and still another that he shall not use opium or drink strong coffee.

There is no limit or qualification to the conditions that may be imposed. In looking upon this law it is difficult to see in what respect this system of parole differs from a pardon by the

Governor upon conditions. Is it not, in fact, a pardon — a release upon conditions? If it is not, if the faith of the board of control is not to be kept, and the convict has no certainty that if he keeps the conditions he will not again be imprisoned, then the whole scheme is a delusion and a snare and unworthy a place upon the statute books. But, as it is, the only guarantee of a person so released of such good faith is the pleasure of the board.

This system of parole is either a pardon upon conditions, and therefore unconstitutional, or it is no release at all, and only a permission to go outside of the walls and stay as long as the board may will. If it is the latter, a simple leave to stay outside until the Board sees fit to call them in, the law evidently does not meet the intention of the Legislature, and is not only undesirable, but indefensible. If this is a pardon upon conditions, as the Legislature no doubt intended it should be, then it is open to all the constitutional objections mentioned in the previous conditions of the People vs. Moore.

The term of imprisonment under this law depends not upon the character of the crime committed, but upon the behavior of the prisoner after he enters upon his sentence. The prisoners are to be classified into different grades, with promotion or degradation, according to the merits of the prisoner, their employment and instruction in industry, and generally as may from time to time appear to be necessary or promotive to the purposes of this act. The hardened criminal may more easily submit to the discipline of the prison than the younger, but more impulsive offender, and therefore get his release sooner. The term of imprisonment depends upon the ability of the convict to please the prison officials in his deportment and not upon the enormity of his offense. This law, if permitted to stand, would be a convenient one for judges who might dislike to perform an unpleasant duty.

When a person of influence or wealth was convicted and the usual pressure in such cases brought to bear upon the trial judge to impose a light sentence, how easy it would be to impose a general sentence and shift the responsibility of fixing its actual term upon the board of control of prisons and let them stand the siege, which would at once commence to secure his release. The law, in our opinion, is not only unconstitutional as heretofore pointed out, but also wrong in theory and dangerous in practice. That such laws have been adopted by some of the States of the Union has no bearing in favor of this act.

A similar statute was sustained in Ohio, but the reasoning of the opinion is not at all satisfactory to us and does not meet the objections raised against the law. The convict is as much under the control of the authorities as is the trusty convict, who is allowed at all times to be outside at work or run errands. Yet, if he violates the condition of his parole after he has been out ten years — if his maximum time has not expired — he can be taken back without trial or any investigation, save by the prison board, and made to serve the ten years beyond the maximum term. It is a wonder that such a law as this, giving such unheard of power to four men not elected by the people, but holding their offices by appointment, could be enacted in view of our constitution and the whole theory of our State government and in the light and example of the history of the establishment and growth of constitutional liberty in this country. In this case the sentence of Cummings is good under our previous decisions for two years. At the end of that period he must be discharged."

It is not necessary for us to make any comment on the highest authority of justice in Michigan in regard to indeterminate sentences.

We will now proceed to review a different state of things, which are more humane in feeling and to conscience.

CHAPTER X
THE LITERARY MEETINGS AND RELIGIOUS SERVICES — THE PRISON CHAPLAIN

ONE of the most beneficial and meritable works of the administration was the literary meetings, which were held four nights during the week and which are conducted on the same plan as those of other educational institutions. The officers are elected by ballot once in three months. During the meeting there are two or three intermissions, when we are allowed to converse with each other, and the programme committee solicits the names of those who desire to participate in the next programme. A special literary meeting is held once every four weeks, during which many songs, whistling solos and musical selections are rendered by the voluntary aid of free people who are ever interested in lifting up the hopes and prospects of men in Michigan's State prison. We will elsewhere in this book give some of the speeches made and essays read during these meetings.

It was customary with Warden Hatch at the end of our literary meetings to say something commendatory or cheering in regard thereto, and he had a task to do to keep us from writing essays and speaking against the convict slave trade. Prisoners are not easily led to believe that contractors are justified in compelling them to do more work in a day than men do outside of prison walls, who are daily receiving good wages for their labor.

One of the main leaders of these meetings is the Rev. George H. Hickox, the prison chaplain. Perhaps no other man in the State is more ardent and zealous in the work of bettering the present conditions and future prospects of ex-prisoners. He has been the chaplain here since October, 1872, and the work performed by him is by far a more laborious one than many persons can imagine. The mental work done by him is surely sufficient to overtax the mind and strength of any ordinary person. He has one of the most retentive memories that we have ever known. He can call nearly two-thirds of the convicts here, both by their name and by their registered numbers. He reads, or superintends the reading, of all the convicts' letters that come in or go out of the prison. This alone is enough work for one man to perform, for it must be remembered that the daily mail here is equal to that of a town of eight hundred inhabitants. But this does not complete the work upon his hands, for there is a sermon for him to preach every Sabbath morning, and prayer meetings for him to conduct on Sunday and Wednesday evenings. He also has to see to the cleanliness of the school rooms and other places of religious gatherings. He is counselor for the men and to him they look to for guidance and sympathy when they receive news of the sickness and adversities of their families. He frequently advances money to convicts to relieve the immediate wants of some one at home and awaits the prisoner's own time and integrity for the return of the borrowed money.

The chaplain emphatically states that in the twenty years' experience here he has not lost a cent by advancing money to convicts. We do not know of any one connected with the prison during our time who stands higher in the estimation of convicts than Chaplain Hickox. He is assisted a great deal in his work by his wife who always accompanies him when he is attending to his duties.

It may not be generally known that the religious professions of prisoners are of great worth in keeping the men in strict compliance with the rules and regulations of the prison. Three or four hundred men attend the prayer meetings, in which the most of them take a lively interest and try to make their daily conduct concur with their professions. About two hundred and fifty of the men are Catholics. Mass is conducted by Father Vicey at nine o'clock, twice a month, during which some very fine singing is done by a choir of young girls from the Catholic church of this city. The 17th of March, St. Patrick's Day, is well remembered and appreciated by the prisoners, and many of them wear green badges and ribbons during the day. At night a very fine programme is given in the chapel, which is finely decorated for the occasion with many of Ireland's saints and martyrs, and many other very fine emblems and tokens of sympathy for Ireland are displayed during the evening.

All of the prisoners are compelled to attend religious services which are held in the chapel at eleven o'clock on Sunday mornings, but it is optional with them about attending prayer and literary meetings. A list of the names of the men is kept who attend school and the other different exercises of the prison. They are unlocked about 5 minutes before the bell rings, which is a signal for them to march from the cells and keep in line as they proceed to and from the places where the exercises are held. This same rule is strictly observed when unlocked for work in the morning. They come forth from their cells by a signal of the bell, each man carrying his night bucket, which he leaves at the bucket ground and goes into the dining room to breakfast, after which they are marched to the shops and begin their daily toil. At twelve o'clock they go from the shops to the dining room for their dinner and then return to their work again. They are not locked in the cells during the noon hour and are not permitted to return to them from the time they leave them in the morning until the bell rings for them to stop work at night, and then they march back to the cells and each keeper locks up the men in his charge.

If a prisoner is missing it is immediately known by his vacant cell and all the guards are at once commanded to hunt for him. The guards are placed on the walls in the morning before the prisoners are unlocked and they do not leave their respective places until the men are counted and locked up at night. If none of the prisoners are absent then a signal is given by the bell for the guards to come down from the walls, but if any are unaccounted for then they do not leave their places of duty until a thorough search is made to see if the missing man is not concealed inside of the walls with the intention of making his escape as soon as the watchmen leave the towers.

CHAPTER XI
GUILTY AND INNOCENT — CANFIELD, THE SLAYER OF LITTLE NELLIE GRIFFIN

ABOUT twenty per cent. of the men once imprisoned here return again, many of them on their third and fourth conviction — and some for life. Convict Johnson is now serving his fourth term here, and two of them were life sentences. He first came here about twenty years ago and was registered number 238. At the expiration of his sentence he remained away for a few years and then returned and was known by the number of 2318 during his five years' sentence. At the expiration of this sentence he was released and remained away for about three years and then came back again under a life sentence, his registered number being 2930. Five years later he again secured his freedom by a pardon from Governor Alger. He was only absent about two years before he committed one of the blackest crimes known to law. While he was tramping through the State he stopped at a house a few miles from town and begged for something to eat. The husband was away from home at work, and his wife being of a kind-hearted and sympathetic nature, at once selected the best food in the house and gave it to the hungry beggar. After having thoroughly satisfied his ravenous appetite, and finding that the wife was unprotected, he committed a brutal assault upon her, regardless of the fact that she was about to become a mother. He was captured a few days later, and it was the narrowest escape from being lynched that a culprit ever had. A mob of excited and determined men at once proceeded to avenge such a horrible crime by taking the criminal's life, and at one time they had the rope around his neck, but the officers of the law succeeded in taking him away from the mob in time to save his life. He pleaded guilty to the charge and was at once sentenced to prison for life. He has already begun to take steps to secure his freedom, but it is hardly probable that Michigan will ever have a Governor that will pardon a man with such a crime against him at present and with such a record in the past.

Henry Zagler was not an unfortunate man. He completed a five years' sentence here, and three years from its expiration he was convicted of murder and sentenced to life imprisonment. But in less than a year after his incarceration he secured a new trial and was acquitted. Four years later he was convicted as a participant in a murder and was again a prisoner, but was pardoned after having served nine years and three months of his sentence. His imprisonments began and ended many years ago and before the present system of registered numbers was in use.

One of the most constant lovers of prison life ever behind the walls is Convict Frank George, No. 5081. The prison records show that he is now serving his eighth sentence. He was released from here in 1889, and at once began a systematic style of robbing his old companions behind prison walls by obtaining their money under pretense of getting them a pardon. Four months later he was arrested and convicted for obtaining money from a convict under false pretenses, and was sentenced from the city of Jackson to three years imprisonment. He is an old man, more than sixty years of age, and has spent more than half of his life behind prison walls.

This class of prisoners sustains us in our opinions given in the first chapters, in which we have stated that the State erred when it abolished hanging and substituted solitary confinement.

But there have been many men incarcerated here who were innocent of the crimes for which they were imprisoned. Convict Edward Murphy was 23 years behind the walls before he was able to prove that he was innocent of the crime of murder of which he was convicted. Eight years of his prison life was in solitary confinement before it was abolished. During the quarter of a century of his prison experience his torturings were beyond human conception.

The sufferings of a man innocently imprisoned are far greater than those of the guilty. A criminal, when suffering for a crime committed, is well aware that he is only being punished for his own perpetrations, and the thought of it lessens the severity of the punishment. But an innocent man imprisoned is ever cognizant and meditates upon the unjust forfeiture of his freedom, and this increases and doubles the severity of prison life. The thought of his innocence alone was sufficient to have created an insane longing for freedom and justice during the many years of lawful and unjust imprisonment.

When his freedom was at last restored to him he was an old man 73 years of age, his constitution shattered, his health destroyed. In 1884 he was allowed a yearly pension by an act of the Legislature, and for seven years he managed to keep life in his frail body by the charitable gift of a great State. But the 25th of January, 1892, he was killed by the cars while crossing the railroad track in the city of Jackson. This ended the life of Edward Murphy, the most unfortunate man ever confined within these walls.

McKay was convicted of a murder committed in Barry County in 1884, and sentenced to life imprisonment. His conviction was secured by the poorest kind of circumstantial evidence, and he ever maintained his innocence. He was the father of six children, the oldest of them only fifteen years of age. He frequently applied to the Governor to thoroughly investigate the case and satisfy himself of the lawful but unjust conviction. But for six long years he was toiling behind these walls before the Board of Pardons concluded to make a final investigation; and when this was done, it was found that in view of the extenuating circumstances the evidence connected with his conviction was insufficient to imprison a man for life. He was pardoned by Governor Luce May 29th, 1890, and received $7.50 for his six years labor behind prison walls.

Another sad case of innocent and unjust imprisonment was that of Tom Allen, alias Tom Conners. He was a salt water seaman, and at the time the crime which we now refer to was committed he was on the briny ocean. A man in Mecosta County was brutally assaulted, perhaps by some personal enemy. Nearly two years after the assault Tom Allen quit the boat at San Francisco and came to Mecosta County, Michigan, to visit friends. He was at once recognized as a stranger there, and was identified by the officers of the law as the man who had made the murderous assault so long ago. He was arrested and jailed. He plead with the authorities to send to the Captain of the vessel for which he was at work and satisfy themselves that at the time when the crime was committed he was on the Pacific Ocean.

His story was disbelieved, and no time could be spared to make an investigation. He was tried and convicted of assault with intent to do great bodily harm, and on November 14th, 1890, he was sentenced to five years and six months imprisonment. As soon as he arrived here he at once began to try and obtain justice and regain his freedom. He at once began to correspond with the proper authorities on the Pacific coast to find the vessel on which he was at work when the crime was committed in Michigan. When the boat was found the Captain and crew corroborated the records of the boat, that at the time the crime was committed Tom Allen, the imprisoned man, was five thousand miles away and on the Pacific Ocean. On December 21st, 1891, he was pardoned by Governor Winans, after having served one year, one month and seven days for a crime he never committed. He was given $7.50 for his unjust confinement and slave labor, and in order to be economical and make his small capital sustain him until he succeeded in obtaining work, he undertook to take a ride on a freight train from Jackson to Detroit, and was thrown beneath the wheels of the cars and sustained injuries from which he died in three days.

There are many others who we could name that have been prisoners here, although innocent of the charge for which they were confined, but for the present we will only name one more of this class.

Louis Grant Wilson (colored) was convicted of murder in Cass County in 1889. At the time of his conviction the Judge gave the jury a very severe reprimand for convicting a man upon such frail and unreliable evidence. His own words to the jury were these: "You have convicted this man upon evidence that is not sufficient to convict a yellow dog. I am surprised at a jury of intelligent men that would render a verdict of guilty upon such evidence as has been produced on this trial. Your verdict compels me to sentence the prisoner to Jackson, but I will see that his case is taken to the Supreme Court, even if I have to defray some of the expense."

Wilson was sentenced to ten years imprisonment, and was without money to carry his case to the Supreme Court. He at once began seeking a plan by which to obtain justice, and well knowing that nothing could be done without money, he at once began to circulate a subscription paper among the convicts. He raised money enough to pursue the proper course to have his case investigated by the Board of Pardons, and they were satisfied of his innocence. He was pardoned by Governor Winans in 1891, after having served two years for a crime he never committed.

The majority of the men here will not associate with a new arrival convicted of heineous offenses. Perhaps this was never more plainly manifested than when Canfield, the slayer of little Nellie Griffin, arrived here on a life sentence.

In this case it is necessary for us to make an explicit explanation of the terrible crime. January 30th Solomon and Clifton Barr, two farmers seven miles south of Lansing, started to cross Grand river on the ice. When near the shore they caught the gleam of something white in the water where the ice had been recently broken. On closer inspection they found that, entangled in the branches of a fallen tree below the surface, was the corpse of a young girl not over fourteen years of age. The ice had been broken and the body apparently tossed in carelessly with the expectation that the swift current would carry it down stream, but the tree limbs had caught it and held it fast.

The body was found seven miles south of Lansing and three miles from the village of Dimondale. When it was removed from the river an hour later, it was evident that it had been thrust into the water but a few hours before, and that it had been disposed of almost immediately after death. The corpse was identified as that of Nellie Griffin.

Nellie Griffin was a slender child with dark brown hair and eyebrows, large brown eyes and a fair and attractive face. She was an orphan, and was an inmate of the State Public School at Coldwater, an educational institution for orphan girls. They can be adopted by reputable persons giving satisfactory evidence to the authorities that the adopted ones will be well cared for.

Canfield appeared at the institution and represented himself as a farmer, and by some means secured the child and started on his pretended journey homeward. But the girl never reached her destination. When her body was found beneath the ice, entirely nude, it was evident that she had been murdered to cover up a more heinous crime. It was well known that Canfield had taken the child from the Orphans' Home, although under an assumed name, and when arrested he confessed his guilt. In less than twenty-four hours after the arrest he was behind these walls for life. It was only the speedy steps taken to avenge the death of his victim and sustain the dignity of the law that saved him from being lynched, for a mob of five hundred desperate men at Dimondale were using every effort to take the culprit's life. When he arrived here among us he was not a welcome companion, for we had already heard of his bloody and unnatural offense. He was not only shunned by us, but was considered by his fellow prisoners as an object of curiosity and a man devoid of human feeling, far beneath the association of most of the men here imprisoned.

It is quite remarkable to notice with what certainty the men of his class make applications for pardons. They have more faith and confidence in their ultimate release than any of the rest of the prisoners.

CHAPTER XII
DIED FOR WANT OF WATER — WILLIAM WALKER'S PETITION FOR A PARDON

IT is terrible to deliberately and coolly take a human life, but this is not the most terrible thing about it. It is the recollection of it, the mental pictures of that death scene that is awful. Generally the murderer, after devoting weeks and months to a careful consideration of his bloody deed, goes insane. When behind prison walls, and calmly reflecting upon the crime, a new light seems to have dawned upon them and they are forced to silently declare they were fools.

The mental punishment of those who shed human blood is far more dire than their imprisonment. Their horrid thoughts has often made them afraid of their own shadows, and to imagine that their victims were softly tramping around with them in the dark and dismal dungeon.

In the spring of 1885, Gabe Brown (colored) murdered his wife at Mason, Jackson County, and was convicted of murder in the first degree and sentenced to life imprisonment. For many months after being confined behind these walls he imagined that his wife was ever present and visible with him in his cell. At night time in his dreams his groans and shrieks were so annoying that he was permitted to let his lamp burn during the night. The tormenting and burning imaginations continued until at last he was removed to another part of the building.

This same hallucination was none the less impressive to a colored convict by the name of Mathews who was sent from Grand Rapids in 1888. He was convicted of the murder of Nancy Curtis, by cutting her throat with a razor. After taking her life he made a feeble attempt to behead himself with the same instrument with which he killed his paramour, but he failed in his attempt and was sentenced to life imprisonment. In his rock-bound home he was frequently heard pleading with his imaginary wife to go away and cease tormenting him, for he did not mean to take her life.

One of the most heart-rending and touching scenes of carelessness and disregard for human suffering ever manifested during our time was that shown toward James McPherson. He was sent from Saginaw County, April 28, 1890, to a term of two years imprisonment for larceny, and had an insatiable thirst for alcohol. He was employed on the Wells & Fargo shoe contract. In this shop a great deal of alcohol is used in the preparations of many different kinds of leather. It is called wood alcohol and is poisonous and unfit for internal use. But regardless of its deadly contents it is often adulterated with water and drank by many of the convicts there employed. In the latter part of October James McPherson and another convict drank of this poisonous liquid. The former succeeded in drinking more of it than his companion and very soon after being locked in his cell at night he was taken with burning pains in his stomach and went insane with misery. He shouted to his cell mates that he was internally on fire and slowly being consumed, and for the sake of a human being, bring him a drink of water.

It is a breach of the rules for a convict to make any unnecessary noise in his cell, and when the convict shouted for water in the dead hours of the night he was guilty of this breach of discipline. On the fatal night in question Mahoney was acting as captain of the guards, and when the dying man called out for a drink of water he was commanded to keep quiet or else he would be reported. It was well known by the captain of the guards that McPherson was under the influence of alcohol and little or no attention was paid to his demands for something to ease his burning stomach. Again and again he called for water and was not only refused a taste of it, but soon thereafter the report was written and, as customary at night time, it was poked between the grates of his cell door. But he knew nothing of this unjust complaint, for he was a corpse when the complaint was written.

The rest of the convicts were very much displeased at Guard Mahoney for not giving their fellow prisoners water when needed, for some of them believed it might have quenched his internal heat and thereby perhaps saved his life.

Their suppositions were well founded, for the postmortem examination revealed the fact that he was internally scorched and blistered and that it was impossible for a human being to survive his condition, unless something was immediately done to cool his flaming tongue. It is generally supposed by the unknowing ones that he died from the effects of his own indiscretion. Perhaps this may be true, but under what circumstances is it meritable for a human being to allow another one to suffer for water when it can easily be obtained? The dead convict had a wife living near Elgin, Ill., at the time of his death, and his mother was also living near West Troy, N. Y. Both of their names were frequently used by him in his last supplications for a drink of water.

There has not been such a sympathetic feeling manifested toward a fellow prisoner since the days of Chrispar Christienell. He was employed on the broom contract, and the thoughts of the adversities and humiliations of his wife and child and the tormenting contract system became so impressive and burdensome to him that he deliberately planned a way by which to get rid of them all. In the broom shop large needles are used in the work of sewing brooms. They are made of the best of steel and are long and slender, varying in length from 6 to 8 inches.

On the 29th of December, 1883, Convict Christienell, while in a despondent mood, seized a broom needle and plunged it up to the hilt into his left side. He did not succeed in striking a vital spot and attempted to withdraw the slender piece of steel in order to renew his deadly purpose, but the keen instrument had torn its way through sinews and muscles and had become fixed and fastened in his bosom and he could not remove it. Two of his companions came to his aid and the needle was removed, and the wounded man was carried to his cell. Soon after being locked up he seized a razor which he himself had made, and nearly severed his head from his body. More sympathy was shown toward him by his fellow prisoners than many people would suppose who are not well versed in convict life and the convict system. We knew of his physical trials during the day, but who can imagine the burning thoughts of his wife and child while locked in his cell at night.

We cannot remember a single instance during our time when the victim of suicide was not employed on contract work. It is the opinion of convicts and free men that the contract system here if not only detrimental to the prosperity of this city, but that it is not enhancing to the financial interests of the State. Many acres of buildings just outside of the prison walls belong to the contractors and are used by them as a place to hoard the golden results of our labor. We were once informed that if all the wagons that were then stored away by the Webster contract were placed in a straight line they would reach a distance of thirteen miles.

It is reasonable and just for us to believe that it would be to the interest of the State to receive a fair remuneration for our work, for it feeds and protects our wives and children.

We cannot understand why the people of the State chose to sell us to contractors for a paltry sum and then compel us to perform such an unreasonable amount of work for the financial benefit of certain individuals. We believe that the daily amount of work performed by us is not just to the innocent men outside the prison walls, who live by the sweat of their brow, and the average amount paid them does not double the seventy cents per day which the contractors pay for us.

The free man out of his daily labor must eke out a living for his wife and children, and the taxation upon his home is the manner in which many of our families are sustained. In the winter time it is calculated that the state has to look after the welfare of more than a thousand women and children, for the simple reason that their main supporters are here in prison and making a fortune for a ring of contract kings. Why not give us a chance to aid in the support of our own children, or else sell our labor to those who are willing to pay a reasonable price for it, and thereby give the State more encouragement and to take better care of our children during the winter months?

It is generally supposed by the knowing ones that the most of our penal institutions are more than paying their way and are not detrimental to the financial interests of the State. But when we consider the State's expenditures for the welfare of our families, we do not believe that a prison can possibly pay its way where contract labor is maintained.

We have previously stated that the men here imprisoned performed more work during the administration of Warden Hatch than ever before in the same length of time during our incarceration. Time after time our tasks were raised, until at last we were compelled to perform the same amount of work during the shortest days of winter as during the longest days of summer. We will give a partial list of the tasks daily performed by the prisoners in shops No. 15 and 16, on the Webster contract. Some of the work in these two shops is very difficult and heavy to handle, and the men are compelled to work in pairs in order to handle the different pieces of the wagons. The task list here given is strictly confined to the paint shop. Each shop in the yard has its own task list.

TASK LIST IN THE PAINT SHOPS.

Two men must prime twenty-five boxes, sides, ends, seats, bottoms and finish twenty-five bottoms.

Two men must paint twenty-five pair of sides two coats.
One man must stencil twenty-five pair of sides two coats.
Two men must stripe twenty-five pair of sides.
Two men must paint fifty-five sets of end seats two coats, or 175 pieces.
One man must stencil thirty-five sets of end seats and varnish fifteen sets of each.
One man must stripe thirty-five sets of end seats, or 175 pieces.
Two men must varnish fifty pieces of gearing, fifty sides and twenty set of ends.
One man must clean and prepare for painting sixty pieces of gearing.
One man must paint fifty pieces of gearing and keep count of the number.
One man must varnish 110 wheels. (No deduction was made in the heavy truck wheels.)
One man must stripe eighty wheels.
One man must clean and nail up eighty wheels, ready for painting.
One man must paint seventy wheels, dust, sand-paper and mark each wheel.
One man must prime 110 wheels.

The above includes all necessary handling, taking from cars, carrying and letting down when finished.

O. C. TOMPKINS,
Acting Warden.

May 6th, 1889.

Under Warden Pond's administration the wheel painters painted forty wheels during the short days of winter and fifty wheels in the summer months for a task. But when Warden Hatch came into power he raised it to seventy wheels per day. Some of the prisoners declared that it was impossible for them to do it. Barbour was employed on wheel painting, and said that it was far beyond his physical ability to perform the amount demanded. He failed to do it, and failure was quickly followed with punishment. He was flogged, kept in the dungeon and hand-cuffed to his door time after time, and a vast amount of his good time earned was canceled. Convict Barbour believed that he was being unlawfully persecuted, and said that at the expiration of his sentence that he would surely bring the prison authorities to trial for damages to his health. He was discharged from the prison November 26, 1891, and at once attempted to have his case brought before the courts of justice. But this was not as easily performed as he expected. He was requested to give security for the costs of the trial, providing he failed to prove the charges made in the complaint. He was unable to give the required security, and consequently his case was dropped.

It was a question among the inmates of the shop in regard to which had the greatest cause of complaint, convict Barbour or his fellow shop-mate Joe Foedor. Foedor is a German, and was sent from Monroe County, to life imprisonment, for a terrible assault upon his own daughter. He has ever maintained his innocence and claims that he was imprisoned by the evidence of those who were very desirous of his conviction. He is now sixty-five years of age, and perhaps the constant reflections of his past life has caused him to become irascible and quick tempered, and he is called by his shop mates a prison crank.

Soon after his imprisonment he was reported for a breach of the rules, and was flogged until he claims it was necessary for him to be sent to the hospital. He is now crippled in his legs, and claims that it is the result of his severe punishment.

Most all of the men here imprisoned for life or a long term of years expect that in the course of time they will be pardoned. After being here a few years they begin to make some kind of an effort by which obtain their release. Those who have neither friends nor money try to win the sympathy of the Governor of the State by writing to him a full explanation of the facts in their case, and thereby perhaps succeed in getting pardons.

Some of the letters thus written are very touching and well composed, and seem to be worthy of great consideration. We will give a synopsis of the letter written to Governor Luce by William Walker, the subject of this book. Governor Luce had seen and talked with the prisoner, and he was sure that he meant to pardon him, and when the Governor sent him word that he did not care to show him any clemency, then the following letter was written:

MICHIGAN STATE PRISON, December 23d, 1889.

To the Hon. Governor Luce:
DEAR SIR — You came to the prison, and on two different occasions, to see me, and I was lead to believe that you would do something in my case before your term of office expired. I paid no attention to what any one else said, for I was satisfied you would not overlook me. I was a slave forty-three years in the Southern States, and have been twenty-five years here imprisoned. Now don't you think that that is enough punishment to pay for any crime a man can commit? I do not think that I am asking anything unreasonable any more than any other life man.

There has been as high as twenty-five life men pardoned since I came here, and I do not think that it is unreasonable for me to ask for one. I have got a wife and two children in Odren County, Missouri, and won't you please do something for me that I may see them before I die?

It is my sincere desire that you will make my sentence a term of years, if you can't grant me a pardon, and if I should live out the sentence you give me I will try and be a good citizen and will ever remember you.

Please call into mind the circumstances under which I was raised. I was born and raised a slave, and was entirely ignorant of the laws of the State at the time I committed the crime for which I have been here twenty-five long years. Where I was raised colored men were no more allowed to learn to read than if they were cattle. I was sold to New Orleans in 1845, and have not seen nor heard of my father or mother since that time. I have had to battle with the world single handed and alone, and never was arrested before.

Please take my case under due consideration, and then do me justice if you won't do anything else for me.

Yours very sincerely,

WILLIAM WALKER, NO. 27.

The convict's pitiful letter did not succeed in procuring his pardon, although many others were pardoned before the Governor's term of office expired, which was only about four weeks later. When Governor Luce received the letter he wrote to the convict that it was impossible for him to pardon or commute his sentence, and could not see any reasons for him to release a man whom so many other Governors had refused.

The old prisoner had been daily expecting a pardon for many years, and has a large box full of prison relics which he has collected from his fellow prisoners, some of whom have long ago been released, or perhaps have been dead for more than a quarter of a century. He has many plans by which to gain a livelihood when some kind hearted Governor shall have set him free. He has constructed a machine of one thousand different pieces, and which has taken him twenty-six years to complete. He believes that his machine will make a fortune for him if properly handled, as everybody will readily pay to see such a wonderful piece of machinery that took over a quarter of a century behind prison walls to complete. He has frequently been disappointed in getting his freedom, and has often been the victim of gullible lawyers, who have succeeded in getting nearly all the money he has earned by doing over-time.

The last time that he was victimized out of his money he became so desperate and despondent that he declared that never again would he pay for his freedom in advance. In 1885 Alex Hamilton, a colored lawyer from Grand Rapids, came to the prison and had an interview with the prisoner in regard to his case. The colored convict placed great confidence in a man of his own race and quickly gave him the money for which he was to work for his release. The prisoner declares that he was left in the lurch, for the colored counselor never even wrote him after he left the prison door.

It will be remembered that the prisoner was sentenced with two other accomplices to solitary confinement. One of the convicts was a woman, Eliza Sholtz, who was pardoned after remaining a few years in the place. The other prisoner died during the rage of the mutton fever. William Walker is now the only one left to suffer for the crime. We have previously stated that the old colored prisoner can neither read or write, and can only pass away the weary hours of his life by making toys and forming plans by which to make a living with his wonderful machine when he shall have left these prison doors.

Another one of the old timers here is John Thomas (colored) No. 626. He was sent from Detroit in 1875 for the murder of his wife and stepdaughter. He was born in Spain seventy-eight years ago. For many years he sailed the seas as a cook. At last he came to the city of Detroit and learned the trade of barbering and then married a woman with a daughter, a beautiful girl about sixteen years old. One Sunday in September, 1875, the mother and daughter were killed with an ax. He was arrested and convicted of the crime and sentenced to imprisonment for life. He claims that he never committed the crime and that it was done by a colored man who was much infatuated with his stepdaughter and could not gain her parents' consent to marry her. The convict declares that the dead girl's lover disappeared soon after the trial and has never been seen since. Convict Thomas is employed on the broom contract and takes great delight in the evenings, while in his cell, petting and playing with his canary birds, always keeping a dozen or more of the best singers that can be found. It is not our intention to give our opinion in regard to the guilt or innocence of any inmate of the prison who was convicted by circumstantial evidence, and we will now leave his case among the things of the past and for other men to consider in the future.

One of the most notable and unfortunate men incarcerated here is George Freeman (colored.) He was born in Hamilton, Ont., and has not seen or heard from his father nor mother in twenty years. He is very illiterate and his reasoning powers are very defective. Thirteen years ago he came to Detroit, where he was hired by a liveryman of the city and soon became competent to earn a living in the capacity of coachman. For a while everything seemed to be working in his favor, but in 1885 a horse which he was driving ran away and fractured his skull. He was discharged by his employer, but soon after he succeeded in obtaining a situation in a private family. He was convicted of committing an assault upon an aged lady where he was employed and was sentenced to life imprisonment.

Soon after he arrived here he was employed by the Webster contract in the shop called the "guillotine," of which which we have previously spoken. He knew nothing about handling edged tools nor fixing whirring machinery. One day while engaged at his work his right hand was caught in the machinery and partially torn out from the socket. He is too simple to even realize the great loss of his hand, and often speaks of his rapid prosperity and wealth when he shall have left these prison doors. It is a question when his day of freedom will come, for he has neither friends nor money, and although he says that he is innocent of the crime against him, yet, who can tell whether he will ever again go forth from these prison doors. He is a constant attendant of the prayer meetings and all other religious gatherings of the institution. In his dreams he feels the fresh air against his cheeks and his blood thrill with the joy of liberty.

CHAPTER XIII
PRISON LITERARY MEETINGS — ESSAYS BY EDWARD HANLAN, IRVING LATIMER AND WILLIAM BUTLER

A GREAT deal has been said concerning the literary meetings during the reign of Warden Hatch and prison reform. There is nothing more that we can add in regard them, only to give some idea of the principal parts taken by the leading literary men of the prison.

One of the leaders of these exercises was Edward Hanlan, No. 4426. He was sent here for three years for larceny from the person. He was an intelligent young man, 22 years of age, and took great interest in the educational meetings of the prison, and often interested us with historical addresses. At this time no one surmised what a terrible ending of his life was in store for him. While here he was very quick-tempered and was frequently engaged in fights and quarrels, but in some way he always managed to be a favorite among the literary men of this place.

Hanlan was well liked by Warden Hatch and was secretary of the meeting of which the Warden was president. His time expired in the month of April, 1891, and he went to Detroit, where he married an estimable, young and beautiful wife. It is said that she did not know of his past career at the time of their wedding ceremony, for he was married under the name of Fitzgerald. Soon after the wedding he informed his wife that he was an agent for a large and prosperous manufacturing establishment in the State of Ohio, and that it was necessary for him to be absent from home for a few days.

The ex-convict left his home, never to return again. Three days from the time he left his home a burglary was committed in an Ohio city, and young Hanlan, alias Fitzgerald, was suspected of having done the burglarious work. Two policemen attempted to arrest him and were fired upon by Fitzgerald, one of the officers being killed. The ex-convict was captured and convicted of murder and sentenced to be hanged. He made application for a new trial and sent a subscription list to Jackson prison for his old companions to help defray the expense of saving his life. He was not very successful, as only a few dollars were sent to the condemned man. He succeeded in getting a respite for thirty days and then he was hanged.

We have stated that he was one of the leading literati during Warden Hatch's administration. The following is verbatim the last essay that was written by him and read before the Saturday night literary society, December 23d, 1890:

"Because men become convicts, either by their own acts or by the intrigues of others, they do not lose their identity. They are still men and more or less humane — still capable to feel and appreciate acts of kindness and to resent insults and brutal treatment.

The convict, well treated, is more docile and better contented to perform the day's labor than when he is taunted and ill used. A sample of nearly all classes and conditions of men, representing nearly if not all of the institutions of the country, find their way to prison and become convicts. With such a diversified class of inmates it becomes a difficult task to govern and regulate all of this vast body of men by any single mode of discipline. Some require kindness while others require forcible means to govern them. It is therefore apparent that all men are capable to act as judges or as officials in the government of our State penal institutions.

It is one of the oldest sayings that there is a medium line in all things, but there is no proposition that is more untrue. There can be no medium between right and wrong. A man must of necessity be radically right or radically wrong — there is no medium ground in this proposition. If we do wrong we cannot be right, and if we do right we cannot be wrong. So the old adage must be obsolete and entirely untrue.

The human race has been so persistently misled ever since the serpent stood on his tail in the Garden of Eden and expiated on the desirability of the fruit of the tree of knowledge that it is no wonder that some are at a loss to tell the real apple from the soft-solder affair tinted over with the russet hues of insincere representations. Circumstances have so combined and operated as to cause every new movement requiring agitation to be regarded with distrust. Owing to past events we are constrained to say that this is both natural and wholesome, providing it is accompanied by reasonable examination into causes, and governed by discretion after opinions are formed. The only way to moralize and christianize the human race is by kind and humane treatment. When a discharged convict commits a new crime all the prison critics in the country hold up both hands and cry out with holy horror against the prison prodigals ever being permitted to return to their homes or to enjoy kind and humane treatment while behind prison walls. Such sentiments from the lips of intelligent people are very unreasonable. Because the lightning every now and then destroys a building, we would not exclude the storm from natural phenomenon. Because the fierce solar rays occasionally overcome or kill a man, we would not do away with the sun.

> When friendship once is rooted fast,
> Its plant no storm can sever;
> Transfixed and heedless as the blast
> It blooms and flourishes forever."

EDWARD HANLAN, No. 4426.

(It was during the time that the warden was being attacked and criticised by many of the leading newspapers that this manuscript of the dead man was read, and many other prisoners during the evening vehemently expressed their opinions in regard to those who were against convicts' rights and prison reform.)

During the evening the following paper was read by Irving Latimer:

"Fellow Prisoners — To hold in one's mind an account of all that has taken place inside the prison walls within the last two years would be almost impossible. However, if there is one he certainly deserves the title of statesman. If my memory serves me right it was almost two years ago that I was advised to take a course in the Hatch labor and industrial institution. You will readily concede that I would have been very foolish to turn a deaf ear to such advice. I reluctantly consented for the simple reason that I did not enjoy the prospect of entering an institution of learning where it required so many years to finish the course. In my youthful days I had taken a four years course in school in company with a sister, but I did not enjoy the thought of taking a course here. But the gentleman who took such great interest in me told me that to acquire a complete knowledge of things, pro and con, it was necessary to sacrifice some pleasure. This statement I am fully realizing at present.

However, I entered the abode of Michigan's selected sons, and was duly received with great courtesy by the clerk in charge. I had received some information in regard to the trip-hammer shop while awaiting my trial, and I assure you I made no effort to secure a position in that department. I had now donned the prevailing uniform, and I took a side glance in the mirror close by. One look and I was nearly paralyzed. I turned and looked around on the floor, hoping to find a hole into which I might glide gently and silently and forever remain in seclusion. I could find none, so I stepped out into the hall. I saw a young man there, so I made haste to ask him what kind of a place this was. It was only necessary for him to use two words in answering. I have forgotten just what they were, but perhaps you can imagine.

But having an eye to business I asked the same gentleman, or convict I should say, if there was a prayer meeting in the prison? He replied that there was. My hope vanished instantly, for I knew it would be impossible for me to try to secure a soft job. I therefore turned my attention to something else, and asked him which contract was the best one to be assigned to. The convict replied that the shoe contract was the most desirable, stating that the majority of the men who engaged in that work generally last until their sentence expires.

A few hours later, during which time I answered many questions propounded to me by the deputy warden, I was taken to the shoe shop. On the way over the deputy told me that he had saved my life, as I had been booked for the polishing department, but he secured a different place for me. The position I secured was a very desirable one, as it placed me in close communication with a gentleman whose cheering words immediately acted as a stimulant on my already weakened constitution.

A few hours after having been assigned to work I was told by him that he would make application and secure admittance for me to the Monday night literary society, which he stated was the best in the prison. A fact which I fully endorse after two years attendance in the societies. But thinking that a very peculiar way to secure permission to enjoy privileges, I asked him if the convicts were running the institution. His reply was that they only had a lien on the place at present, but were going to run it after a while.

A few days later another gentleman of commanding presence and a determined look came up and was heard to say that he was going to interview the Board of Inspectors and get gray clothes for the men. This statement led me to believe that there was some truth in the expression of my first friend. This was the beginning of the remarkable change I am about to speak of. However, time will not permit me to enumerate all the changes that have taken place in that time. Some for good and some for bad. But dwelling for a brief period upon present movements in the prison, I can only say that none deserves the attention of the men who are desirous of receiving instructions more than the system known as the lecture house. Whoever conceived the idea conceived a good one. Professor George White, who delivered the first lecture, selected an idea which we all consider an excellent theme. Though few will doubt that his remarks were such as to elicit just criticism from a person well versed in penology.

The observant listener who was animated with the desire to also absorb all of the meaning of his discourse, readily detects the fact that a portion of it was intended to convey to his audience the truth that a man is nothing more or less than an animal, until he exercises that divine attribute known as reason. I admit that the statement was true in all of its details. But in the following statement that he made, which was an attack upon the press, including the daily and weekly journals, he completely ignores his former statement and contradicts himself. For instance, the drift of his remarks was nothing more or less than an expressed desire to exclude from the prisons a large number of papers that are now read by the inmates. He contended that a great amount of news as inserted in the colums of the press was not only detrimental, but was to a great extent the cause of the mental and moral faculties of man deteriorating. Now that part of his discourse meets with my approval. For I admit that to fill the mind with criminal news is to weaken the intellectual powers of perception.

Now the point I wish most to impress upon your mind is this. Man is but an animal until he exercises his power of reason. But how are we to presume that he is to exercise his power of reason unless matter is placed before him that will allow him to choose the good or the bad.

The press declares that no confidence can be placed in convicts, that they can not be trusted, that the privileges now granted should be taken away from us who are earnestly striving to help ourselves and others who need help. We are told that our schools should be discontinued, and the ignorant fellows who were filled with the hope that they might learn how to read and write, locked in their cells.

Convicts here in general are losing hope and interest in themselves. Why should they not? They are the victims of ridicule at the hands of disgruntled and unscrupulous men. To elevate a man's thoughts he should be granted the privilege of reading newspapers, regardless of some of their worthless contents. To deprive men of reading matter is to force them to be an animal still, because you have removed the cause that called into action their intellectual and moral faculties. The Associated Press places before us accounts of nearly everything that occurs, good and bad, from a prize fight to a sermon, and yet it is recognized by society as the great educator of mankind. I have met men who stood high in the social and commercial world who were the possessors of no school education, some could scarcely write, yet they were able to conduct an interesting conversation on any of the principal topics of the times, and their knowledge was acquired wholly by reading newspapers and other periodicals.

Nearly all of the writings and sayings of our most intelligent citizens, including lawyers, statesmen and ministers, are first brought to our notice through the columns of the press, afterward placed in book form, and to deprive the men in Jackson prison from reading newspapers is to keep them from reading the gospel. We have a man at the head of this institution whom I believe is honestly and sincerely desirous of bettering the condition of the men who have been so unfortunate as to be placed in prison. Outside of these walls our warden may have many bitter enemies, but we should be his best friends. Some of his political enemies outside of these walls are possessed of a sufficient amount of manhood to fight him and his principles openly, but as yet they have been unable to annihilate him or prove that his statements regarding prison discipline are erroneous. His enemies, however, who are inside the walls have and are now taking an entirely different course to defeat him in his efforts, and their progress in this direction during the past year has been far below their expectations.

But certain events have occurred during the past few months which have enabled them to secure a better hold of the strings they have been gently pulling during the period I have mentioned. The hammer of revenge is descending on every hand. Blows are being directed toward this administration which are quite harmless at present, but are bound to have a lasting effect in the future, and I am persuaded to believe in the near future. When we consider the fact that the reports of Warden Hatch's methods of conducting a prison have been flashed through all the States of the Union, and perhaps to foreign countries, one can not think too seriously upon these all important matters. It has been admitted by the leading officials of the prison that nearly all the movements in the prison have originated in the minds of the convicts. Not only that, it has also been admitted that many of the inmates have materially assisted in controlling the actions of the men and preserving good discipline.

We have also been led to believe that confidence was placed in us to a certain extent, in fact we have been allowed to assemble at different intervals for the purpose of talking over matters relative to reformatory work. Special schools have been in operation for some time, wholly among the inmates. And permit me to say that better results have been obtained in the special school in the two years we have conducted it than in any other two years since the erection of the school room. May everything end all right; may no event occur that will ruin our work here and forever put a stop to Warden Hatch's method of reform; may the feeling of discontent and enmity that has been engendered among the men die out and be forgotten.

IRVING LATIMER."

The night the papers were read by Convicts Hanlan and Latimer, there was quite a feeling among the men in regard to the criticising attitude shown by some of the leading newspapers in reference to Warden Hatch's system of prison reformation.

After Latimer concluded his speech he was followed by Jim Butler, colored, who spoke in substance the following words:

> "Fellow Men and Fellow Sufferers — I have not appeared before you tonight with the intention of relating the virtues of my past life, for it has been a complete failure. I am now thirty-seven years of age and twenty years of it I have been confined behind prison bars. On all previous occasions on leaving prison doors, I have left them with the intention of again pursuing my old way of committing depredations for a living.
>
> Of all my prison history I have not seen such encouragement manifested for men to lead pure and happy lives on leaving penal servitude. I have only a few months longer to remain here before I shall have fulfilled the demands of the law in expiation for my crimes, and when I shall have left you I expect to earn my living by the sweat of my brow.
>
> I have two or three different methods by which I can earn an honest living. You all are well aware that I am not unskilled in the art of shoe making, for I not only perform my daily task at making shoes on the shoe contract, but I also earn from ten to fifteen dollars per month doing over-time. I am not entirely ignorant in the art of tailoring, having followed it in many different cities for a living, and can do manual labor to perfection. With all of these advantages to the road of wealth and happiness at my command, I can not see any reasons for me to travel on the road of ruin and death after I shall have bid this place a long goodbye.
>
> I have made arrangements to work here for the same firm I now work for, after my time expires, and when I asked the warden if he would allow me to pass in and out of the prison to my work he quickly answered, yes, sir, and I was very much surprised in the confidence he could place in an ex convict. Fellow men, I am no scholar nor a public speaker, and for the present I bid you farewell."

Perhaps the last speaker might justly be called one of the shrewdest men ever confined in this place. In 1886 Butler and two other convicts planned a most daring escape. They were all employed on the shoe contract, whose shops are situated only a few rods from the gate through which all all the manufactured products of the yard pass.

The daring prisoners waited for the gates to open, and one afternoon in the month of August of the year mentioned, they ran through the gates and made their way toward the suburbs of the city. They were quickly run down by the guards and after being flogged and put through other modes of punishment, they were set to work.

Butler was an exemplary prisoner during the rest of his sentence and gained the confidence of those by whom he was employed. At the expiration of his term he was employed by the same firm which he worked for during his prison life. For a time he was a model workman and gave the best of satisfaction, but this state of conduct was irksome and short-lived. A few months after his release from prison a great burglary was committed in the city and Butler was arrested for having committed the crime. He was arrested and jailed. But a few days thereafter he made his escape and fled to Canada. He was extradited and brought back to this city, and was tried and convicted of burglary and sentenced to eight years at hard labor.

Butler declared that he would never serve his sentence and that he would surely make his escape. He kept his word. One morning in the month of March, 1892, when the men were going to the dining room to breakfast, the prisoner quickly left the ranks unnoticed by the guards and climbed upon the kitchen, and then ran along the west wing of the prison and let himself down with a rope to the ground outside of the walls. Ten days later, when again heard from, he was in Windsor, Ont., where he was arrested and jailed as an escaped convict. He refused to return to his old home without being extradited, and employed the best of counsel in his defense, but it was of no avail. He was given up by the Canadian authorities and was brought back to the place from which he so cunningly made his escape. A twenty-five pound ball and chain was securely fastened to him and he was again set to work on the Webster contract.

At the time the prisoner committed the crime for which he was imprisoned he had an accomplice by the name of William Hitchcock, alias William Howard, colored, who turned state's evidence against his partner and was set free. Butler swore vengeance against his old companion, but the informer was then enjoying his freedom and beyond the reach of his partner's wrath.

A few months later a robbery was committed at Canandaigua, Michigan, and Hitchcock was suspected of having done the deed. He was arrested by Sheriff Baldwin, but escaped from him before he was brought to trial. Soon after his escape from the sheriff at the village of Sturgis, he was hauled in at Ann Arbor and carried back to the place where the crime was committed. When he was convicted of the charge of burglary and asked if he had any reasons why the sentence of the court should not be passed upon him, he begged the judge to send him to the Ionia Reformatory in preference to Jackson prison.

The prisoner was well aware that Butler was here, and that there would be trouble when the two convicts met. Hitchcock was given seven years in Jackson prison. He is a hard character and his pal is confined here be reason of his turning state's evidence in the watch robbery in Jackson. No doubt that if the two crooks meet there will be war.

CHAPTER XIV
LOVERS OF PRISON LIFE — BEGGING TO BE RETURNED TO PRISON

A GREAT deal has been said about men returning to prison after having once been set free. Many persons are of the opinion that only confirmed criminals prefer to follow the same wrong road. It is a great mistake to form any such conclusion. A majority of the convicts think they will live honest lives when they get out. Some who have money or friends to look after them do, but others who are thrown upon the world branded "ex-convict," have a hard time trying to make an honest living, and it is not to be wondered at that they again commit crimes.

When they are released they are furnished transportation from whence they came. They have no money and with no object in view they do not know what will become of them. Everybody knows they are ex-convicts, and as they have no one to recommend them they have a hard time securing employment. People are naturally supicious of them. They finally become discouraged and in their desperation commit a crime, are hunted down by the officers and sent back to prison. While this is the case with some, there are others who would not lead an honest life if they could, and could not if they would.

But in order to give those a chance who desire to reform this State lacks nothing. There is a Home of Industry for ex-convicts at Detroit. Then when a prisoner is released he goes to this home where he works for wages. When he demonstrates he is willing and can work, an effort is made to find him employment elsewhere. If employment cannot be found immediately he has a home anyhow and is making a little money, while at the same time the home is profiting by his labor. He may have friends in a remote part of the country who would help him if he could get to them. He stays in this home until he earns enough to get to his friends and then they will not know that he has been in prison and are entirely ignorant of the misfortune which once befell him.

We have said that some men once imprisoned can not, or will not, refrain from the same old road of sin, and Charles Temple (colored) must surely be one of the number. This model lover of prison life is thirty-eight years of age. He was born in Detroit, and his life has been one of sin and crime. He has served five terms in prison. He was behind the walls of the Columbus, Ohio, prison for breaking and entering a dwelling house in the night time. When he left the prison doors of Columbus he was next heard from in Indiana, where he began the same old way of living that he had followed in days gone by. He was sentenced to three years in the penitentiary at Michigan City. At the expiration of his sentence he left the State of Indiana and went to Illinois, where he was sent to Joliet for two years for assaulting and cutting a man with a razor. When next heard from he was in the State of Michigan, where he entered a dwelling house and got off with the light sentence of one year in Jackson prison. When his time expired here he went to Kalamazoo and committed another burglary, and was sent back to Jackson for seven years.

His term expired the 18th of January, 1892, and he left here for Detroit. A few days after his arrival there he walked into the police station and said that he wanted to be sent to the State prison for life in order that he might get his old job back on the Webster contract. The desk sergeant thought that the man before him was a fugitive from the lunatic asylum, for never before had he heard of such an unreasonable request. The sergeant was well aware that it was impossible to send a man to penal servitude without him having committed a crime, and when he informed the prisoner of that fact he replied that there was a burglary attempted here a few nights ago, and that he was the man that had made the daring attempt. The sergeant knew that there was an attempt at robbery only the night before, and the prisoner's words only confirmed his guilt. He was locked up, and at his trial he plead guilty and was sentenced to five years imprisonment. He begged the Judge to make his sentence a little more severe, in order that he might have a home, but the Judge refused to impose a heavier sentence.

He is now employed on the same work on the Webster contract that he has done on his previous confinements. Convict Temple is naturally of a queer disposition. He seldom has anything to say to his fellow prisoners, and when out in the yard he always keeps aloof from the rest of the men. When in his cell he never has any love for music or takes any interest in any of the literary societies.

CHAPTER XV
SUNDAY IN PRISON — MUSICAL PRISONERS — THE DYNAMITE EXPLOSION

IT is generally supposed by the unknowing ones that the Sabbath must be a long and lonesome day for men behind the prison bars. But this is a great mistake. Sunday is one of the most enjoyable ones for the men incarcerated here. After the services in the chapel they have nothing else to do but to sleep and play on their musical instruments, of which there are many among the men.

Did the reader ever have occasion to visit the State prison on Sunday afternoon? If not, providing you desire to experience a sensation the like of which you have no idea, you should call at the institution at the time mentioned. Immediately after dinner on Sundays the men are marched to the cells, where they indulge in any pastime which they may fancy. The largest part of the inmates make Sunday a veritable day of rest, and after seeking the seclusion which their granite tomb-like apartments truly offer, stretch themselves on their beds and pass an hour or two in slumber. This is the time you should visit the prison. One cannot imagine the extremely large and varied assortment of snores, whistles, wheezes and groans that are to be heard. From all sections of each wing come the most awful sounds. The deep bass, foghorn-like snores are plainly heard, accompanied by several grunts and a penetrating whistle. Several variety of wheezes are also discernible. In its entirety the collection is extremely difficult to beat, as one can understand when he considers that the noises emanate from about 800 throats. The ludicrous sounds from the mouths of tired mortals continue until about four o'clock. By that time nearly all are awake, and sleep beyond that hour is entirely out of the question. From a far away cell suddenly comes the twang, twang of a banjo, followed by the ting, ting of a guitar, and in less time than it takes to relate the incident the air is laden with the sounds of musical instruments. Every convict who has "music in his soul" and an instrument in his cell proceeds to play. The noise is deafening. There are violins by the score, accordions, mandolins, flutes, clarionets, and in fact nearly every musical instrument known to the age, with the exception of brass band horns. The mouth-organ, apparently, has the preference, for there are a dozen of them used to one of any other instrument.

There are many really good musicians, both vocal and instrumental, incarcerated at the prison, several possessed of national reputation on the theatrical stage. The famous "Charley" Seamon accompanies his fine baritone voice with the same banjo which he used to delight the thousands of theatre goers throughout the United States. Mr. Seamon is known as "Jolly Charley" by his comrades, and he is like Mark Tapley, "jolly under all circumstances." The music continues until supper is served, and it is a great and noisy ending of a sabbath afternoon.

Perhaps nothing ever occurred among the inmates of the prison that created such excitement as the dynamite bomb which was exploded in a window of the west wing Monday evening, October 13th, 1889, by John Donovan and Daniel Griffin.

Donovan was sent from Wayne County to ten years imprisonment for robbery. He had attempted to escape prior to this, but was foiled, and after being locked in the dungeon for thirty days besides undergoing other kinds of punishment, he was set to work. But the prison authorities were aware that he was a cool and desperate man, and he was constantly being watched. On the night in question the convicts which we now refer to were unlocked with the rest of the prisoners who attend the night school, but they did not go to the school room with the other men. As soon as the rest of the men had gained the school room Donovan and his pal quickly seized their dynamite cartridge and laid it upon the base of the window sill and touched it off.

The concussion was so great that many convicts throughout the prison were lifted from the floor and thrown around in their cells. But the men did not succeed in blowing out the large stone by which they were to make their escape, and when they found out that their plans had failed they ran to their cells and shut the doors. The noise made by the explosion quickly brought the guards to the spot, and just in time to see the two convicts rapidly leaving the window. The huge stone was cracked and moved from its place, but not far enough for them to pass through. Donovan was kept in the dungeon for three months, and then he was again sent back to the Webster contract and set to work.

But the desperate man was determined to have his freedom, if possible, and was ever on the alert for any way by which to make his escape. Two years passed by before the opportunity was offered by which to gain his freedom. Walter Briquelet and Charles Keehne were employed in the same shop with Donovan. Briquelet was born in Monroe county, Mich., and is a young man of twenty-three years' experience in this world. More than two-thirds of his life has been spent among criminals and is as shrewd in their line of work as they are generally found. He was sentenced to eight years here for the crime of incest, and had two years longer to serve.

Charles Keehne was born in the State of Pennsylvania and was sent from Muskegon county to fifteen years imprisonment for assault with intent to do great bodily harm. He was one of the most intelligent men here. He could fluently speak three different languages and was a rapid stenographer, often taking down the speeches made by Warden Hatch to his subjects.

These three men planned and executed one of the most unique escapes that was ever attempted within prison walls. They were all employed in shop No. 14 on the Webster contract. Briquelet and Keehne were shipping clerks and bookkeepers and could go about the many shops on the contract wherever their work called them. But their partner, Donovan, was compelled to labor on a machine close by the keeper's desk ever since he made his attempt to escape by blowing out the window. It was impossible for him to be of much use in the plan by which they were to make their way to freedom, but it was he that engineered the plot. The shop in which they were at work is on the ground floor and there are many different rooms and stalls where iron and other kinds of stock are kept for wagon making. It is thirty feet from their shop to the outside of the wall. A tunnel was dug by the two shipping clerks and the dirt was secreted in one of the rooms used for keeping stock. When the way to liberty was completed the signal was given to Convict Donovan and the three men went forth to freedom. When they emerged from the tunnel they were all disguised as common laborers and passed close by the guard on the wall unnoticed.

After the escape the question arose among prison authorities in regard to the source the clothing came into their hands, and by some means suspicion was cast upon Aaron W. Hamacher, the foreman in the shop, as having been the man who furnished the clothing and aided them in making their escape.

Hamacher was arrested and was brought before Judge Peck in the city of Jackson for trial. He was defended by Attorney Ware and ex-Governor Blair and son, and Thomas A. Wilson and Prosecuting Attorney Parkinson represented the people.

It was brought out at the trial that there was a convict at the prison who was cognizant of all the facts connected with the escape of the prisoners. They asked that his testimony be taken. It was not deemed advisable to bring the prisoner to the court room to testify, so the attorneys and stenographers adjourned to the prison.

Daniel Griffin, the convict in question, testified that he had worked with Donovan for some time. That he knew that those who had escaped by means of the tunnel had made a portion of their clothing and that a portion of it they had secured in the shops; that a kind of dye had been made from paints and clothing colored therewith; that the pails which the prisoners were seen carrying contained apple butter and had been brought into the prison with grocery orders. Griffin admitted that he had been disciplined for having been connected with Donovan in the dynamite plot, and that he had talked with Hamacher and others about the escape. There was a great deal of controversy about some of the clothing that was found in the tunnel and which was proven to once have been in the defendant's possession. Letters were produced in the defendant's handwriting, which were of a very damaging nature. It was a long and well tried case and the prisoner was convicted. He was arrested for having aided Convict Donovan in making his escape from the prison, and when found guilty of the charge his case was appealed to the Supreme Court.

The Supreme Court decided that Donovan was not legally detained, consequently Hamacher, the defendant, had not committed any crime even if he had aided the convict in his escape. The case of Convict Donovan, the prisoner, in which it was said the suit arose, was exonerated from having committed the crime and would have been legally set free if he had pursued the proper course.

Hamacher was much elated at the decision of the Supreme Court and said that he would do all that he possibly could to secure the release of the convict who had so truthfully sworn in his behalf.

To prevent escapes in a place of this kind is almost impossible, it being necessary for the prisoners to be employed in many different places outside of the prison walls, and while thus employed they frequently betray their trust and run away.

Samuel Hamivan was sentenced February 10th, 1890, from Oakland county to five years' imprisonment. He had been a "trusty" for eight months, having acted as Deputy Cellum's errand boy. In this capacity he has been accustomed to go to all parts of the yard and shops, and even to the home of the deputy. He grew restless under this pageship and one morning after he had mopped the floor of the guard room in the most approved way, and made a few preliminary arrangements he took his departure, his exit being made out of the front door of the hall where he was engaged at work. This was about seven o'clock in the morning, and his whereabouts are as yet unknown. It was supposed that he would make a bee line for his uncle's, Jeremiah Hamivan, who was then plying the spectacle trade in Detroit and who at one time ran a pawn shop in the city of Jackson.

Jeremiah's boy Sammy is a bad one. Several years ago he lived in the city of Jackson and broke into a clothing store, for which he made the Ionia house of correction his home for some time. After he left Ionia he went to Lansing and set himself up as a receiver of stolen property. He had not received a large amount of things before he was caught at it and sent to the prison for two years. He behaved himself in a most exemplary manner that time and officiated as "trusty" for awhile. When he left the prison he managed to secure a term in the Detroit house of correction. Then he drifted to Oakland county, sinned some more, was sent back here and remained until he ran away. Hamivan is twenty-six years old, but looks much younger, and bids fair to give the prison authorities a long chase before they shall have overtaken him.

CHAPTER XVI
DESPERATE PRISONERS — MACHINERY DEMOLISHED WITH A SLEDGE HAMMER — PRINCE MICHAEL

THERE are some desperate men confined in this place, as there is in any place where criminals are confined. Some of them would not hesitate to take the life of a keeper or a convict. On October 24th, 1891, convict Burns made a most daring attempt to kill the keeper by whom he was then being guarded. He was sent here from Saginaw County for five years for an assault of this kind. He was classed among the most dangerous men in the place.

Burns was working on the new buildings that were then being erected for the State on the Withington & Cooley contract. On the afternoon of the day we have stated the convict became hungry and took something to eat out of one of the dinner pails that belonged to one of the free men, who was also working at the same place. Keeper Burns, who had charge of the gang of prisoners, reported the convict for pilfering another man's dinner. A short time thereafter the reported one crept up behind the keeper, threw his arm around his neck, drew his head back and with the open knife in his hand he tried to cut the keeper's throat. He was partially successful. The keen blade made a terrible gash that reached from ear to ear in the keeper's neck, but did not succeed in severing the windpipe and he recovered. For this daring attempt at murder the prisoner was most severely punished. He was flogged most unmercifully, and then kept in the dungeon for many days. He swore that he would kill the guard before the year was out, and perhaps this might have had something to do with his separation from the prison. For he quit the prison soon after the convict was brought out of punishment.

Another attempt at murder occurred between two convicts, Thomas Cassidy, No. 4664, and Robert Meecham, alias Muhun, No. 4633. Meecham was sentenced from Detroit for breaking and entering a store in the night time, for which he is doing a five year sentence. Cassidy is undergoing a three year sentence for larceny. They were both employed on the broom contract and the latter's time expired the next day after the cutting. They had assumed a hostile attitude toward each other for some time, and the day the cutting was done they came to blows. Meecham seized a long bladed knife, used in cutting broom corn, and plunged it into the side of his adversary. The blade struck a rib and glanced away from a vital part.

The above illustrations only partially shows the bloodthirsty character of some of the inmates of this place.

Billy Smith (colored) was doing a three year sentence for assault in the city of Detroit. He was employed on the Webster contract, which is by far the most slavish combination in the yard. One day in August, 1890, convict Smith became dissatisfied with his continual burden, and seizing a sledge hammer began to demolish the machinery of the shop. Three guards were in the shop when he began his destructive work, but none cared to lay hands upon him while he was so frantically swinging the heavy hammer. In less time than it takes to relate it, he had demolished three machines and done hundreds of dollars worth of damage. The damage to the machinery was so complete that the blacksmith shop was shut down, and the men were locked in the cells until new machinery could be obtained.

The colored convict was assigned to the dungeon for three months, and received a terrible flogging besides. At this time he only had about three months more to serve, and it was a question in his mind, whether or not he had not violated the law and laid himself liable to a prosecution for the destruction of property. After being released from punishment he was set to work in the hall and attended to the wants of the men in the west wing of the prison. As the end of his sentence drew near he was much worried in regard to whether, or not he would be arrested at the door. He made many inquiries among the men, to see what they thought about the chances for his arrest. Several of his fellowmen concluded that he was liable to be prosecuted for the deed. Smith declared that he would not take any chances, for he believed that a man was just as liable to be prosecuted for a crime committed in prison, as on the outside of prison walls. He was the boss of the gang of men that kept the wing in proper condition for the rest of their fellow sufferers, and was admitted to pass through the door of the prison that leads to the bucket ground, on Sundays, in the discharge of his duty.

The first Sunday in November, of the year already mentioned, he was admitted through the door of the prison to the bucket ground as usual in discharging his duty. As soon as the prisoner passed through the door, he scaled the wall of the prison, (which on Sunday afternoons are unguarded) and has not since been seen.

The shortness of his time, thirty days, which he had to remain in this place, and the boldness of his attempt, is sufficient to satisfy us that he never would have taken such chances when freedom was near at hand had it not been for fear of being arrested when his sentence was completed.

Perhaps the example of convict Smith was followed by two other colored convicts, William Close and George Woods. The latter has perhaps justly earned the name of being the most obstinate and stubborn man ever confined in Michigan's penitentiary. He was sentenced from Detroit in 1890, to ten years imprisonment for burglary. He has a record of being the only man in this place that could not, or would not, be made to work. It is said that while undergoing his seven years confinement in the Ionia Reformatory it was impossible for the prison authorities to compel him to do six months labor during his incarceration. When he came here and refused to work, day after day, and withstood all manner of punishment, it was thought that surely he was insane. But after being well informed of his actions while confined in Ionia prison, the warden believed that he was only dealing with an incorrigible man, and at once began to use the most severe methods of subjugation. He was confident that if he yielded to the will of the stubborn man that his example would soon be patronized by a majority of the men under his command. When the prisoner refused to work it brought the Warden's forbearance to a climax, and he was sent to the dungeon, where he remained many days before he would make any concessions to the Warden's demands for work. They soon found out that they had the most willful man to deal with that they had ever met. He seemed to care no more for flogging and the dungeon than if he was enjoying the very best of freedom on the outside of the prison walls. Time after time he underwent more punishment than any other man whom we could possibly name. He was fed on bread and water for weeks at a time, flogged, handcuffed to his door, and at last he was put on the stretching machine, which is by far the very worst punishment ever imposed within these walls. But he still remains the same impregnable and unyielding prisoner. Sometimes, after weeks and months of this kind of punishment, he takes a notion to work for a few days — probably for exercise — and all at once he assumes the same old routine of disobedience and goes back to his old home — the dungeon — and lives on bread and water. Convict Woods was nearly a match for his incorrigible companions, and in many respects imitated their examples. Soon after the machinery was smashed to pieces on the Webster contract by convict Smith, Woods attempted to follow his example. One morning when marching to the dining room, he left the ranks and went into the shop, seized a sledge hammer and began to destroy the machinery. He was prevented from doing much injury by the guards, who came upon him just as he had fairly commenced doing the work. He was compelled to put on a suit of striped clothing, as a mark of his disgrace, and whip-lashed most severely, and then locked up in the dungeon for thirty days.

At the present time Michigan's State prison has in its custody some notable men. Among the number is Dan K. Sartwell. He is a third termer. He was arrested at Port Huron in April, 1892, on a charge of burglarizing several business places and residences in that city, wagon loads of miscellaneous stolen property being found on his premises. He was convicted of the charge in the month of June, and Judge Vance sentenced him to prison for ten years. The prisoner is a very cool and nervy man, but the sentence was more than he expected, and he broke down completely and cried like a child.

His incarceration has no novelty for him, as he has previously served two terms in this place. In the early seventies he did a short term for larceny. In 1876, the centennial year, he was sentenced to four years for burglary. In the year following, 1877, he escaped. This was under the regime of Warden Humphrey. Chief of Police Winney took after Sartwell and chased him to the Thousand Islands, in the St. Lawrence river, where he lost the scent. New York officers finally captured the fugitive, but he was too slippery for them and escaped the second time. After awhile Sartwell came to Howell, where his wife was living, and was captured and returned to the prison by Sheriff William Goodrich, and served his time.

Another very prominent man among our number here is David Strange (colored). He was sentenced from Detroit in September, 1891, to twenty years in prison for murder. It is a question in our mind whether or not he ought to have had to serve a sentence, for the man he killed had twice attempted to take the prisoner's life.

The quarrel originated about a colored damsel, of whom the murderer and his victim were infatuated. William Loomis, the victim, was quick-tempered and very desperate, and previous to the murder he attempted to cut his rival's throat. For a while Strange succeeded in keeping out of the way of his angry foe, but on this fatal night he was partly intoxicated as well as the one he killed. It is said that the prisoner was in a saloon when William Loomis came in and said, "Now I have got you," and drew a knife or some other sharp instrument from his pocket and struck at his rival. Strange drew a pocketknife and plunged the keen blade up to the hilt into the side of the aggressor, and he fell dead.

David Strange was tried and convicted of murder in the second degree and sentenced, as we have stated. He is both a vocal and instrumental artist of ability, having been employed for years by some of the best musical companies on the road. He is the best singer of the place, and frequently cheers our despairing hearts with his many funny songs and comical gestures. David Strange has a colored quartette for the benefit and interest of the literary societies of the prison, and seldom do they sing a song that they are not heartily encored. He is a fine banjoist as well as a professor of the guitar, and has a class of prisoners to whom he gives musical instructions once a week. He is assisted in his vocal and instrumental work by William Howard, a colored man from Kalamazoo county. He is doing a sentence of twenty-five years for assaulting an officer with intent to murder. Howard was intoxicated at the time and when the officer attempted to arrest him he cut the officer with a razor. He was given the unreasonable sentence of twenty-five years in Jackson prison. He was sentenced in 1885, and soon became a favorite among the men for his superb singing and his fine guitar solos.

Howard and Strange are employed on the Withington & Cooley contract, from which they are anxiously striving to get away, for they believe it is the hot-bed of serfdom, and not many men could be able to live a quarter of a century and work for the Withington & Cooley firm. On this contract the men are at work grinding hoes, pitchforks, etc., and there is more or less steel dust flying through the polishing shop and these particles of dust are not prolonging to life when daily inhaled into the lungs. One day during the winter of 1891, Convict Howard became enraged at John Shaw, the foreman of the shop, and struck him a powerful blow with his fist. This was considered one of the greatest acts of disobedience that it was possible for him to perform. He was called over to the hall and put in striped clothing, a mark of disgrace, and then cat-whipped, after which he was handcuffed in the dungeon.

Convict Howard has a guitar class in the doctor's office on Friday evenings. Men of good conduct, who are desirous of studying music, are allowed to do so, and can belong to any of the musical classes of the institution by paying the required sum of one dollar per term of three months.

Professor Mills, a music teacher of great reputation, has a very large class of convict students under his tutorship. Some of them are taking banjo and guitar lessons, and others are learning to master the clarionet, flute, horn and many other instruments. This musical class generally meets once a week in the evening, from half past six until eight o'clock.

There are also classes of foreign languages. A German convict has a class of prisoners studying German, and a French prisoner gives lessons in French for two hours once a week. There are also scholars in painting and photography. This class of fine art is taught by John Mitchell, who is quite an expert and is now serving his fourth term. He was released from here in August, 1884, after having completed a four years' sentence for robbery. At the expiration of his sentence he went to the State of Ohio, and for awhile was employed in the business of selling crockery on commission. Mitchell soon disappeared from Toledo, and when next heard from he was in Windsor, Ont. A few days later he was employed by a photographer in that place, but soon thereafter he disappeared from Windsor, and some jewelry belonging to his employer could not be found. When next heard from he was living in the suburbs of Detroit, near Wyandotte, and was arrested for the latter theft, convicted and sentenced to four years in Jackson prison. While here imprisoned he gained quite a reputation as a photographer and painter, and made quite a handsome sum enlarging photographs and painting pictures of mothers, wives and relatives of his fellow men. Convict Mitchell was frequently visited by many people in this city in their anxiety to have him paint or enlarge the pictures of some relative or friend. He was discharged in March, 1892, and remained in the city of Jackson. Four weeks later he was arrested for another crime he committed, was convicted of the offense and again sentenced to four years' imprisonment.

The special barber shop is another feature of the prison worthy of mention. All men in this place are entitled to a shave once a week. But the special barber shop is in one of the small rooms of the prison, and the men who wish to shave can do so by paying the sum of two dollars, which entitles them to a shave twice a week for three months. This extra shaving is done in the evening and by colored barbers, who use the money thus earned for their own benefit. They generally earn from fifty to sixty dollars a month. A list of the men is kept who are on the barber's shaving register and they are unlocked one at a time in the evening and shaved.

Perhaps the greatest job the barbers ever had of shaving and hair-cutting was that of Prince Michael. He was sent from Detroit in June, 1892, to five years imprisonment for having too many women under his control. Michael was posing as a saint in the City of Detroit and soon succeeded in winning the confidence of many feminine followers. They contributed to his financial wants and he was living in ease and splendor. His followers were compelled to wear their hair hanging down to their shoulders, and to otherwise distinguish themselves from the common herd.

It hardly seems possible for a man in this age of christian intelligence to succeed in making any class of people believe that he is a supernatural being, and that they must do according to his will. But such is the case, and the long haired imposter soon had many people under his charge. His conduct became so ungodly that the citizens of the neighborhood called him to account. He was arrested for having young girls and women doing his will, regardless of the fact that he had a lawful wife living under the same roof where these crimes were perpetrated. He was convicted and sentenced as stated.

From the very beginning of his trial until the prison doors shut him in the outcome of his case was, perhaps, as eagerly watched for as any murder trial that the State has ever had.

The crime for which the prisoner was convicted was committed in the City of Detroit, but his case was tried at Ann Arbor, that he might have a fair and unprejudiced trial.

The day after his conviction the following item appeared in the columns of one of our leading newspapers: "The trial of Prince Michael Mills at Ann Arbor yesterday was a shame to that city and a disgrace to the State. It was concluded and the beast in human form convicted. Michael Mills was on trial, charged with the most revolting of crimes on little Bernice Bechel, aged fifteen. Eliza Courts, Mike's spiritual wife and the chief of his harem, was by his side during the trial. The entire day was devoted to the speeches of counsel. The court room was crowded to suffocation and hundreds were unable to gain admittance. Prosecutor Burrows finished the closing argument at 5:35 in the afternoon. Judge Kinnie at once delivered his charge to the jury, concluding at 5:48, when he ordered a recess until 7 o'clock. At 7:20 the clanging of the big court house bell announced that the jury was prepared to render its verdict. Then ensued a scene that beggars description. The jury had deliberated just fifteen minutes, the time between the adjournment of court and 7 o'clock having been occupied by the jury in eating supper and stretching their limbs. In answer to the question of the clerk of the court the foreman of the jury announced that they found the prisoner guilty. The verdict provoked the hundreds that crowded the court room to the wildest enthusiasm, and it was some minutes before quiet could be restored. When this was done Judge Kinnie immediately sentenced the prisoner, giving him the maximum penalty, which is five years in State prison. The cheering and applause of the vast audience was deafening at the conclusion of the sentence, and amid the din court was hastily adjourned, thus ending the most remarkable case on record. The startling and sensational scene presented in the court room, however, was followed by a scene wilder and more thrilling than any that has been witnessed at Ann Arbor for years. Even though justice was meted out by the court, the indignation and hatred of the crowd did not abate, and in his brief journey from the court room in charge of four officers, Prince Michael, with Eliza Courts at his side, was surrounded by a mob of many hundred people, who conducted him to his prison, hooting, shrieking and yelling like fiends. When he vanished into the jail the surging wave of humanity rolled back to the court house. Then followed another scene which shall become memorable.

William Bechel, the father of Bernice, the complaining witness, whose position throughout the trial has been a most peculiar one in turning against his own daughter, was seen for a moment in the doorway of the court house, and became the object of the crowd's wrath. He saw his danger and with two companions sought refuge in an office of the court house. In abject terror he and the other two Israelites were taken to the depot in charge of officers and sent to Detroit.

The prince was safely landed at Jackson and was commanded to sit on the same seat in the hall master's office where all prisoners sit when beginning prison life. The bench upon which they are commanded to sit upon is called the mourner's bench. While Mike was thus seated upon the mourner's bench preparatory to donning the prison garb, it began to thunder and lightning and the rain came pouring down in torrents against the window of the hall master's office. The hall master remarked to an officer of the prison, that Michael must have been the sign of damp weather? "Yes," replied the prince, "and it shall rain every day until my time expires." The first three days of his prison life, it rained every afternoon, and it was thought by some of the officers that his predictions for rain during each day of his imprisonment were coming true and a farmer suggested that so much rain was ruining the crops, and that it would be best to take the prince out of prison and hang him.

While Michael Mills was seated upon the mourner's bench, Warden Davis came into the hall master's office, and observing the new prisoner, inquired who he was? Mr. Mosher replied: "Why, warden, is it possible that you are not acquainted with the famous man, Michael Mills, the Detroit prince?"

The warden replied, "Why, Mr. Mosher, is this the man we have all read and heard so much about. He is entirely welcome to the choicest viands in the kitchen and the strongest bed in the prison." The prisoner replied that the warden's will was law and by which he would abide in the most exemplary manner during his five years' imprisonment.

After the noted man was deprived of his hair and whiskers, by the prison barber, it was gathered up and it is said that it was speedily sent to the Wonderland Museum at Detroit.

One of the members of the colored quartette composed the following song about the new convict:

> When Michael came to prison
> He prophesied the rain,
> But the barber drawed his razor
> To cut his hair just the same.

Prince Michael says, Mr. Shaver
What are you going to do?
You keep still, says the barber,
Or I'll cut you half in two.

Then the Prince he looked up
With his eyes full of tears,
And then the prison barber
Reached out and got his shears.

Then Michael shed his coat
And stepped through the door,
When the barber clipped his hair
And it fell upon the floor.

It is the opinion among the leading men of striped clothing in this place that the prince will soon deliver one of his famous lectures that has won him so many followers. The prison chapel is the place where the monthly literary meetings are held, and it is generally filled and over crowded with anxious spectators, to listen to the words of the lecturer, and it is predicted that on the evening the lecture is to be given, an unusual number of visitors will be present long before the speaker steps upon the rostrum.

CHAPTER XVII
CANDIDATES FOR THE HOSPITAL — CAPITAL PUNISHMENT — SINGULAR MURDERS

IT would be an interesting sight, to a stranger, to see the scores of men going into the doctor's office in the morning when marching from the dining room. Morning is the time the medical wants of the men are looked after. Those who are unable to work are excused and return to their cells or are sent to the hospital. Others who are unable to do a full day's work are permitted to do only half of the regular task.

It frequently happens that the doctor refuses to excuse the patient, believing he is playing the truant or that he is not unable to perform his daily labor. Sometimes the prisoner when told to go to the shop after the doctor has examined him, refuses to comply with the doctor's request, and then trouble is at hand.

But the physician's judgment is not always correct in regard to the prisoner's abilities to perform the work of the day, for we have known them to fall down in the shop from weakness and ill-health and were carried to the hall, and then perhaps to the hospital.

The hospital is situated over the chapel and in the dome of the prison. When a prisoner dies here he is kept for a certain length of time, and then if his body is not called for by his friends it is liable to be sent to the medical college at Ann Arbor.

On Sunday, the 19th of June, 1892, convict Mourer died here after having served four years of a life sentence. The crime for which he was incarcerated was a peculiar one. He killed his sister-in-law, Mary Mourer, at her residence in Detroit July 27th, 1888. The murder occurred at 11:30 in the morning, while Mrs. Mourer was dressing preparatory to going down town. Mourer approached her from behind and shot her in the back of the head without the slightest warning. A daughter of Mrs. Mourer entered the room where her mother had just been shot, and Mourer fired two shots at her. At the trial it was shown that Mourer was sober at the time of the shooting, but it could not be developed that the murderer and his victim had ever quarreled, and the motive that prompted the crime has always been a mystery. Now that the assassin is dead his object in committing the murder perhaps will never be known.

Soon after the shooting of Mrs. Mourer murders were of an every day occurrence, and the people and the press were talking strong about re-enacting the law of capital punishment. But one of the leading newspapers of the State, when speaking of the brutality of the gallows, printed the following item: "The talk about capital punishment is on tap in Michigan. Murder is active, but whether exceptionally so or not we are unable to determine. It is always occurring with more or less frequency in semi-civilized society. We doubt if there has been an unusual number of murders this year. If there has been the conclusion is hardly avoidable that the average moral condition of society is not improving. Social crimes are certainly on the increase. Crimes against property are also more frequent than they used to be. Let us ask, in all seriousness, if it is for this that the people of Michigan are spending five to six million dollars a year for what is called education? If it is we had better return to simpler and more primitive methods. Our elaborate system of educating away from manual labor does not seem to have produced the desired moral results. Labor and morality are the best safeguards against crime. In the system of State education these two elements are sadly overlooked. The dominant idea among advocates of capital punishment is that hanging will lessen crime. The only other motive for recommending it is revenge, and that itself is of a murderous nature. A cruel society will resort to cruel methods, a humane society to humane methods. Like produces like everywhere. We have no faith in killing as a preventative of crime. If society is of such a character that a majority desire to hang, shoot or imprison murderers, so be it. When society improves, murder will diminish, and not till then, whatever the punishment may be, and society will not be likely to improve much under State regulation of morals, religion or education. We have no faith in the State as an agency for uplifting society in any respect. It is not creditable, however, that the gallows is an emblem of our so-called civilization. Under the discipline subjected to the inmates of our State prison they are better behaved than are the inmates of our State capitol. For the accidental or spasmodic murderer there is a chance for reformation in the prison. But for nearly all murderers, belonging as they do to the hereditary criminal class, there is not much hope — generally not any. Still the question arises, can society afford to cheapen human life?

This is a serious question. Since our civil war, with its numerous victims, while it evoked some of the noblest virtues as well as detestable passions, human life has not been regarded with its old-time sacredness in this country. It has been cheapened. Society is greatly demoralized. If society engages in killing men and women for crime, will not the effect be to still further cheapen human life? The cause, or causes, for the increase of crime must be sought, not in the mode of punishment, but in the conditions of society itself, in the lowering of its ideals, in the selfish aims that control, and in the efforts that are made to perpetuate the criminal and defective classes. Some one has wisely said that society prepares crime; the criminal executes it. Justly, we think, the prevalence of crime is largely laid at the door of society. To lessen it more attention must be paid to the cultivation and stimulation of the social and moral virtues, rather than the intellectual faculties of the rising generation. The gallows and hang-man are not reformatory agencies and never can be, nor can the State, divorced as it is, from morality and religion, set up any machinery that will diminish crime. Even so, every good tree bringeth forth good fruit; but a corrupt tree bringeth forth evil fruit. A good tree cannot bring forth evil fruit; neither can a corrupt tree bring forth good fruit.

The effort of all science and invention is to foster, preserve, and better life. It is true that the crime of murder is committed in Michigan, but not more so than in the States which punish by hanging or electrocution.

The extermination of one man for the killing of another originated from a desire for vengeance, of which the law does not and cannot take cognizance. Justice is the demand of the people and the purpose of the law. Certainly there is neither justice nor its essential adjunct — mercy — in the killing of a human being. We have no right to take a man's life. Our efforts should be to regenerate it and make it better. The day of the dungeon is past, and this horror has been consigned to oblivion with the rack, thumb-screw and like implements of torture. Our prisons are no longer prisons according to the old definition of the word, but reformatories in which the combined efforts of the officers and charitable institutions tend, not to turn out prisoners more hardened in crime than when they entered, but men, better for the discipline and training they have received and the knowledge they acquired, ready to once more take their place in the world as law-abiding citizens and do their share of the work directly for their own good, and indirectly for the benefit of the world at large. That this effort is not always successful is no argument against it.

It is right in principle, and as time goes on its results prove more and more gratifying. Punishment for crime should be swift, sure and just, but vengeance should have no place in it. No crime has ever been committed by which the world has been made better, and the legal murder of one man for the criminal murder of another neither replaces the dead nor helps the living. Crime is the result of passion and ignorance. The only way to obliterate it or reduce it to a minimum is by education, enlightenment and progress, and the greatest, longest and best step in this direction at the present time, is to conduct our prisons on a moral and a conscientious basis. Make the punishment sure, but make it reformatory; let justice replace vengeance and education do away with the necessity of physical suffering legally inflicted. It is true murders have increased in the last few years, but not only in Michigan, but all over the United States, and crimes of all kinds will increase as long as the gulf between the classes increases.

The great well-to-do middle class which is now being diminished and impoverished, is the moral class. Crimes and dissipation are to a great extent confined to the extremes of society. The right way to diminish crime therefore is to better the condition of the producers. Give them a fair chance, wipe out the unjust laws, re-establishing justice, prosperity and morality will be increased.'

In order to diminish crime the classification of criminals is necessary. In Jackson prison young men and old men — first time offenders and hardened criminals are indiscriminately mixed together. They are mixed together on contract work and sleep side by side in the cells at night. The building is so constructed and the arrangement of the cells is of such a character that it is almost impossible to prevent communication between the young and first time offenders and the most daring criminals whose hands are stained in blood.

A German boy, thirteen years of age, was confined in this place for three years for committing a slight offense. He had been in this country only a short time and could speak no English, knew nothing about the laws and customs of this country. He was arrested for some slight offense, convicted and sentenced to three years' imprisonment, in the company of robbers and burglars of the most daring kind. It does not require a connoisseur in the science of penology to appreciate the baneful influence of such companions upon an innocent youth.

The cells of Jackson prison, especially those of the west wing, are of such an unhealthy construction that it is a wonder that the death rate is not enormous. In some parts of the west wing there is no ventilation to the cells other than the grated doors. The cells are as dark at midday as they are at midnight, and the prisoners are compelled to burn oil in their lamps from morning until night. Perhaps there is not a man in prison who has been incarcerated for a number of years in the base of the west wing but what is full of rheumatic pains as a result of living in the dark and dismal cells.

The new wing of the prison was built under the administration of Warden Hatch, for the purpose of bettering the condition of the inmates, but when it was finished it was no benefit to us, because it was not used during the administration. For some reason or other the heating apparatus of the new wing was not in running order, but when Warden Davis came into power he had a new heater put in, and the place was filled with prisoners.

Cleanliness is a potent factor in the reformation of criminals, and when men are compelled to live many years in a dark and ill-ventilated cell it has but little effect toward improving their moral and vicious inclinations.

The contract system is a powerful stimulus towards irritating and discouraging its serfs, for it is utterly impossible for a man to be employed on contract work without meeting many disappointments, and many of them find their way to the insane asylum.

Emory Nye was sent from Battle Creek in 1875 to twenty-five years' imprisonment for murder. He has been employed in nearly all of the contract shops in the prison, and two years before his time expired he went raving mad and was sent to the insane asylum for criminals at Ionia.

Convict George Palmer was sent from Calhoun county to six years' imprisonment, and six months before his time expired he was taken from the Webster contract and sent to the asylum, having been pronounced a lunatic by competent physicians.

John Helmes was sent from Barry County to four years imprisonment for larceny. He was employed on the Webster contract, and two years from the time of his arrival he was pronounced insane and sent to the asylum. Helmes has had a hard time of it here.

There was scarcely a day that he was not reported for not having done enough work. At last his mind became so affected with his unenviable position that he would frequently quit his work and go screaming through the shop.

Insanity is more prevalent among the married men than the single. Many of them have families in destitute circumstances. Wm. Brown was sent from Detroit to ten years imprisonment for robbery. He had a wife and six children, the oldest a girl seventeen years of age. His wife was an invalid, and the main support of the family was the oldest daughter who was a cigar maker, and for a while she succeeded in keeping the family from hunger. During these prosperous times the prisoner was as contented as the general run of men when in prison. But at last the daughter — the bread winner of the family — took sick and died. The mother also died and was buried three days after the death of her child. The only protector of the prisoner's five remaining children was a boy, only fifteen years of age. The prisoner attempted to aid his children by doing over time here, and for a few months he succeeded in making six or eight dollars per month. But at last the task was raised, and the prisoner's only source of revenue was cut off. Then he began to worry about the poverty of his children, and he soon had enough to worry about, for the son was arrested on a charge of breaking into a mill and stealing flour. He was sentenced to one year imprisonment. The convict's four remaining children were soon scattered. The oldest, a girl was sent to the Industrial School at Adrian for disorderly conduct. One of the three remaining boys was sent to the Reform School at Lansing, and the other two found homes in respectable families in the city of Detroit. The family of convict Brown was widely separated, and in three years from the time he entered these walls he was a raving maniac in Ionia's insane home for criminals. His reason had forever fled and he died in the maniac's home.

George Lovely (colored) was sent from Calhoun County to life imprisonment for the murder of his wife. He was one of the most wretched and mind disturbed human beings that we have seen during our time. If it is possible for the dead to taunt and tease the living, then George Lovely was terribly annoyed by the unseen presence of his wife. She was stabbed to death and terribly mutilated with a knife, on a Sunday evening at eight o'clock. The quarrel arose over an apple pie which he wanted made for dinner, and which she refused to make. Lovely was born a slave in Kentucky, and made his escape from there just before the war. He brought with him one of the old fashioned Kentucky bowie knives about eighteen inches long. At the time he murdered his wife he used this knife and plunged it into her body fourteen times. After his incarceration, and on Sunday evening about the time the crime was committed, he imagined that his wife was with him in his cell, and he could be heard arguing and pleading with her to take his life in exchange for her own, and he would die and she would come back to life again. Very often the fatal fracas would be revived and his cell would ring with oaths and curses over the imaginary dinner table. These tormenting Sabbath scenes continued for four years, and finally one Sunday evening he had a frightful quarrel with his imaginary visitor. The fight lasted for more than an hour, and was distinctly heard throughout the wing. All at once the insane man sprang aside to dodge a blow from his dreaded persecutor, and a stream of blood gushed from his mouth, and bespattered the walls and the floor of his cell, and the convict reeled and fell to the floor. He was dead in a very few minutes. The insane man had bursted a blood vessel in his desperate struggle and his spirit had gone to meet its tormentor.

One of the most singular murders ever committed in Michigan was the one for which Stevens is now serving a life sentence. Convict Stevens was engaged to be married to girl in the city of Detroit, and the night before the wedding was to take place her throat was cut from ear to ear with a razor. Her body was found early in the morning, lying just inside the gate of her home, and Stevens could not be found. He was captured the next day many miles from home, while walking along on the railroad, trying to make his escape. It was well known that the night the crime was committed the two lovers were together and had a long conversation while standing at the gate. When arrested he admitted that he was present at the time when the deed was done, but said that it was not the work of his hands. He claimed that his intended bride and himself were standing at the gate discussing their future prospects and good results which must follow after when they were made man and wife the next evening. The prisoner says that while they were thus conversing she playfully put her hand into one of his pockets that contained a razor, and after having opened it she held the keen blade close to her neck and said that if she drew the keen edge across her throat that there would not be a wedding, but a funeral, on the coming day. Stevens says that he reached for the razor for fear that she might cut herself while handling it in such an awkward manner. When he snatched after the keen instrument she quickly jerked her hand away to prevent him from taking it away from her, and in some way or another the keen blade came in contact with her throat and severed her jugular vein. The prisoner declares that when she fell to the ground a corpse, that he fled through fear of being arrested for a crime accidentally committed by her own hand. Stevens was convicted and sentenced to life imprisonment. He stoutly denies that he had anything to do with the murder, and declares that she accidentally killed herself. When he had been in prison two or three years he had his case investigated by the Board of Pardons, and they visited the scene of the crime and concluded that it was impossible for them to discover any motive for the prisoner to have committed the murder, but yet they refused to recommend him to the Governor for a pardon. Whether he is innocent or guilty, it is surely a wonderful case. Why he should take her life, and only a few hours before they were to be married, is a mystery to us. Stevens is quite a young man, twenty-six years of age, and is employed on the Wells & Fargo shoe contract.

Perhaps his case may have a parallel in that of James M. Mathews (colored). He came from Cass County under a life sentence for murder. Mathews was infatuated with a colored damsel, and one night during the summer of 1890, while they were together, three pistol shots were heard in quick succession. It was soon discovered that the girl had been instantly killed, and the prisoner was lying a few rods away from her with a bullet hole in his left breast. The bullet struck a rib and turned aside from his heart, at which it was aimed. He was arrested and jailed until he had recovered sufficiently to be brought into court and stand trial for the capital crime. Evidence was produced that loud words were heard between the murderer and his victim just a few minutes before the shooting. It was shown that the revolver belonged to the defendant, and that he had offered to bet one of his companions that before the week passed by he would take his own life. The prosecution endeavored to show that the prisoner killed the girl because she refused to elope with him, regardless of the fact that he had a wife and child living in the same neighborhood.

The prisoner's defense was a very peculiar one. He claimed that the girl was very anxious for him to elope with her, and on several different occasions had threatened him with violence if he refused. On the night of the murder they were together and she emphatically demanded that some satisfactory explanation be given to her demands. Mathews claims he replied that he could not be her husband, for he had a wife and child whom he dearly loved, and scarcely were the words uttered before she thrust her hand into his pocket where she well knew he carried a revolver. She drew out the deadly weapon before he realized her intentions, and placing it to her side she screamed, "This is the last of me," and fired. The prisoner declares that as soon as he saw her fall to the ground he took the smoking revolver from her hand and placing it to his side, pulled the trigger.

Mathews was convicted of murder in the first degree and sentenced to Jackson for a term of ninety-nine years and one day. We believe that his sentence is equal to life imprisonment, as he is now thirty-five years of age, and if he serves his sentence his good time will expire about the year 1947.

Mathews is one of the most restless and dissatisfied life men confined in Jackson prison. He is ever speaking of his aged mother and father who are yet living. He was not here a year before he began taking steps to procure his release by executive clemency. He has frequently written to the judge and prosecuting attorney before whom he was tried, to intercede in his behalf. But he does not receive much encouragement from them. The prosecuting attorney in answering the convict's letter informed him that he was convicted without prejudice and perhaps it was impossible for a jury of just men to arrive at any other conclusion than that of his guilt.

We do not know whether the prisoner is innocent or guilty; we have only stated the facts as gleaned from his own lips, together with the incidents of his trial.

There are many innocent men confined in Jackson prison, and who can tell but what James M. Mathews may be one of the number. The prisoner is employed on the Cooley contract, and has a record of being one of the most exemplary convicts in the prison, and if innocent of the crime for which he is now serving a life sentence, may his innocence soon be brought to light and the bondman set at liberty.

The principal aim of society is to protect men in the enjoyment of those absolute rights which are vested in them by the immutable laws of nature, but which could not be preserved in peace without the mutual assistance and intercourse which is gained by the support of our penal institutions. Our prisons are an unavoidable necessity for the protection and benefit of society. Crime is the result of error or ignorance, and every criminal will be benefited and society better protected and improved when these facts are heeded and indelibly impressed upon the convicts' minds. It is quite surprising to notice the mass of uneducated men confined in our State prison. Twenty per cent. of them can neither read or write, and forty per cent. of them were never in a school room as a pupil.

Every Wednesday evening those who cannot write their own letters are unlocked and march to a room where writing material is kept, and then the most intellectual convicts are sent to the same room to write letters for their fellow prisoners. There are generally from thirty to forty men every Wednesday evening anxiously waiting to have a letter written to their home and friends. Many of the letters written on these occasions are addressed to lawyers and other persons of note to intercede in the prisoners' behalf for clemency or a new trial. One hour is allowed for letter writing and then the men are marched to their cells and locked up.

Letters written to lawyers are generally speedily answered and they nearly always ask for a part of their money for their services paid in advance. There is generally from eight to ten thousand dollars here in the warden's office that belongs to prisoners, and which they can expend for any reasonable cause. Much of this money is used in buying groceries and paying lawyers' fees. Any convict that desires to purchase groceries can do so by giving the order to the keepers of the shops, and at the end of the month the groceries are delivered in their cells. They generally purchase sugar, butter and apples. Nuts and candies, oranges and bananas, are in great demand. The money thus expended by convicts generally averages from a hundred and fifty to two hundred dollars per month. Much of the money among the men is made by making toys and trinkets in their cells in the evening and selling them on the toy table to visitors passing through the prison. Some of their wealth is made doing over-time, but there is very little money made here at present in that way, for the tasks have been raised so often that only a few of the prisoners can earn any money for themselves after their day's work is finished.

It is a sight worthy of the reader's time and patience to take a stroll through the prison in the evening after the day's work is done and the men are locked in their cells. By the aid of the electric light in the cells an observing person can plainly distinguish how the inmate spends his time after working hours until the prison gong signals the hour of bed time. They have many different ways of passing away the weary hours while locked in their cells. Some of the men spend their evenings by playing on musical instruments; while many others are making toys, painting pictures or making fancy boxes. Others are engaged in writing essays, reading papers and books, and some of them are pacing too and fro. Some are lying curled up and fast asleep upon their cots and perhaps dreaming of home. But what shall we say of those who are sitting upon their stools in the corner of their cells, with their elbows resting on their knees and their hands supporting their chin, whilst their eyes are gazing at the floor. Perhaps they are the cold blooded murderers whose consciences are their burning companions and they are being harrowed by their nightly presence. Who knows but what those silent and thoughtful prisoners may be the desperate criminals planning an escape, and would not hesitate to slay a dozen guards, providing they could thereby secure their freedom.

CHAPTER XVIII
THE SUNDAY SCHOOL — PAPER READ BY IRVING LATIMER AT A SABBATH SCHOOL EXHIBITION

WE have previously spoken of the religious meetings of the institution. The Sabbath school, which is held at 9 o'clock every Sunday morning, numbers about 300 convicts and is run and regulated by the chaplain of the prison. The Sabbath school teachers are generally composed of our own number, some of them being well versed in Scriptural knowledge. Both scholars and teachers are well supplied with religious tracts, Sunday school papers, etc. The Sunday school is in progress one hour, and a few minutes before the allotted time expires the Rev. George H. Hickox reviews and explains the difficult parts of the Sunday school lesson. Once every three months we have a general review of the lessons passed over during the last quarter. For these Sunday school exhibitions the chaplain selects some of the scholars to write papers, or select some choice religious reading for the occasion.

Irving Latimer was a leader in Sunday school work long before he came to this place as a prisoner. He was selected as the director of the evening of a Sabbath school exhibition held on Jan. 2, 1890. He was introduced to the audience by Chaplain Hickox and read the following paper.

"There is an ancient legend of a king in a certain eastern country, who besides being both wealthy and wise, was respected and loved by all the people throughout his vast domain. He made just laws and the people obeyed them and were content, and the fame of their content and of their prosperity spread through all the countries roundabout. And the' ruler of these countries because of their clamor and discontent of their own people, convened together and said to one another, 'let us go to our neighbor, the wise king, and ask him in what manner he rules over his people, for our own people are discontented and have no peace.' And when after many days' journey they came to the palace of the wise king he met them very kindly, and, having listened to their questions, said; 'Come with me, and on the morrow I will show to you that which you ask.' On the morrow he took them to a distant part of the capital city and they entered a huge building, within which were many children, youths and maidens, and many teachers were instructing them. And the wise king said unto the other kings: 'Thus do I have the children of my people instructed, that when they reach years of discretion they may know the laws and obey them.'

The advantages presented, the good influences exerted by the Sunday school cannot be over estimated. Between the infant class of our Jackson Sunday schools and our own school there is a vast difference. Not the one of age merely, nor that of freedom and incarceration, but a greater still. They, in their youthful innocence, entering upon a study of those precepts, which, closely followed, shall guard them from such a fate as ours. We — you and I — who, whether innocent or guilty, have forfeited our liberty, because we know not just how to use it, find in the same precepts that instruction, which, implicitly obeyed, shall enable us when freedom is again ours, to re-enter life clad in an invulnerable armor which shall render every evil attack against us harmless.

Man is a creature of destiny. His life is what he makes it or permits others to make it.

Within many of our minds the memory of those scenes when we, as children, listened to the interpretation of the living word, is still fresh.

But the past is forever gone, and though years have elapsed, we again assemble and renew our studies, possibly at almost the very same point we so long ago left them. But why speak of the past? It is the future with which we have to do. When the iron gates shall swing open for us again our future thenceforth shall be our own.

Let the clang of the closing gate be the funeral of the evil of the past. Let your exit into the free world be demonstrative of a change in your career, a desire for which you evince by your continued attendance here, Sunday morning after Sunday morning.

> Once to every man and nation
> Comes the moment to decide,
> In the strife of truth and falsehood,
> For the good or evil side.

Though a man attain to the age of one hundred years, though his life be one of ever changing experiences among many people and many nations, yet all this experience is as naught, unless he be guided by something higher than human laws to fit him for the simple duties of every day life.

The study of the Bible is a never ending source of wonder. This single volume (to quote from that little pamphlet distributed among us this morning) is in reality a library filled with history, genealogy, law, ethics, prophecy, eloquence, medicine, sanitary science, political economy, art and perfect rules for the conduct of personal and social life, and from its study may be derived all that knowledge necessary for us to attain the perfect happiness of the future.

This great guide, the only guide to that unknown future, is offered to us. We are not asked to labor for it, it is ours for the asking.

May the Almighty help us to receive and believe his divine word, and may we all be benefited by the knowledge gleaned in our Sabbath School."

CHAPTER XIX
EXPIRATION OF WARDEN HATCH'S ADMINISTRATION — A CHRISTMAS PRESENTATION

IN November, 1890, the people of Michigan elected a Democratic Governor and the administration of Warden Hatch expired on the first of January, 1891. It was proposed by some of the leaders among our number that we present to him something valuable as a token of our gratitude for his energetic and untiring work of prison reform. Thomas Navin, was authorized to circulate a subscription paper among the men for the purpose of raising the money with which to make the desired purchase. We concluded that six hundred dollars would be required to buy that which we wished to present to him who had for six years advocated prison reformation.

A good and kind-hearted officer is seldom found behind prison walls, for it seems natural for the minor officers of the prison to be cross and indifferent to our welfare. But when a man is found who is kind-hearted and tries to do by us as he would wish to be done by, he is called a model guard and his name soon spreads throughout the prison and he is well known among all the convicts. A guard, John Dunn, was one of the most human and just men that we have had, and we concluded that we would also remember him in this act of kindness and make him a present of gold coin to the value of one hundred and fifty dollars. About seven hundred and fifty dollars was raised with which to purchase a silver tea set for Warden Hatch, and present the sum of money agreed upon to our favorite guard, John Dunn.

On Christmas evening, 1890, the prison chapel was packed with spectators anxiously waiting the last act in the administration of Warden Hatch — the presentation of the presents already spoken of.

The audience was much surprised when Tom Navin stepped upon the rostrum and uncovered the valuable silver tea set, which cost five hundred and fifty dollars. It was a magnificent gift and a present worthy to present to a king. The silverware, all of which was lined with gold, shone with such a brilliancy while under the electric light that it was almost impossible for the eye to behold it.

Thomas Navin stepped upon the stage and spoke as follows: "Fellow men and fellow prisoners — We have met here tonight upon the greatest occasion in the history of penal institutions. He who has been our long and well tried friend is about to leave us, and we are here to make a lasting manifestation of the many benefits derived by us during his administration. We are about to be severed from him, whom we all know has battled single-handed and alone; battled long and well against public sentiment and against the press while advocating the invincible principles of human rights and prison reformation. We do not believe that in any land, nor in any age of the world's life, have men in penal institutions been called together to witness a more beneficial, nor a similar event. The separation of our leader from his followers, is severing us from him who has defended us against the criticisms of the people. He is now about to leave our sight, but we will retain him in our memories, and we cannot let him take his departure from us until we have made a lasting impression on his mind, that we are satisfied that we have met with an irreparable loss, and one upon which hangs the destiny of our future happiness. Warden Hatch, in the name and with the consent and best wishes of the men in Jackson prison, I now present to you this Christmas present, for which every man under your charge has contributed. The departure from us of your estimable wife and child is a great and very sad loss. We, who have families, were compelled to think of our own little children when we looked upon the fair and loving countenance of your own darling little child. She has frequently distributed lillies and roses among us as we were marching to our cells after having completed a hard day's work. And may the prosperity and peace of the blessed remain with you and your family wherever you may go."

At the conclusion of Navin's speech Warden Hatch stepped quickly forward and spoke as follows: "Men — For six long years I have strived to do my duty, regardless of the opinions and the criticisms of men. I know that I have made many mistakes while conducting the prison, but I have done my level best. Surely this is the most regretful moment of my life. I have been with you so long that I have become attached to you, and feel as though my happiness was not disconnected with that of your own prosperity and contentment. During the remaining years of my life it will be a pleasure for me to think of the men in Jackson prison. Not of their conditions nor their sufferings, but of the noble struggle they are making to rise up out of their past ways of life, which has only brought upon them sin and sorrow. Men do not cease to continue to pursue the upward course. Broaden out and get out of the channel of your past mistakes. The course you have taken in presenting to me such a valuable present is more impressive upon my mind and more valuable to me than any language at my command can express. I am glad that you have given me something that I can enjoy with my wife. You have unexpectedly made me a Christmas present long to be remembered and one that cannot be forgotten. No man has a greater right to be more rejoiced and feel more encouraged in his feeble efforts than myself. I have frequently met those on the outside world, and who were once here as prisoners under my charge, that were married and living in in an humble home of happiness and peace. It always gave me great pleasure to meet those who were once prisoners, but were then freemen, and I could predict by their sun-burnt countenances and husky hands that their freedom was not short-lived nor jeopardized.

Men, broaden out and do not abandon the great and natural principles which bring peace and happiness to all, and which are more than impregnable and independent of the laws of men.

I consider the principles which are embalmed in the desires of making the presents tonight of more real worth than the presents themselves. And I hope and believe that there are men here tonight who are held as prisoners that will rise up to the standard do unto others as you would have them do unto you.

The change that has come among us has been the will of the majority of the people of the State, and surely the change of administration which is about to occur, is for the best, or else it would not happen. Men, whatever you do, do not relax your hold nor forsake the principles of prison reform. Many have already prophesied that the great change that is about to take place in the penal institutions throughout the State, and especially Jackson prison, will be the end of your just intentions and the death of prison reformation. It is left with you to decide whether or not their prophecies will yet be fulfilled. Men, it is impossible for me to portray my feelings, nor express my heartfelt thanks for this magnificent present which you have made.

I sincerely believe that the steps you have taken tonight will not only change and ameliorate the governing of the penal institutions of this State, but will have a tendency toward bettering and changing the governing of the prison in all countries."

John Dunn, the guard previously spoken of, received his present of solid gold, and perhaps we never have expended money to a better purpose than that which we contributed to him who had ever been just and unchangeable while ruling over us during the many years of his connection with this prison.

John Dunn had a sweet little girl about six years of age and whom we all dearly loved. Her name was Winnifred Dunn and she became acquainted with us by so frequently bringing her father's dinner to the prison. She was always sure to come into the dining room and remain there during the dinner hour. Many of the prisoners' eyes would fill with tears while she was with us at noontime, for they were reminded of their own sweet child that was left at home without a father's care.

But earthly joys, we know, are fleeting, and earthly sorrows are ever with us. The child was taken sick and died on the 11th of June, 1891. When it became known among us that she was a corpse a feeling of sympathy and love for the child was visible in the countenances of the men throughout the prison. One of the most desperate men in Jackson prison, when told of her death, remarked that if it was possible he would gladly give up his life if he could by so doing call Winnifred Dunn back to life, so that she could take her place and be the same living ornament to us in the dining room.

CHAPTER XX
WARDEN DAVIS' ADMINISTRATION — EMANCIPATION DAY ADDRESS — CONCLUSION

IN the month of February, 1891, Warden Davis took control of the prison. We anxiously waited to see what changes would follow the new administration.

We were soon convinced that he was not a believer in the reformation of criminals while they were confined behind prison walls, but he did not put any obstacles in the way of the men who were inclined to uplift and rise up out of their past ways of sin and folly. Warden Davis sincerely believed that the prisoners should be kept steadily at work during the day, but he did not sustain the contractors in any of their unjust claims for more work and less pleasure from the men in their employ. There were seventy-five per cent. less reports during this administration than during any time of a like period since our incarceration.

Much of the good time lost by convicts by being reported under other administrations was restored to them, and they left the prison when their short time expired. Convict John Hatfield, No. 2556, was a fifteen-year prisoner. He came here in 1883, and in the latter part of the year made his escape in a very peculiar way. He was employed on the cigar contract as shipping clerk, and he made the packing cases in in which the cigars were shipped. One day he made a box which opened by means of a trap door with a catch on the inside of the box. In the morning when the box was shipped to the depot the convict was in it instead of the 150 boxes of cigars. He made the box in such a manner that it would be of the same weight while he was in it as it would be when filled with the boxes of smokers. When the box arrived at the freight house he opened it by means of the spring on the inside and escaped. His fellow prisoner who aided him in this model escape, informed the prison authorities of the refugee's destination. He had been given a letter by him who aided the escape, to carry to his sister in Boston, Massachusetts, and the police authorities were informed to be on the lookout for him.

He was captured when he arrived in Boston while he entered the house to deliver the letter given to him by his false friend. He was brought back here and served his time, and when his short time expired he had lost nearly one thousand three hundred days of his good time. But Warden Davis concluded that the prisoner had been in confinement long enough and only detained him five months longer after his short time was ended.

The new warden has done much toward adding to the financial worth of the State's property. He erected the new building for the Cooley contract, which is by far, the finest building in yard. The new wall on the west side of the prison, and the fine cemented sidewalks inside the walls were erected by his command. He started a toy manufactory in the State shop, and set the cripples and old men at light work making toys that find a ready sale and at a financial profit to the State.

There are some of the most humane and conscientious guards connected with this administration that we have had during our prison life. None of them seem to have any other motto, only to do that which is justice to us, and justice to their positions.

Warden Geo. N. Davis is not a favorite among all the men under his charge. They have various causes for complaint. For many years they had been taught the principles of prison reform every other night during the week in their literary meetings, but under this administration these meetings were not held only every other week and the time allowed to hold them in the evening was much shorter than they were under the previous reign.

The class in ethics which was once held in the school room once a week has been done away with. There are many other minor grievances upon which some of the prisoners form the basis of discontent. But the unprejudiced and the unbiased minds will admit that the present ruler of the prison will not infringe upon convict's rights himself, nor permit it to be done by any of the officers, nor the foremen inside the yard. He is a patient listener to comic songs and sweet music, and frequently has the colored glee club unlocked in the evening for the purpose of singing some of their sweet melodies that he, and some of his invited guests, may listen to the funny songs and pass away an hour of solid pleasure.

For many years the convicts have had a literary league, and of which we have already stated, held their meetings in the prison chapel once a month. Under this administration the league was remodeled, and was called the Progressive Thought Association.

There has been many of these public exhibitions in the chapel during this administration, and on various occasions the papers read and speeches made by prisoners were sufficient to satisfy the skeptical minds that the reformation of criminals is not a hopeless task, and that some men in our State prison are striving to rise up out of the old channels of past mistakes and be law-abiding citizens.

The 1st of August is Emancipation Day among the colored people of this country, and it is strictly observed here among the colored prisoners. They have public exercises in the chapel, and on one of these occasions, August 1st, 1891, a colored prisoner, the author of this book, made the following address:

> "Fellow men — You have observed the dates of 1834 and 1863 stamped upon the cover of each programme. They represent the birth of events that will be remembered, and perhaps commemorated, as long as the African race exists. And tonight we challenge stone walls and iron bars to erase those events from the records of memory. Many of the great events recorded in history are fading, and only a few of them are producing annual fruit. Tonight we commemorate one of the latter named events. Ancient pyramids and Egyptian monuments that have withstood the shock of earthquakes and the storm of time's erasing finger for innumerable centuries, are at last crumbling away. Earthquake shocks and land slides will in the course of time dislodge the very basis of the solid rock. Meteors and shooting stars burst into light, but they disappear into darkness. But tonight we commemorate an event that is impervious to the erasing finger of time, and immortal to darkness and decay. The emancipation of a race, the remodeling of a great government, until every man born or nurtured on American soil became its prime factor. But freedom does not erase our obligations to the law nor wipe out our responsibilities to our country. Freedom resolves that industry and reflection must accompany freedom and human rights. The grand principle of freedom is that liberty shall be turned into culture, brain and skill, and every freeman of this great nation has the problem before him that he must solve, how to render life more happy, more reflecting, more virtuous, to the great surrounding mass of humanity. We must not weigh men and render our final verdict until their life shall have ended. Why, there are men here tonight, although buried under this avalanche of iron and stone, who may yet become free men. Men again, and take adverse fortune by storm, for honorable ambition and just intention is the only true success in life. And there are men here erecting a kingdom of morality and integrity for future use, and so firm are they laying each corner stone that no scheme or machination in future life will ever be able to disturb or dislodge them. And no grove ever produced a flower that can compare with the laurels that fame places on the brow of the adverse, but ambitious conqueror. But some of us here are well aware that this world is a great campaign against color, trast and cantrast, and we must daily expect a skirmish, but this nation has thrown its helmet to us, and we will wear it on our front until we shall have swept away the dark circle of every imaginable prejudice. We never can forget the anniversary of our freedom, although we do not seek retrospection, for it leads our minds into rivers of sorrow which are foam-flecked with blood. We do not wish to review some of the real facts which are connected with our bygone serfdom. Facts, some of them so hideous in their nature and so revolting to human belief that history has failed to note them, and the world will never learn them, for some of those dread secrets every

slave will forever keep. And years after the hounds have ceased to bark and the horn has ceased to blow, after both master and slave have faded from sight and partially from the memories of men, in our dreams we are slaves again. In our dreams we are on the same old plantation, sitting in the same old log cabin or using the same old hoe. In our dreams we imagine we are in the midst of the dismal swamp, with no torch except the north star in heaven, with no compass but the thought of freedom, we are again wandering northward. In our dreams we are startled at the rustle of every leaf, and the chirping of every cricket seems to cry out, "Stop him!" "There he goes." And in our dreams we can hear voices whispering in the still midnight air. In our dreams we are standing on the auction block, and in our dreams we can hear our mothers shriek, "Oh, give me back my child!" Why, servitude struck an awful blow. It paralyzed the intellect of the slaves, foundered the intellect of the masters, and wiped out the freedom of the whole race. Hope may wither but never dies in noble breasts, confine the men where you may. And hope never left the breast of the panting slaves, although they did not know how near the huge cup of servitude had filled up the measure of its iniquities. But they did know that somewhere under the north star there was a free country. And nights so dark, dark as any night that ever smothered the land of Egypt, found some panting slave wandering northward.

But years have changed that scene. Every day works a revolution — a change. To-day trembled before the approaching footsteps of to-morrow. Why, all manner of tortures and solitudes are dying, dying dizzy with awful memories of their past, when the present looks forward and sees the living future come sweeping up. Why, freedom, it a flower, yes, it is a rose that is indigenous to every clime, and will yet bloom in every country; in 1834 it blossomed out in the isles of the West Indies; in 1863 it bloomed in United States; in 1884-5 it matured away down in South America, and I predict that before this century shall have ended that freedom's mother (Home Rule) will sweep old Ireland.

Don't you doubt it, Home Rule is freedom's fruit, dead ripe in Ireland — and ripe fruit must fall, why there is a message by the Atlantic cable — it is due now, and must soon scorch the ocean in its lightning speed to tell the world old Ireland is free. For torture — oppression, has no permanent home, it is a wandering skeleton, it is a moving vampire, and the constant hound of freedom will surely track it down. Wherever torture or oppression nestles, it is sure to meet an adversary. Why, if standing there, (pointing) you could see a thorn or thistle. Why, right over here, (pointing) you would surely see a little rose. That rose is watching them, and whenever servitude is hiding, freedom, its master crouches, and eyeing it, cannot escape; for long before history was born, long before any cringing form of society or government was organized, there went forth a royal fiat — a sacred proclamation, which has never yet been amended or revoked. Why, the echoes are yet quivering in the air from that proclamation which said that all men, (that means both slaves and master, landlord and tenant, all men, both convict and contractor) shall live by the sweat of their own brow. There are events extraordinary, for they never appear but once and the brilliancy of their approaching extinguishes the records of our world's greatest heroes, but America has produced one man that was more than the coming of a great event, for he was the event itself, and he never had a predecessor, he never had a rival, he will never have a parallel. In the world's great catalogue of extraordinary events there is one name that will stand green through all the muffled march of time, and when the name of all other great heroes shall have rot in oblivion, for he gave freedom to the slaves. It is no dream, for we will never have another Lincoln, nor will we ever have another slave. It is no dream, for our freedom lives and servitude is a corpse, for we hellots heard its three dying groans up-heaved from its burnt-out carcass at Gettysburg, and when wrapped in the rebels' fallen stars and broken bars for a shroud, we saw it buried at Appomattox. We have ploughed our way through dark days and awful nights, but at last we are anchored safe on freedom's rock, and all the coming future owes us hope, and to all the dead and buried past we are under no obligations."

— — — — —

We have said within these pages that ignorance was a great induction to crime, and our experience of a quarter of a century behind these walls confirms the fact that education cancels the criminal's past views of life and directs him on the future road of honesty and integrity, and impresses upon his mind that christianity is absolutely necessary to live a long and happy life.

Footnotes

1. It is the largest bell in the world. Weight 386,000 pounds. It fell down during the great fire at Moscow, Russia, and lay buried where it fell until 1837. It was twenty-one feet in height and the same in diameter.
2. It will be remembered that slaves only had their first name; the last was the same as their master's name and always changed when sold.
3. The burial ground was in the same lot where many score of hogs were kept.

www.ingramcontent.com/pod-product-compliance
Lightning Source LLC
LaVergne TN
LVHW011950070526
838202LV00054B/4874